Damien opened the bedroom door a crack—and blood lust welled up within him.

Shannon lay there, sound asleep. Naked, relaxed, alive. Beautiful. With everything in him, he wanted to go to her, touch her, run his trembling hands over her flesh....

The thirst raged. The hunger. And he knew, too well, that if he denied his savage nature too long, the craving would build and build until it took over.

He tore himself away from the sight of her as the hunger called again. This time, he wouldn't deny its power over him. He couldn't let it grow until it reached the point of madness. Not again. Not with Shannon in the house. So near. So sweet.

She'd be succulent....

"No!"

Damien slipped out into the night, whirled until he became only a gray blur to human eyes. And then he flew, a dark streak across the sky....

Dear Reader,

We have two especially eerie books for you this month. Just think of them as our New Year's gift to you. As a toothsome treat, both books feature vampires—though in completely different ways.

Maggie Shayne continues her popular "Wings in the Night" miniseries with *Twilight Illusions*. Vampire hero Damien is revered by all as the greatest of his kind, but he risks everything—not just his power, but his very existence— for the love of a mortal woman. Whether this is your first foray into the spellbinding world this author creates, or whether you've been there from the very beginning, this is a book you won't want to miss.

In *Dark Obsession*, Amanda Stevens makes a welcome return to the line. Heroine Erin Ramsey at first thinks vampires are merely fiction, but then her sister is found dead, all the blood drained from her body. Suddenly vampires seem all too real. And just who is Detective Nick Slade, the man assigned to her sister's case, the man who might want to kiss Erin—or kill her!

Start the New Year by taking a walk on the dark side of love, and then come back again next month and every month for your chance to find love in the shadows— Silhouette Shadows.

Enjoy!

Leslie Wainger
Senior Editor and Editorial Coordinator

Please address questions and book requests to:
Silhouette Reader Service
U.S.: 3010 Walden Ave., P.O. Box 1325, Buffalo, NY 14269
Canadian: P.O. Box 609, Fort Erie, Ont. L2A 5X3

MAGGIE SHAYNE

Twilight Illusions

Published by Silhouette Books
America's Publisher of Contemporary Romance

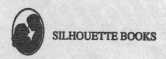 SILHOUETTE BOOKS

ISBN 0-373-27047-X

TWILIGHT ILLUSIONS

Books by Maggie Shayne

Silhouette Shadows

* *Twilight Phantasies* #18
* *Twilight Memories* #30
Kiss of the Shadow Man #38
*Twilight Illusions #47

*Wings in the Night

Silhouette Intimate Moments

Reckless Angel #522
Miranda's Viking #568
Forgotten Vows...? #598

MAGGIE SHAYNE

lives in a rural community in Central New York with her husband and five daughters. She's currently serving as president of the Central New York chapter of the Romance Writers of America and has been invited to join the National League of American Pen Women. In her spare time, Maggie enjoys speaking about writing at local schools and conducting a romance writing workshop at a local community college.

To Jena, who gave Damien his magic.
I love you.

CHAPTER ONE

It is an old story
But one that can still be told
About a man who loved
And lost....

Shannon took copious notes, swearing at the inefficiency of a penlight for writing in the middle of a pitch-dark theater. She swore again at the narrow arms on the seats, which were no good at all for holding a notepad. Especially when the jerks on either side of her seemed to think they owned exclusive rights to them. She growled a sigh, shoved the meaty arm to her left out of the way and whispered loudly, "Hey, do you mind? I'm trying to *work* here."

Anger was good. Anger would keep her mind away from the images burned into it. Tawny, with hair and eyes that matched her name, and a porcelain-doll face, and a smile that lit up a room. Her dreams of becoming a star, her overly dramatic way of expressing herself. Her fearlessness. Her stubbornness. Shannon wanted to remember the vibrant upstart actress by day, call girl by night, best friend forever. Not the pale, naked body sprawled on the rumpled sheets, with its vacant-eyed stare. Not the twin gossamer strands of scarlet meandering over her paper-white neck. God, not that.

The guy in the next seat grumbled and shifted as far away from her as possible. Shannon wrote, only vaguely aware of the spreading applause. The gradual quieting. The sense of expectation in the crowd. The deep, melodic voice of the man at center stage announcing that he would need a volunteer from the audience. A sudden burst of movement and loudly voiced offers from the female spectators distracted her only for a moment before she adjusted the dim penlight and continued writing.

"The women here are practically drooling. It would be easy for him to lure one anywhere he wanted. Still no one who can tell me where he was last Wednesday night between..."

Her pen stopped on the pad and a cloud of frigid air seemed to envelop her. She glanced up, toward the aisle three seats away. *He* stood there, a tall, shadowy form draped in black satin. An instant later the spotlight caught up with him, illuminating his hair, until it gleamed blue, and making his ivory skin seem even paler. His arm was outstretched, his hand reaching toward her. And his eyes, huge and round like an owl's, seemingly holding the wisdom of the gods and the pain of a thousand hells, focused on her, keeping her prisoner.

"You, miss."

She wished her heart would stop racing. There was still no shred of evidence that the man was a twisted murderer. Only a matter of circumstance and her own suspicions. "Me, what?"

His lips curved upward. His gaze fell to the notepad, the penlight and the pen she'd been juggling all evening, then jumped back to hers again. "What's your name?"

"Sh-Shannon... but, I—"

"A round of applause for the lovely Shannon, our courageous volunteer."

He said it loudly, waving toward her with a flourish and a ripple of that shimmering cloak. The spotlight obeyed him, instantly dousing her in a pool of hot white brilliance that did nothing to chase away her ominous chill. She squinted as the applause swelled. His hand closed on hers, big, warm, hard. He pulled, none too gently. The notepad, penlight, purse, everything, avalanched to the floor as she was jerked to her feet.

She gave her hand a tug, but his grip was as good as any pair of handcuffs ever invented. He pulled her along at his side. Her protests went unheard beneath the noise of the crowd and the accompanying music. He dragged her up the steps far to the right and onto the stage. She could either fight him and look like an idiot, or accept this fiasco with a modicum of grace. She decided on the latter, though she thought the vain bastard could use a good kick in his over-size ego.

He looked into her eyes, and again, his lips curved. It didn't go far enough to qualify as a smile. More like an "I know what you're thinking and find it amusing" kind of a look.

She glared at him, her mind exchanging his black eyes for Tawny's light brown ones—wide open, glazed, forever blind.

His grip on her wrist eased. He frowned down at her and his hand slid down to clasp hers. They stopped center stage. Behind them, a red velvet curtain rose as silently as a ghost. Shannon glanced over her shoulder, saw a clear pane of glass balanced across the backs of two chairs.

"The lovely Shhannnon—" he drew the consonants in her name out until it sounded like an incantation "—is about to assist me in defying the very laws of nature...of Mother Earth..."

She told herself not to lose her anger to the ever-growing tide of uneasiness that could easily become fear. Killer or not, he couldn't very well hurt her right in front of thousands of onlookers. She stiffened her spine. "If you think I'm letting you saw me in half, forget it," she rasped, teeth grated, mouth barely moving. She glanced sideways at him, saw the twitch in his lips, felt his hand tighten on hers.

"Of gravity itself," he went on.

He had a way of speaking that was utterly mesmerizing, each word enunciated slowly, his mouth seeming to caress every syllable before releasing it. It made you focus on his lips as he spoke, against your own will.

"This way, Shannon." Mist shot up from the floor, encircling their legs to twist and writhe in time with the erotic music, if music could be that. Slow, sexy, with an urgent beat. He led her to the makeshift table, waved an arm over it, then took her hand and guided her up a pair of wooden steps as the silken music swelled, his every movement in perfect synchronization with the beat. "Lie down, Shannon. And prepare to be swept away."

She shivered a little, wondering if he spoke in those slow, measured tones all the time or only onstage. She lay back on the cool glass, her gaze never leaving his face. Even his breaths and the blinking of his eyes were grace epitomized, as if they, too, had been choreographed. He circled her once, one arm extended, cloak swirling as he moved. Then, with a flick of his fingers at his throat, he whipped the cloak from his shoulders, swung it outward, draped it over her. He drew it up from her feet, covering her right up to her chin.

The fabric was heaven, satin inside and out. She wanted to rub it against her cheek. The scent that invaded her mind was dusky and potent. Like nothing she'd smelled before.

His hand touched her forehead, sweeping downward. His fingertips closed her eyes. She stiffened, again thinking of Tawny.

"Relax, Shannon. Don't move. Let your muscles melt at my command. Break the bounds of earth. Free yourself from the constraints of gravity."

She sighed hard, blinking away the angry tears the image of her friend had brought to her eyes. Damien Namtar knew how to put on a show, if nothing more. Of course, he wouldn't be the hottest magician in the world if he didn't. Damien the Eternal. She'd have rolled her eyes if they'd been open. More like Damien the Master of Optical Illusion. But maybe she'd learn something about him if she paid attention. Maybe she'd manage to stop thinking about Tawny long enough to find a hint of who'd killed her.

And how? For the love of God, how?

She focused her mind, lying still as he'd instructed. She didn't want to break this contraption and get dumped on the stage.

Nothing happened. Shannon heard a collective gasp from the audience and opened one eye. Damien stood near her feet, holding a chair in one outstretched hand. She frowned a little. The chair that had been propping up that end of the glass? But her body was still horizontal.

He set the chair down and walked to her head, pausing to lay that feather-light hand over her eyes again, closing them once more. She popped them right open again, though. She'd paid to see the damned show. She certainly couldn't see it with her eyes closed, and she wasn't about to miss what might turn out to be a clue.

He was standing at the head of the makeshift bed now, looking down at her face. He pursed his lips when he saw that her eyes were open, but she didn't close them again. His gaze grew intense, probing, piercing. He bent, and she knew he was pulling the other chair from beneath the sheet of glass. When he straightened he held the chair, whirled around and threw it off stage right.

When she could see him again he had a plastic hoop in one hand. He ran it over and under her, then around her body, back and forth to demonstrate no strings held her aloft.

The hoop was tossed aside, as well. He leaned over her face. "Concentrate with me now, Shannon. There is nothing to fear."

With a look of glee, he pulled the cloak over her head. That would teach her for not keeping her eyes closed, she imagined he was thinking.

She heard him mutter words in a language she didn't recognize. Then there was a strange sort of vibration. She felt the glass under her back move. It slid to one side. She instinctively began to clutch it with her left hand, but his caught hers and held it still. Her chilled fingers, surrounded by his graceful, warm hand. She almost squeezed it, almost turned her palm to his and laced fingers with him. Weird notion. Luckily, he released her before she had time to follow through.

She felt the glass slip out from beneath her. The music faded as the beat of drums grew louder, faster. She remained where she was, lying in midair above the stage. How the hell—

The cloak was moving now, satin rasping against the denim of her jeans as it slipped down her body. Damien stood there, stark-white shirt opened at the collar to reveal a muscled column of throat. Gleaming dark curls showed on his chest. He stood a few feet behind her, arms outstretched, palms up, eyes closed as if in concentration. He had incredible lashes for a man. In fact, everything about him was pretty incredible. Shannon knew Tawny better than anyone, and she had a feeling Tawny wouldn't have left the theater that night without at least offering . . .

As he lifted his hands and the drums pounded frantically, Shannon seemed to rise on a cushion of air. She caught her breath. Higher and higher she floated, until she had to close her eyes to keep from getting dizzy.

Then she just stopped, far above his head. She dared a peek downward. He was staring up at her. He stepped forward. "To me, Shannon," he called loudly, firmly, in a deep voice that would be tough to argue with. Then he bent his elbows, snapped both fingers. The music stopped all at once...and she fell. It lasted an instant, the sensation of plummeting full-speed through space, the certainty that the landing was going to hurt like hell, the urge to scream out loud. She bit her lip...and landed in his arms.

She blinked in shock. He stared down at her, and his smile was just a bit fuller. His banded arms cradled her tight to his chest, and the sensation was alien to her. She thought she might be just a little closer to understanding Tawny's alley-cat morals after tonight. He lowered his head, touched her forehead with his lips. She was sure he'd burned a brand into her skin by the touch of his mouth. But that was stupid. It was the music, and the mist and the magic making her feel ripples of pleasure race up and down her spine. Not the touch of a man. Never the touch of a man.

The crowd's roar almost deafened her. He looked away from her, out toward the audience, and she followed his gaze. They were on their feet...every last one of them, and their cheers went on and on, vibrating right to the rafters.

But her attention strayed back to the man who held her. His strong profile, the elegant line of his jaw, the aquiline nose. And the light gathering brilliance somewhere deep within those jet eyes. He loved this. He absorbed the adoration of the crowd the way the desert absorbs the rain. He was in sheer ecstasy. He almost glowed.

The curtain lowered in front of them and he set her on her feet. His hands caught her shoulders, turned her to one side and pushed gently. "Offstage, Shannon. Watch from there." A stagehand hustled toward her and Damien leaned over, whispering close to her ear, "You were wonderful." Then the short redhead gripped her arm and led her offstage. He pointed to a folding chair and ran out of sight, a clipboard clutched in one hand.

Shannon glanced back to see the heavy, rippling curtain rise as if weightless. Damien stood center stage, fastening the ties that held the cloak at his throat. When the curtain stopped its spectral ascent, the crowd beyond it still stood, still cheered.

Sketching an elegant bow, he held his hands up for silence. "Thank you. Thank you all. I'm afraid the fair Shannon won't be rejoining you. I've decided to have her for dinner."

Laughter rippled through the theater.

Damien opened his arms to his sides, the edges of the cloak held in his hands. "Farewell, my friends."

A drumroll pattered across her heart. The crowd went utterly still. He lowered one arm and swept the other over his face in typical Dracula style. He whirled in a circle, once, twice, faster, three times.

Cymbals smashed. The cloak fell, a satin puddle. He'd vanished. Shannon came to her feet, squinting, searching that shimmering black mound. She saw movement and frowned harder. What the hell was that little . . .

The bat launched itself from its satin nest, fluttering wildly, swooping in crazy patterns before soaring out over the crowd. It dove low, eliciting shrieks of delighted horror, gasps of surprise. Then it turned and headed back to the stage. It angled left and flitted right past Shannon's face and out of sight.

The curtain fell again and the theater shook with applause.

The noise went on and on before it slowly died. She heard people in the crowd shifting, moving. The activity backstage increased. Shannon shook away the spell the magician had briefly cast over her, and looked around her. She had a mission, despite that his mystical illusions had made her lose track of it for a few minutes. She crossed her fingers and started off in what she hoped was the right direction. She wasn't finished with Damien Namtar yet. She had questions and she wasn't leaving here until she got some answers.

A tap on her shoulder made her spin around, half expecting to see the magic man himself smirking at her. Instead it was the same red-haired man who'd led her offstage. Her purse dangled from one pudgy, freckle-smattered hand. "Damien said I should give this to you. Said all your stuff's inside."

"Thanks." She took it, her gaze busy looking beyond the man. "Where is he? I need to talk to him."

"No chance of that. He's gone already."

"He's...gone?" She felt exactly like a balloon being slowly deflated.

"Long drive to that palace of his in Tigris. And it's raining."

"Palace?"

The redhead looked at the floor, shaking his head slow. "Like somethin' outta 'Life-styles of the Richer-Than-I'll-Ever-Be.' Know what I mean?"

She did. She'd seen the photos in the entertainment magazines, which couldn't get enough of the world-renowned, millionaire magician. Nor could his legion female fans. She tilted her head. "I heard he was a recluse. You'd think he would keep where he lives secret, keep the fans from hounding him."

"Everybody knows about that place, but there's no danger of him bein' hounded. He's got a security system like Fort Knox. *Nobody* could get in there."

"Nobody, huh?" She thumbed the strap of her bag over her shoulder and turned to go.

Damien,

Once again, I write you and hope for a response. And this time, I'll make an effort to explain my motives more completely, and perhaps ease your misgivings about me. I am a vampire, like you, and a scientist.

I devote my time, over two centuries now, to the study
of our kind, in an effort to better understand the pe-
culiarities of our existence. Why are we here? To what
purpose? And also, in the hope of easing some of the
less pleasant aspects of our lives. I study the Chosen,
as well, those humans with whom we share an inexpli-
cable psychic link. Those we're drawn to, and whom we
instinctively try to protect. Those who can be transformed, and who have the same elusive antigen in their
blood as all of us had at one time. My studies have
yielded a great deal of information. But I crave more.

    You, Damien, I've been told, are the most power-
ful, the most ancient of us still in existence. You're said
to have abilities beyond those of younger immortals,
and I've no doubt your wisdom exceeds ours, as well.
I wish only to meet with you, talk to you, learn from
your vast aeons of immortality. Your wisdom could
benefit us all, Damien. I should like, very much, to be
your friend.

    Yours in darkness,

                                        Eric Marquand

Damien crumpled the letter with its formally patterned
sentences that, in his opinion, made it clear to anyone who
cared that the author wasn't from this time, and tossed it
into the cold ashes of his modern, marble hearth. This
Marquand ought to learn to sound as if he belonged here
and now. Damien had always thought that was the most
important part of fitting into any culture—sounding as if
you belonged. No sense drawing attention to yourself.

He grimaced, remembering the last line of the note: *I
should like, very much, to be your friend. Friend.* The word
disgusted him. He didn't want or need to be anyone's friend.
He'd lived through that debilitating pain once, and didn't
have the slightest urge to repeat it.

This Eric Marquand, this infant of an immortal, this vampire who called himself a scientist, wouldn't learn much from him, anyway. Marquand had probably gained more knowledge about the undead in his mere two hundred years of existence than Damien had in almost six thousand. Damien had existed in solitude. He wanted no contact with others of his kind, and most of all, no contact with the Chosen.

The Chosen. They scared the hell out of him. This irresistible instinct he knew all vampires felt, to watch over them, to care for them—it shook him to the bone. It threatened his solitary life. He didn't want to care for anyone. Not ever again. The only way to avoid the mental tug of those rare humans was to avoid them, and that was exactly what Damien had always managed to do.

That is, until tonight.

He'd sensed her presence in the audience from the second he'd stepped onto the stage. He'd felt her there, and there'd been that pull, magnetic, powerful. Some demon inside had urged him to see her, talk to her, touch her and feel the power snap between them. He'd felt that urge before, when he'd chanced to cross paths with one of them. He'd always been able to resist it. Not this time, though. He'd wanted to touch her, and he had.

Maybe a little too much. Damien deliberately kept his mind closed, like pulling shutters tight over a window. He didn't want or need to open himself to the thoughts and feelings of others. He didn't care about them, wasn't the least bit curious. But tonight, in the brief moments of physical contact with the woman, he'd felt an avalanche of emotions pouring from her mind to his, emotions so powerful they'd shaken him. He'd felt her pain, her anger. Most of all, her grief. Anu, for a second he hadn't been sure if it was hers or his own, resurfacing to cripple him one more time. It was so similar. The ancient instinct to make things better for her had leapt to life, forced itself to the front of his mind. He'd doused that blazing urge with an act of will, and made a greater effort to shut her out. But it had been close. It had been too damned close.

He'd need to be more careful from now on. And he'd most definitely need to avoid any more contact with this particular woman, who affected him the way no one ever had.

She wore a black spandex bodysuit and leggings. A black nylon face mask, taken from a Cat Woman costume she'd bought one Halloween, covered her face. Only her eyes and mouth showed. The thin gloves that covered her hands were black, too, as were the lightweight tennis shoes on her feet. She even wore black nylons so her ankles wouldn't stand out in the darkness.

She'd given the man a chance. She'd phoned his house three times. He'd answered the first time, and as soon as she'd told him who was calling, he'd barked at her not to bother him and hung up on her. It had been busy ever since, and she suspected the hermit had taken it off the hook. Fine. He wanted to do this the hard way, then she'd oblige him. Hell, she had nothing to lose. His refusal to talk to her was a roadblock. She wanted to find out who'd killed her best friend and how. This guy was effectively stopping her in her tracks. Too much like being controlled. Too much like letting someone else pull the strings that ran her life. There wasn't much that could make her angrier, more defensive, more ready to do battle. The last time anyone had controlled her life, she'd been sixteen years old, and the results were not pretty. It hadn't happened again.

She scanned the big hulk of black that was his mansion, and wondered what was so great about this setup, anyway. No motion detector on the fence that surrounded the place. Just an alarm that would sound if the locked gate were tampered with, and a couple of surveillance cameras mounted up top. "Big, fat, hairy deal," she muttered.

She slipped the coiled rope from her shoulder, tossed the grappling hook to the tree limb that hung right over the fence—how could *Mister Security* have missed that?—and climbed up. Walking farther out on the sturdy limb, she attached the hook again, and lowered herself to the ground inside the fence. Simple. A kid could break into this place.

Two spotlights came on, aimed right at her. She hit the dirt facedown, her heart thudding in her chest like a jackhammer. Damn!

The lights remained on for several seconds before going out once more. So there were motion detectors. Anything moved within their range and those damned lights would come on again, giving her away if they hadn't already. Okay, think.

The sensor had to be aimed at the movement in order for it to work. She was assuming it wasn't aimed right at ground level or the lights would snap on with every rabbit or field mouse or stray leaf that blew past. Okay. It was worth a shot. She hadn't heard a sound from the house so far, so maybe magic man was asleep.

She slithered toward the house on her belly. She hadn't had much of a look at it yet, in this gloomy darkness. She knew only that it was huge, and utterly dark. Not a light glowing from a single window.

She'd try the door first—not that she expected to find it unlocked, but there might be a doggy door or something she could crawl through. As long as there wasn't a doggy to go with it. She crossed her fingers and humped her way up the broad flagstone steps like an overgrown inchworm.

When the door was right in front of her face, it slowly opened, and her vision was filled with a pair of calf-hugging black boots.

CHAPTER TWO

"What, exactly, are you doing here, Shannon?"

His anger vibrated in those low, measured tones, but seemed to be held in rigid control. She opened her mouth to answer, still staring straight ahead at his gleaming skintight boots. No words came out.

"Much as I might fantasize about the implications of your present position, I think you ought to get up now."

She did, quickly, and she felt her face heating beneath the mask.

That's right, the mask. How the hell did he know it was me?

She tugged it off and glared at him. "Look, I tried to talk to you at the theater, but you left. When I called, you hung up. You really didn't leave me much choice—"

"The choice I left you with was to leave me alone."

His dark eyes burned with some inner fire. Black fire. Dark light. How was that possible? She blinked and shook herself. The wind picked up a little, and it made a deep moaning sound when it passed through the branches of the big oak tree. Perfect October night wind. She faced him, and tried to ignore the shiver of apprehension. How could a man as attractive as this one make her feel so afraid? Nothing scared her. Not even death. Not that she'd admit it, anyway. She couldn't afford to, in her present condition. "I'm afraid I *can't* leave you alone."

"Why not?"

"Let me in and I'll tell you." She watched his face, and knew when he didn't refuse that he was wavering. "It's important."

"It must be." He glanced down over her attire as he said it, and his sarcasm couldn't be missed. Just when her chin rose and a few choice set-downs jumped to her lips, he nodded once and stepped aside. "Ten minutes, Shannon. Then you either leave on your own or I call animal control."

She sauntered past him, feeling triumphant, glancing back over her shoulder. "Who do you think they'd pick up? Cat Woman or Batman?"

He grimaced, as if her little joke had been so bad it was painful, but he couldn't hide the twitch at the corners of his lips. She wondered, for a second, why he'd want to. Then she turned to see where she was going, and all her thoughts stampeded from her mind like cattle from a burning barn.

The short hall she'd traversed opened into a circular room that would put the Oval Office to shame. Black marble fireplace with two arched openings. One for the fire and the other to hold the neatly stacked logs. The mantel stretched the length of it, and was littered with artsy objects encased in clear-glass cubes of varying sizes. The floor gleamed, the same swirling black marble as the hearth, accented here and there with colorful Turkish rugs. Their patterns were wild, orderless, vivid. Were those black eyes peering up at her from behind swirls of scarlet and gold? God, these things, with their braided tassels and secret meanings, could pass for Aladdin's magic carpet. One lay near the fireplace, all but invisible under a mound of pillows. Round, square, oval, satin, silk, velvet, blacks and reds and golds.

A chaise lounge the color of goldenrod, and big enough to hold a crowd, held court to one side of the fireplace. Its shimmery fabric would glow with the firelight when there was a fire. There was a couch, but it wasn't really. It had no back. The plump red cushions angled upward at either end, curving over scrolled wooden arms. Long strands of red fringe hung to the floor all the way around it. The wooden legs and trim were engraved with obscure shapes and symbols.

She blinked and gave her head a shake.

"Not what you expected?"

It was as though an icy wind had just blown over her, the way she shivered.

But it wasn't an icy wind. It was a warm breath, and four simple words spoken softly, close to her nape.

She drew a breath, closed her eyes, calmed herself. She wouldn't let the man's mystic demeanor shake her. After all, it was only part of the act. A persona he put on and took off like the satin cloak he wore. An image. He took it further than she'd anticipated, but that wasn't proof he'd taken it to the ultimate extreme. Was it?

"Perfect setting to keep the image intact, Damien." She continued scanning. There were two wide, arched doorways, at ten o'clock and two o'clock if the fireplace was noon. Neither of them had a door. Instead they were draped with countless strings of beads that looked like onyx. "Although," she went on, trying to keep the amazement from her voice as she found one wondrous item after another, "I don't know why you bother. I was told few people ever get past the front gate. So, who are you trying to impress?"

"The room is for me. I like it this way."

The walls and high ceiling were plastered, their surfaces rough, like stucco, and slightly yellowed, as if very old, although she was sure they were new. The lights were recessed into the walls, with half circles of intricate plaster work shading them from below. The effect was a muted glow that seemed to emanate naturally from above.

She stepped closer to the mantel, eyes widening as she looked more closely at the items within the glass cubes.

Small figures of bearded, almond-eyed men. What looked like a billy goat standing on its hind legs, apparently plated in gold. A chipped piece of pottery shaped like a glass, with animals and designs painted in dulling colors and perfect symmetry. An uneven, rather rectangular hunk of stone with line after line of tiny, detailed marks. Writing? "Are these things as old as they look?"

"That depends on how old they look."

She faced him, frowning. "They're artifacts, aren't they? You collect them. But where do you find things like this, in some pharaoh's tomb?"

"Nice guess. Try a bit earlier and a little farther south." She bit her lip, racking her brain, but he cut her off. "It doesn't make any difference, Shannon. I've given you ten minutes, and you've wasted the first three gawking at my living room. Are you going to tell me what it is that drove you to dress in that ridiculous outfit and break in?"

Her anger returned, and with it, her awareness of why she was here. "You think it's some silly thing, don't you? That I'm an obsessed fan and all I want is an autograph or a souvenir of *Damien the Eternal*."

He tilted his head to one side, crossing his arms over his chest as if waiting patiently for her to get to the point. It was infuriating. She unzipped the small fanny pack that was snapped around her hips. The manila envelope she pulled out wasn't sealed. "How often do you do that levitation routine, using an audience member as a volunteer, Damien?"

His gaze dipped to the envelope, then met hers again. "It's new. Tonight was only the third time I've done it. I like to keep the act varied."

"This was the third time," she repeated. "Do you happen to remember your volunteer last week?" She pulled out the photos, not giving him time to answer. She kept her eyes on his, careful not to glance down at the pictures she held out to him. She'd seen them too many times already.

He looked at her for a long moment, brows creasing. She saw some kind of war going on in those glittering black eyes. When he took the stack, his fingertips brushed over hers and she shivered. She turned away from him, paced to the piece of furniture that looked like Cleopatra's bed and sat down.

She refused to look at him. She gazed, instead, into the cold hearth, noticed the crumpled bit of paper there, wondered what was on it and whether he'd leave the room long enough for her to get a look.

She never heard him approach, so it shocked her when his hand closed around her wrist and he jerked her to her feet. His grip was like iron, and he glared down at her with a fire in his eyes that was potent, and dangerous.

"What in hell is this garbage?" His other hand clutched the photographs.

Fear should have taken over. That it didn't wasn't on account of her unshakable courage. More that she had nothing to lose. Nothing at all. What was the worst he could do to her? Kill her? So he'd beat the disease to the punch. Big deal. It was laughable.

"Don't you recognize her, Damien? I'll admit, it's tough with her skin white as candle wax and her eyes glazed over like that. Still, her hair is the same. Tangled, but basically the same. She was an actress, you know. At least, she wanted to be."

His grip tightened. "What kind of sick prank are you trying to—"

"You *do* remember her. Good. It's no prank, Damien. Tawny Keller is dead. She died in her bed, a few hours after she performed for the last time, as your audience volunteer."

His gaze narrowed. His grip on her arm eased, then his hand fell away. He turned slightly, shook his head.

Shannon reached into the fanny pack again, pulling out several stapled-together pages. "Don't believe it, huh? Well, try this, then." She thrust the papers under his nose. "Medical examiner's report, autopsy results."

His gaze rose to hers again. Anguished. She had the brief sense that he was bleeding inside, but it vanished as fast as it came.

"How did you get these things? Are you a cop?"

She squared her shoulders. "Not a cop, a PI." He hadn't taken the papers, so she tossed them aside. They spread their pages like wings and fluttered to the floor. Silence stretched tight between Damien and her. She didn't want to live it again, didn't want to feel it again. "I found the body." The memory rushed over her, even though she fought it with everything she had. Pounding on Tawny's door. Worried because she hadn't answered the phone, and they always talked first thing in the morning. The door hadn't even been locked. God, she was careless!

Shannon felt a cold hand grip her heart as she recalled walking in, calling, hearing no answer. But she'd known, she'd felt that dread even before she'd entered the bedroom and seen what no one should ever have to see.

She turned to hide the pain from him and paced away. "They're keeping the whole thing quiet. There'd be a circus if the apparent cause of death leaked to the press. But I saw her. I knew. I traded my silence for the photos, the reports. I've worked with this ME before, and he's a stickler for the rule book. He wouldn't have let me have these things if I'd given him a choice." She stared into the darkened fireplace, battling tears and eventually winning. "They threatened to pull my license if I got involved in this, but I don't really give a damn. She was my best friend."

He cleared his throat. "I'm sorry." He'd moved closer to her, stood right behind her now. He must walk like a cat. "But I still don't see—"

She whirled on him, poking his wide chest with a forefinger. "Don't you? She bled to death, Damien. And the only injuries found on her entire body were those two little marks on her throat. You tell me how the hell anyone could do that to her, *and then* you tell me who *you'd* suspect if you were in my shoes."

He closed his eyes as if he were in some kind of physical pain and turned slowly away from her. "It's impossible. There had to be some other injury, or—"

"Read the damned autopsy report if you don't believe me. The cause of death is listed as extreme blood loss. They can't explain it. If this were an upstanding citizen instead of a hooker-slash-actress, they'd be probably call the FBI." She closed her eyes. "But it was just Tawny. Just some nobody who grew up on the streets and did what she had to do to survive. Just my best friend since I was sixteen years old. I'd have never lived to see seventeen if it hadn't been for her."

He said nothing, only stood with his back to her, one hand shielding his eyes.

"The police think I'm crazy. They say there's no evidence to point to you. But I'm *not* crazy. I'm good at what I do, and right now the only goal in my short, miserable life is to get to the bottom of this." She sniffed, and tried to erase the waver from her voice. "I'm trying to track down the woman who volunteered to be your assistant the week before Tawny did. Rosalie Mason. But you know something, Damien? I'm not having much luck. And my gut tells me I'm not gonna find her, or if I do, she won't be in any shape to tell me a thing."

She heard his slow, long sigh. "So, you came here to accuse me of murder. You've done that. Maybe you ought to leave now."

"Rosalie was a prostitute, too, you know." She paced back and forth in front of the fireplace, ignoring his words, going a little faster with every lap. "She attended the show that night with a john. No one's reported her missing. No one wants to talk to the cops about where she might be. They're ignoring the fact that she just isn't around anymore, because no one cared. But it's different with Tawny. Someone cared about her. And I'm not letting this go."

"Go home, Shannon."

His form appeared in front of her, stopping her pattern. She stared up at him.

"So, which is it, Damien? Are you insane enough to believe you *really are* what you pretend to be onstage? Or is this just a publicity stunt? A few vampire killings while you're in town to entice the populace. Oughtta work wonders at the box office." Her brows drew closer as she studied him. "How much did Tawny suffer before you killed her, Damien? Just how the hell did you *do that* to her?"

His anger pounded down at her like a physical force. "What do *you think?*"

If his tone and his threatening stance were supposed to intimidate her into cowering silence, it didn't work. She thrust her chin up and held his gaze. "*I think* this is a pattern. And if I'm right and it holds true, then I'm next in line, aren't I? I'll know for sure, then. And you know something, Damien? I almost hope you do come for me. Because I'll be waiting."

She felt his rage. It seemed to zap and spark in the very air between them. If it did, then it must be wrestling with her own, because she was furious. He hadn't denied a thing.

"Oh, will you?"

"You're damn right I will, and you'd better take me out on the first try, because I won't hesitate. And I never miss."

"Going to shoot me, are you?"

"Blow your head right off your shoulders. I don't know how many other girls you've left lying dead in your wake, but you messed with the wrong one this time. Tawny was my best friend in this world. It ends here. So give it your best shot, magic man. It's gonna be your last one."

She turned away from him, started for the front door, but his hand shot out to grip her arm and he twisted her around to face him again.

"You're not going anywhere."

Her eyes widened, eyes the exact color of very old amber. He felt the rush of dread that passed through her. But she didn't show it, didn't cower or even lower her head. Her golden blond hair framed her face so she looked like an angel. At the moment, a fiercely angry, avenging angel. He opened his mind, deliberately opened it, for the first time in aeons. The bombardment stunned him. He released her, his hands automatically pressing to his temples at the force of all that hit him. Voices, thoughts, emotions, sensations. Thousands upon thousands, pummeling him all at once. Too much. Too many.

He closed his eyes, took a staggering step backward. The noise of countless voices pierced his eardrums. Feelings of pain, pleasure, heat, cold, sickness, exertion, trampled over his body until it vibrated as if electrified. Visions flashed in front of his eyes, blinding him. A thousand scents assailed him, a thousand tastes coated his mouth before he managed to block them out, slamming the door of his mind like the lid of a casket. Closing it, sealing it.

For the love of Inanna! It had been so long since he'd attempted to receive the sensations of others…he'd grown in power, in strength, in the ability to do the trick, and at the same time, neglected the taming of his own abilities. He'd need to work on it, relearn the ways to filtering the vibrations, to home in only on the mind in question.

Which, at the moment, was hers.

He opened his eyes, blinking the room into focus. He was alone. He turned to stare down the short hallway. The door stood wide, with only the night beyond it.

Gone. As if she'd never been there.

Damien closed the door and stood for a moment, still trembling with the aftereffects of the blow he'd just taken. He made himself move back into his comfort room. The haven he'd created for himself. The place he felt the most relaxed. The sunken eyes of the dead woman stared up at him from photos scattered over gleaming black marble floor. The marks on her lily-white throat seemed to taunt, to laugh at him.

You think yourself the enemy of death, Damien? You think wrong. I've won at last, you see? You've surrendered. I own you now.

He lunged forward, snatching the horrible pictures from the floor, falling to his knees in front of the hearth, throwing them down on top of the cold ashes. "I didn't kill her." The words came as if on their own, in a harsh whisper. The face of the once-beautiful young actress stared at him, accusation screaming from the silent depths of her sightless eyes. He focused the beam of his thoughts, and the photo burst into flames. Red-orange tongues danced and licked, spreading to the other photos in the hearth and then to the letter he'd thrown there earlier. Damien watched them burn and wondered what more he could have done to prevent this.

The thirst—the damned need—had grown stronger with every year he'd lived. It raged now like the Bull of Heaven, sent down to wreak the vengeance of the gods on mankind. It was impossible to deny, or to deprive the hunger. Animals no longer sufficed. The cold plastic liquid stolen from blood banks couldn't fill his burning need. He couldn't ignore it.

He'd tried. In fact, he'd made it a ritual of self-torment. Whenever the hunger came, he refused to feed, fought the bloodlust, resisted it until it became all powerful. He'd thought that by resisting it, he'd be the one to grow stronger. It hadn't worked out that way, though. Every time he tried, the lust raged more potent in his veins, until every cell of him screamed for the elixir, until his mind left the realm of his control and he hunted, swathed in a bloodred haze of mindless need.

And even then, he'd thought he'd kept a modicum of restraint. He'd fed only in sips, and only from those women who'd hounded his steps after a performance. The groupies. The ones who slipped uninvited into his dressing room, baring pretty necks and offering themselves to him, sometimes begging him to take them.

Fantasies, he knew. And he'd laugh off their offers, only to appear in their bedrooms—in their dreams—a few hours later. There, twined in their warm, mortal arms, he could sate his roaring lust. And by his simple command, these willing victims would remember the entire exchange as an erotic, pleasure-filled dream. As they drew their first breaths, bathed in sunlight, the marks on their throats would begin to heal. If they noticed the wounds at all, they'd remember a minor accident to explain them. One that had never happened. He thought he'd been so careful. Always leaving them asleep, looking utterly tranquil and contented, having gained as much satisfaction from the exchange as he had.

Had he gone too far? Had that desire inside him overwhelmed him to the point that he'd drained one of them and not even been aware of it? Could it?

That's right, Damien. I've won. You've not only surrendered, you've joined my army. Joined it alongside sickness and war and famine. One of my horsemen now, Damien. An instrument of death.

He moaned in agony and folded his arms around his middle. No one despised the shadow of death more than Damien. No one. Death was his enemy. His greatest foe. If he'd reached the point where feeding his own demon meant feeding death another victim, then he'd end his existence tomorrow. He'd walk naked into the sunrise. He'd...

No.

He straightened his body and stared into the blackened remains of the photos in the hearth. Red still glowed around the edges of the letter, and bits of white showed amid the charred paper. Before he did anything, he needed to learn the truth. If he'd killed, if indeed he had taken a life, then he deserved to surrender his own.

But if not, then there was someone else.

He paced the floor, deep in thought. Someone who, perhaps, wanted the world to believe Damien was guilty.

His steps stopped near the first archway. Someone who was doing it by preying on the women whose blood he'd tasted?

No, how could anyone know that? He would have been aware if anyone had seen him, wouldn't he?

Preying on the women who'd assisted him onstage, then?

His gaze flew to the spot where he'd last seen Shannon.

If he didn't go after her, watch over her, and his theory was on target, her life might very well end tonight.

If he did go after her, as his every instinct was screaming at him to do, and his greatest fears were true... her precious life might end anyway. *Anu,* how could he risk killing someone he wanted only to protect? How could he risk his need for solitude by giving in to the urge to protect her, when his mind was telling him to run in the opposite direction?

What the hell was he going to do?

CHAPTER THREE

The raven soared into the night, its glistening blue black wings spread as it rode the wind, spiraling upward, ever upward. Then, folding those gleaming wings to itself, it dove at dizzying speeds, until anyone watching would have caught his breath in alarm, fully expecting to witness the death of a once-graceful bird. Instead, though, the wings unfurled. The bird slowed, arched upward and, with gentle flapping, alighted upon the rail of a balcony on the twenty-third story.

She slammed the apartment door, turned the lock, shot the dead bolt, fastened the chain. Breathless, she leaned back against the door, closed her eyes. The courage, the defiance, had been flawless right up until he'd grabbed her and told her she wasn't leaving. At that moment, with that iron manacle of a hand gripping her arm, those cold, sure words hanging in the air and those unnaturally gleaming, jewel black eyes holding her captive, she'd felt pure, undiluted panic.

Instantly his image flashed into her mind, a snapshot of the way he'd looked at that moment. What had happened to him? He'd released her all of the sudden, his hands going to his head as if it were splitting in two. His eyes squeezed shut tight in apparent pain.

And she'd run like a rabbit.

She'd climbed over the fence to make her escape, no longer caring how many alarms she set off. Her rope and grappling hook still hung from the monster of an oak tree out front. Her Cat Woman hood probably still lay on his front step. She'd forgotten the photos of Tawny and the autopsy report. She'd forgotten everything except that she didn't want to die. When he'd grabbed her arm and told her she wasn't leaving, she'd thought she was about to.

She squeezed her eyes tighter to prevent the stupid tears that tried to leak through, and shook her head at the bitter irony. Her, running from death. Her, not wanting to die. God, what a joke! Not for the first time, she heard herself cursing fate for its idiotic mistake in choosing Tawny as the victim of this sick killer's whim. It should have been Shannon. Tawny had a future, a life waiting for her. A career. She'd have made it happen, too. Shannon knew she would have. She had a way of willing things to go the way she wanted. Shannon swore and swept a hand over her damp eyes.

It shouldn't have been Tawny. It should have been me. God, why wasn't it me? At least one of us could have gone on, lived, maybe had a family someday....

Blinking, she crawled out of the self-pitying puddle she'd stepped into. If she didn't get herself together, it *would be her.* And it would end any chance she had of bringing Tawny's killer down before her time on this planet ran out. If he was coming for her, it would probably be tonight. Tawny had died the same night she'd volunteered as his assistant. And as far as she could tell, the other woman, Rosalie, hadn't been seen since the night she'd taken her turn in the spotlight. So he would probably come tonight. Probably pretty soon.

She was tired. Damn, but she was tired.

Shannon dipped her hand into the fanny pack for the stubby .38 revolver. It had been with her the whole time she'd been at Damien's. She'd never *really* been in any danger. She could have dropped to one knee, pulled out the little black handgun and pumped all six rounds into him in under three seconds. Sure, it would've been tough to prove self-defense, when she'd broken into his house and he'd been unarmed. So, she'd have done some time.

Not a hell of a lot, though.

She took the gun into the bathroom with her, set it on the little sand-colored counter that surrounded the shell-shaped coral basin. Within easy reach. No one was going to sneak up on her. Not even someone who walked as quietly as he did.

She stripped off her clothes, quickly and not too neatly, tossing them and leaving them where they landed. Then she stepped beneath the hot, pounding spray and just let it soothe her aching muscles. God, it would be good to take a break from all of this. Relax with a good book, or a bowl of popcorn and an old Bogart movie. Jump in the car that often cost her her grocery money and head south until she hit sand and sun, and just bask for a while. But she knew she couldn't. Not now. She'd set the wheels in motion and she had to see things through to the end. There wasn't a lot of time. She was all too aware of that.

Even with Tawny's death and all its repercussions, all the questions screaming for answers, Shannon still couldn't stop her mind from wandering where she least wanted it to go.

Damien Namtar.

The image of him floated into her brain again, damn him. He was a murder suspect. Not to the police, granted. But in her mind he was. Right now he was the *only* suspect. So she shouldn't think about the odd awareness she felt around him, the prickling sensations that encompassed her, the palpable touch of those eyes. "Physical distractions," she muttered, and tipped her head back to let the hot water drench her hair. She inhaled the moist steam, hoping it would put some sense into her head. He was utterly handsome, in a dark, exotic kind of way. Add to that the fact that his performances were always loaded with sexual innuendo, and it was no wonder her libido was responding this way.

Or was it? She'd thought herself immune to sexual desire. She'd had little experience; the clumsy, drunken gropings of the man who was supposed to be her guardian, the foster parent she'd been sent to when she was sixteen. She'd had no choice about going to live there. Orphans, abandoned children didn't have a hell of a lot of choices, and God knows she'd had none to speak of up to that point in her life. Certainly no choice over what that bastard had tried to do to her.

From that day on, though, the choices had been all hers. No one had ever told her what to do again. No one ever would.

Only one good thing had come out of that time in her life, and that was that she'd met Tawny. They'd been sent to the same foster home, from different orphanages. They'd suffered the same abuse, albeit for a short time. They'd fled before the bastard's attempts could lead to the ultimate violation. They'd had little choice. Neither Shannon nor Tawny had trusted authority enough to turn him in then. Whom would they have told? The same pencil pushers who'd sent them to him? And where would they be sent next? Someplace worse?

Later, Shannon had written a letter to the social worker, recounted everything, even signed her name—but she hadn't told them where to find her. She couldn't risk losing control of her own life again.

The results of their brief stay with that man had been totally different. For Tawny, there was no more respect for her body. It became a means to an end, and she used it that way, laughing inwardly at the men foolish enough to pay her for something they could get at home free. Idiots, she'd called them. If they were dumb enough to hand over their hard-earned cash, that was their problem. She'd always said the johns didn't know it, but they were the ones being used.

For Shannon, it was different. She'd made up her mind that she would never want to be touched by a man. Never. She couldn't even think of sex without remembering the disgust, the humiliation, the stench of his breath. How could closeness with any man ever bring her pleasure? She'd shunned Tawny's methods of survival, taken a menial job cleaning hotel rooms, instead.

It had been a long time, though. And for some reason, she wasn't recalling all that revulsion when she thought of Damien. She probably should be.

She sighed and tried to put him out of her mind, but she couldn't. She remembered his performance tonight. Scantily dressed beauties running their hands up and down his body to some frantic jungle beat as he prepared to perform the next feat, seductively touching and caressing him as they fastened chains around him for an escape trick. It was little wonder he had groupies throwing themselves at him. Little wonder he seemed to exude some mystical allure to her. He probably had the same effect on most women, which surely accounted for the gossip she'd read in the fan magazines about the ones who were constantly offering to take him to bed after a show.

The question of the hour was, did he murder them after obliging them? Had Tawny been taken in by his sex appeal and offered herself as others did? It was something Tawny wouldn't have hesitated to do. Was that why he'd killed her?

Or maybe the opposite was true. It might be the ones who seemed indifferent to him that suffered the ultimate punishment. Maybe Tawny had turned him down. Maybe that was why he'd killed her.

But why do it in such a grisly way? And how? How the hell do you drain the blood out of someone, leaving only two tiny wounds in her neck? How do you do it without a drop of blood spilling on the sheets, or the pillows the person is lying on? What the hell do you do with it after you've taken it?

She lathered her body, rinsed it, washed her hair, and still felt no closer to knowing what had happened to her friend.

There had been precious few other cases demanding her attention. She'd referred them to larger investigations firms, hating to have to give away business when she'd fought so long and so hard to get established. But this took precedence, and besides, she wasn't exactly saving up for retirement. It wasn't as if she was going to be spending much money. All she needed was enough for the next few car payments, and another month or two's rent, if that. She wouldn't be taking on any new cases. She kept the office open only for her own case now. And when she found Tawny's killer, she'd close it for good.

She intended to focus solely on Tawny's murder from here on. She couldn't afford a single distraction. She would use every second of the time she had left to—

Dizziness swamped her and she reached out blindly, clutching the shower curtain to keep from falling. She let her body rest against the cool, wet tiles of the shower stall, held her head with one hand and shut the water off with the other. She waited for the vertigo to pass, but it didn't.

Damn! Why now? Why the hell now?

She groped for a towel, twisted it around her and staggered out of the shower, pausing only to clumsily pick up her gun before continuing through to the living room. She had to get to bed, had to lie down, rest until it passed. It would pass. It always did. God willing, the bastard wouldn't show up to kill her before it ran its course.

She needed the bed, and she fought to keep her balance until she got there. She had to huddle into the blankets, because the chills would come next. And then she'd shiver and shake and run a fever until they finished with her. They usually lasted only an hour or so. But they'd been coming more frequently lately. Her body's little alarm clock, reminding her every so often that time was nearly up.

She made it just to the doorway of the bedroom before she collapsed. She felt her legs melt from her ankles to her hips, and then the floor rose up to greet her. She pulled her arms under her to push herself up, but they'd become useless, heavy, nearly impossible to move.

The shaking kicked in. Her body jerked with the chills, and she could hear her own teeth chattering. God, she was so cold. She felt the goose bumps rising on her arms and legs. If she could just get to the bed. She'd always had time to make it to the bed. The damned episodes were hitting faster, harder, than before, she realized, as well as more often. She didn't want to think about what that meant.

But why the hell did it have to happen tonight?

Concentrating fiercely, she managed to tighten her hand around the gun, though the effort cost her. She broke into a cold sweat, fought to catch her breath. She couldn't lose the gun. She had to cling to it in case he came for her. He'd kill her if he found her defenseless like this. God, she hated being helpless, weak, not in control of her own body. She focused on the feel of the cold wood grips in her hand, made herself feel the trigger, kept her mind on where the barrel was pointed, even as she strained to make her arms function and struggled to pull her shuddering body across the floor. Every muscle in her throbbed and ached in protest, burned with an unseen fire. Then the damned convulsions tried to tear them from the bone.

Someone bent over her, lifted her, and a familiar scent invaded her awareness. Dusky. Subtle. Somehow erotic. The arms around her, the chest against her, felt familiar and warm and hard. She forced her eyes open, tried to focus her vision, but saw only a blurred outline. It didn't matter. She knew perfectly well who held her, who carried her across the room and lowered her to the bed. Covers were tugged over her, tucked tightly around her. The electric blanket she'd so recently purchased for just this kind of occasion was plugged in, turned on. She knew, because she felt it begin to heat her chilled skin. He gently worked the gun out of her trembling hand and set it aside. His hands, those big, hard, magic hands with their long, elegant fingers, pushed her hair away from her face.

"Do you want me to call an ambulance, Shannon?"

She heard the words, heard that soft voice, which had been harsh the last time he'd spoken to her. It was still like velvet music on her ears, but so gruff now. So hesitant.

She tried to form an answer, gave up and shook her head, instead. Even that small effort took every ounce of energy she could summon.

"Your family, then?"

"N-noo. There's ... no one."

"What is it? What's wrong with you?" The low, level timbre of his voice seemed to have deserted him. He spoke quietly, as if he might hurt her ears if he used his normal tone. She felt the strength of his hands on her shoulders. The warmth of them. The pressure of each fingertip, pressing urgently into her flesh.

Fear tried to make itself heard in her mind, but there was too much else there in the way. She knew, somehow, that she ought to be afraid of him right now, but she wasn't. And it had to be because of the illness. It must be dulling her intellect, or she'd be scared to death.

The electric blanket's heat seeped a little more deeply into her body. The shaking slowed. The chills eased, just a bit, but left that aching that made her feel as if a steamroller had just mowed her down. She felt his weight leave the bed, heard his steps.

God, she was so groggy when these spells came. Why hadn't he killed her yet? Where was her gun? Why wasn't she screaming for help, or reaching for the phone or dragging herself to the door?

He returned, the bed sinking when he sat on its edge. Pills touched her lips. Then cool water. She swallowed as he held her head up, his long fingers curled around the back of her neck, threading up into her hair.

"Ibuprofen," he told her. "For the pain and the fever."

She nodded. He lowered her to the pillow again. The shaking eased further.

"Better?"

Her eyes could not stay open, no matter how she strained to look at him, to see what he was thinking, what he'd do next, whether there was murder in his jewel black eyes.

"You care to tell me how you planned to take on a crazed killer in this kind of shape?"

He sounded angry. She wondered why.

"Did-didn't . . . plan this."

"Is it better? Is it easing?"

She started to fall asleep, only to feel his hands tighten on her shoulders and lift her from the pillows.

"Tell me!"

Her eyes flew wide. Here it was, her fogged mind told her. The end. And they'd find her in the morning the way she'd found Tawny. Drained of her blood, lily-white, eyes staring sightlessly at the ceiling. Dying of one of these attacks didn't seem so terrible when she considered the alternative.

She had to do something. She focused her mind, the strength of every muscle, into one small act to save herself. One all but limp hand swung outward, toward the nightstand. That was where he'd put her gun, wasn't it? She connected with the lamp and heard it crash to the floor.

He stilled, then gently lowered her back down to the pillows. Her vision was clearing. She saw his black eyes search her face, saw him reach out. Then his hand was pressing something hard and cold into hers.

"This what you're after?"

She closed her fist around the cool wood grips, breathed again.

He pushed a hand through his dark hair. "Keep it, if it will ease your mind, Shannon. But I didn't come here to kill you."

She drew the handgun close to her chest, covered it with her other hand, relaxed a little. The barrel pointed in his general direction. Her finger just barely touched the trigger. Her eyelids drooped. She popped them open again.

"It is getting better, isn't it?"

She nodded. "What...why are you here?" Her voice was slurred, as if she'd been drinking. "If you d-didn't come to kill me, then why..." Her lids tried to close. She fought to keep them open. It was getting harder.

He smiled a little. "You can barely stay awake. It's all right, Shannon. Sleep a while."

"No. Not...until you...you leave..." She licked her lips, forced her gaze to fix on him, to get her message across. "Get the hell out."

Damien had seen her eyes spit golden fire at him. And for just a second she'd reminded him of his oldest friend, the only man who'd ever had the nerve to stand up to him, and he smiled.

She was afraid, but she had the courage of Inanna. She saw him as a demon, but she challenged him to battle. Much as he'd once done. She was like him. And like Enkidu.

Damien licked his lips, hearing the ragged, shallow way she breathed as her body surrendered to sleep's unstoppable invasion.

The demon he'd once sought to vanquish had been death itself. But fighting death was a sad exercise. Death always won in the end. Hadn't he searched endlessly for the key to immortality, only to find, instead, a perpetual living death?

He did not want to do it. With the will of every second of his nearly six thousand years, he did not want to do it. But he left the bedside, went to the little bathroom and dampened a cloth with cool water. He brought it back to bathe her heated face, her sweat-slick forehead, her fiery-hot neck. He'd keep an all-night vigil, not out of affection or even a passing fondness, but out of simple decency, and in a sort of remembrance.

The sight of her burning up with fever, shaking helplessly on the bed, brought back the worst moment of his existence, when he'd watched his best friend die in such a similar way. He'd felt so helpless then. Crying out to the gods for mercy, only to have them answer in vengeance.

He reminded himself that Shannon was not his friend. She was a stranger. And these were not death throes racking her slender body, but simple fever chills. Already they were easing.

"Don't . . ."

He glanced sharply down at her, but she wasn't talking to him. At least, he didn't think so. "It'll help the fever," he told her, and settled the cool cloth on her forehead again.

"Don't touch me." She whimpered, and twisted in the bed. "Tawny, make him stop!"

Fat tears rolled down her face, and Damien couldn't help the lump that came into his throat when he saw them, though he knew it was stupid, senseless. He didn't care about this woman.

He touched her face. "It's all right, Shannon. No one's going to hurt you."

It shocked him when her small hand shot upward to cover his where it rested on her cheek.

"Don't leave me," she whispered. "I'm so afraid . . ."

She wasn't talking to him. She was asleep, still burning up with a fever and half out of her head. She was dreaming. *She was not talking to him.*

Even so, he knew he'd stay with her. How could she possibly defend herself in this kind of state? If it was true that some maniac was preying on the women who'd assisted him onstage, then she was in danger.

He did not want to believe that was possible. And yet, part of him did. Because if someone else hadn't killed that other one, it must have been him. *And it couldn't have been him.*

He barely recalled her face. There'd been so many over the centuries, so many who'd sated his eternal hunger. Young, beautiful, all too ready to sink with him into a well of ecstasy. But he'd never killed them. Never. He *hated* death.

He forced himself to remember Tawny. She'd come to his dressing room after the performance. She'd slid her warm palms slowly over his chest and stood on tiptoe to kiss him. And she'd tucked a piece of paper into the waistband of his pants before she'd slipped away. Her address. And he'd known he would visit her there. The bloodlust that night had reached the height of its power. He couldn't fight it anymore. He'd fought it through the entire evening, forcibly wrenching himself from the luscious dancers who were his assistants in the act. Dragging his gaze away from their pulsing jugulars time and time again, as the roar in his mind grew deafening, and the hunger writhed inside, and his will weakened.

So he'd gone to her. She'd been half-asleep in her bed, and he'd awakened her with a kiss, but never spoken a word. She'd stripped away her nightgown and pulled him down to her in the rumpled sheets, hidden by the darkness of midnight. And as he'd pierced her body with his, as he'd assuaged the burning hunger at her throat, as he'd reached the precipice of blinding, urgent desire, there was that instant of insanity. That single heartbeat in time when he was no longer inside his mind.

And when he'd pulled away from her he'd felt the same flood of guilt he always felt. He'd stared down at her lying still, sinking into sleep. He'd pulled blankets over her, and silently commanded she recall the experience as nothing but a dream. Then he'd fled into the night, his conscience too raw to stay there another second.

Now he paced, beside the bed of another beautiful woman, Tawny's friend and would-be avenger. And he questioned the accuracy of his own mind. She *had* been sleeping when he'd left her there, hadn't she? Or had she been dying? Was there a chance he'd taken too much, that he'd snuffed out a young life? He'd believed the spark of decency that his soul still had left wouldn't allow him to sink to that level. And he knew, beyond doubt, that he did have a modicum of decency left. If he didn't, he wouldn't be here with Shannon right now. He'd leave her to whatever fate had in store and save himself the anguish of starting to care. It was a big risk. He knew that more every time he looked at her.

He pushed the golden blond hair away from Shannon's face, felt the silken texture of it between his fingers, against his palms. He'd make sure the threat to her was eliminated, even if he himself turned out to be that threat, and then he would run to the farthest reaches of the globe and never, *never* set eyes on her again. Never so much as *think* of her again. And he'd do it without letting himself care about her. Damien Namtar cared for no one. It had been that way for centuries, and that was the way it would stay.

He could see, though, that he had little choice except to try to find out what had happened to Tawny Keller. For if he *had* become a man who could no longer exist without taking the lives of others, he knew he had to end it.

All of these things circled like a cyclone in his mind as he sat with her, watched over her, took care of her. He was doing exactly what he'd sworn he'd never do. Taking on the roll of protector to one of the Chosen. Acting on impulses that were purely physical, instinctive, like a goose flying south in autumn.

It was only as dawn approached that he realized he couldn't leave her there alone, unprotected.

Anthar watched that building and a smile curved his lips. Just before dawn, the being once called part man, part god came out, carrying the woman in his arms. Unconscious? Or asleep? Perhaps entranced? Whatever, it didn't matter. The pagan had come to care for someone . . . again. He rubbed his hands together in glee. It was too perfect. Too utterly perfect. Ah, the destruction of Gilgamesh—soul and body, mind and spirit—was at hand. At last, the tools to carry it out had been given. He'd awaited them long, but patiently. For it was not possible to completely demolish a man who cared for no one. The caring, that was the key . . . the weakness.

As long as it truly *was* caring.

Anthar dared not attempt to read the pagan's thoughts, lest he tip his hand. It was vital he remain undiscovered, unknown, unsensed, as he observed Damien's every move. He had to be sure before he could proceed.

A test, then. Or several. Whatever was necessary to be sure. And then the slow torture and ultimate destruction would begin.

CHAPTER FOUR

She awoke feeling as if she'd been in a fight with a freight train and had lost. Her head throbbed. Her body ached. Her throat had been scrubbed with steel wool. Her tongue had doubled in size and dehydrated. She squeezed her eyes tighter against the shimmer of sunlight that glowed red against her lids, and burrowed more deeply into the big downy pillow. Its satin case caressed her cheek. When she inhaled, her lungs filled with potpourri-tinged air. She hugged the luxuriant, fluffy comforter more closely around her—

Her eyes opened wide. She stilled utterly as a snowball of foreboding rolled up and down her spine. This was not her bed. She'd never owned white satin sheets or a down-filled comforter. She rolled onto her back, sitting up and blinking until her bleary eyes focused. This was not her room, either. The black lacquered headboard, the huge matching dresser with its gold trim, the little copper potpourri pot, simmering over a white candle on the stand near her head. None of this was hers.

"What in hell..." She tossed the covers aside and got up. Plush white pile hugged her bare feet, enveloped her toes. She blinked and shook off this through-the-looking-glass sensation. The room was a triangle, and the tall, gleaming black door opposite her was its point. Where on earth was she? For the briefest second she wondered if she'd died and proceeded on to some waiting room between heaven and hell. But that wasn't it. That couldn't be it. She felt too damned miserable to be dead.

She went to the door, gripped the knob, twisted. It refused to budge. She jiggled it, tugged again and pounded on the wood. "Hey, what's going on? Let me out!" Her heart pattered harder as she awaited a response that didn't come. Only silence. A heavy, smothering silence that closed in around her like a shroud. She willed her pulse to slow, pushed a hand through her hair, tried to calm herself. It wasn't a dream. She was sure she was awake. Okay. So what happened?

The memory of the night before returned slowly, but clearly. She'd had an episode. A bad one, worse than any so far. And then Damien had been there. A slow breath worked its way into her lungs. She'd been afraid he'd come to kill her. But he hadn't. He'd actually... he'd tried to help.

"Yeah, some help. As soon as I was out cold, he kidnapped me." She glanced around the room, having no doubt it was somewhere in Damien's modern-day palace. The guy must have something against plain old square rooms. She walked the perimeter, flinging open the door in one angled wall and seeing a triangular bathroom. The door in the opposite wall revealed a triangular closet. Actually, the whole thing *would* have been a square if the three rooms hadn't had walls dividing them.

The huge bed, black lacquer like every other piece of furniture here, reclined like a decadent goddess in the center of the triangle's base. Tall narrow windows stood sentry duty on either side of it, their livery, black satin, held apart by white bows. She parted the luxurious drapes and glanced outside to confirm her suspicions. The tall fence she'd scaled the night before stood watch in the distance. Sloping roofs, at varying heights, loomed at right angles, and the vine-covered brick walls were familiar.

It was his place, all right. And the window was no good as an escape route. Looked as if she was at least three stories up, with nothing but sheer wall and the grassy ground, carpeted in decaying autumn leaves, below her. The sun was low. She'd slept most of the day.

"Damn him." Shannon jerked the drape back into place, and stalked back to the bathroom in search of a way out. A hidden door. A heating duct. Anything.

Nothing. Just gleaming porcelain, glittering chrome and sinfully thick terry cloth. Spotless. Expensive. The hot tub was big enough to hold the Democratic National Convention inside. And the robe that hung from the wall was...wait a minute, that was *her robe!*

Charging back into the bedroom, she yanked open the door of the closet, only to see more of her clothes hanging neatly inside. A pair of jeans, a button-down blouse, her brown suede jacket. Her favorite running shoes stood innocently on the floor. Her purse perched on a shelf.

"That son of a—what the hell does he think he's doing?" She paced back toward the bed, and that's when she saw the picnic basket on the floor beside it. She narrowed her eyes, moved cautiously closer, flipped it open. A pile of fruit. She looked closer, lifted the other lid. A half-dozen assorted muffins. A thermos bottle. A sugar bowl. Her stomach rumbled. Part of her wondered if he'd put something into the food. Another part wondered why he'd bother. If he'd wanted to hurt her, he'd had his chance last night.

She disliked this situation. Everything in her rebelled against it, and if she'd cared to analyze herself this morning, she would know why. Her choices had been taken away. It was almost as bad as if she were a child, a ward of the state, again. She was not in control of anything at this moment. *He* was. He'd brought her here without her consent, locked her in for some insane reason, chosen the clothes she'd wear today, the food she'd eat for breakfast, the soap she'd use in the damned shower.

When she saw the bastard again, she would probably kill him.

In the meantime she was starved. The hell her body had been through last night had drained her. And while he had chosen the food, it was entirely up to her whether or not to eat it.

She threw caution to the wind and reached for a muffin, then the thermos, praying it held good, strong, ultracaffeinated coffee.

It did, piping hot. Aromatic steam rolled from the brew as she poured. It tasted even better than it smelled.

She looked around the room again, shaking her head in frustration. "I don't know what you're up to, Damien, but you aren't going to get away with it."

Damien had decided there were only three possibilities. One, that he'd lost control of his own mind, that he'd become the harbinger of death, his hated enemy. Two, that there was another vampire hunting the streets of Arista. Or, three, that an ordinary mortal with a twisted mind was responsible for the killings, and for some sick reason, wanted them to look like the work of a vampire. Though *how* any human could manage it, he still couldn't guess. The killer might be someone who wanted Damien to be blamed for *his* kills. If that was the case, then Shannon was in grave danger. And much as Damien had sworn never to do it, he was inclined to protect her. The blood ties, damn them straight to hell, were impossible to ignore. He could hate the instinct all he wanted, but he couldn't resist it. No more than a human can resist the gravitational pull of the earth, and go floating off into never-never land. He had no choice, no matter how he looked at it. And he resented the intrusion on his solitude.

"The lady's awake, sir."

Damien pulled himself from his ponderings to glance up. The deck of cards he'd been shuffling went still in his hands. Netty tilted her small head to one side and the other, like a little, curious bird. He forced a smile, and her face crinkled with her answering one. She had the frail build of a music-box dancer, and the temperament of a saint. Where else would he ever find someone to take care of the everyday needs of this place, to deal with the repairmen and the gardeners and the salesmen, to put up with his bizarre hours and strange requests, all without question or complaint? What the hell would he do when death crept up to claim Netty?

"Thank you, Netty." He pursed his lips, wondering what he'd say to Shannon when he went up the stairs.

"Been awake for quite a while, now. Pacin'. Nervous-like."

Her head tilted again, and he knew she'd like nothing better than an explanation for the unheard-of circumstance of a stranger, much less a woman, in the house. She'd never lower her proper British ways enough to pry, though, no matter how curious she was.

"You left the food for her?"

"Oh, yes. Sleepin' like the dead, she was, when I went in. Lovely thing, don't you think? All that angel's hair spread around her—"

"You can go now, Netty. You're through for the day."

She bit her lip, bobbed her head and hurried from the room with quick little steps. Seemed wherever she went, Netty was always hurrying. He heard the back door, then the motor of her car.

He stiffened his spine and glanced toward the staircase. He didn't have to open his mind or try the trick of scanning hers to feel the fury emanating from Shannon. It was palpable. It filled every recess of the house, and all of it was directed toward him.

He sighed heavily, cut the deck one-handed, then fanned the cards facedown on the table. With exaggerated grace, he extracted four cards and flipped them over. Four aces. One more card trick to add to the repertoire. He grimaced as he rose and started for the stairs.

When he reached the door, he paused, startled to realize there was something warm surging like a South Sea tide in his belly. Anu forbid, he was looking forward to seeing her! That worried him. "She's nothing to me," he whispered, willing his mind to remember it. "Nothing."

He freed the lock with his mind and stepped inside. The first thing that hit him was the clean, moist smell of her. She'd bathed. He could feel the steam in the air, smell the water drying on her skin, almost taste it. Her hair was still damp, curling at the ends. She wore jeans and a green button-down cotton shirt. She was in the process of rolling the sleeves, when she whirled to face him. The fact that she hadn't fastened a single button didn't seem to faze her in the least. Her amber eyes flashed gold and her jaw went taut beneath the smooth skin. There were glistening droplets still clinging to her lashes.

"It's about time you showed up. Just what the hell do you think you're doing, bringing me here! Locking me in! That's unlawful imprisonment, mister, and I can tell you, you'll find yourself in a cell the minute I—"

She broke off, glancing down, apparently having finally noticed where his gaze was focused. The frilly white edges of the bra caressed the mounds of flesh they cupped like adoring fingers, and he couldn't for the life of him look away. She was beautiful. He hadn't taken the time to really appreciate feminine beauty in too long. He satisfied his needs in darkness, with hurried encounters and no words exchanged. He realized just what an oversight that had been, as he traced her flat belly, the dark well of her navel, the swollen curves of her breasts, with his eyes. He stared long and hard at the darker circles at their centers, just visible through the white material. Their peaks came alert as he stared and he felt the razor-edged blade of desire run him through.

She turned her back to him, buttoning up. "I want a phone. I'm calling a cab and then I'm getting the hell out of here, and when I get back to my apartment, I'll probably call a cop."

He said nothing, just watched her. She tucked the shirt-tails into the jeans before facing him again. "Well?"

Her cheeks were pink with rage and her eyes sparkled. Her breaths came a little too fast, and her fists were clenched.

"You look a lot better. How do you feel?"

She threw her hands in the air, rolled her eyes. "Fine. Perfect. Where the hell's that phone?" She walked past him, through the door and into the wide hallway. She looked up and down it, obviously not sure which way to go.

"Do those attacks come often?"

She started, as if she didn't know he'd walked along behind her. "None of your business. Which way is the phone?"

"Answer my questions and I'll take you to it."

If her eyes could shoot daggers through his heart, they would have. When she spun on him again her hair flew out around her like a wet halo, spraying his heated face. "Why did you bring me here last night?" Her eyes widened slightly for just an instant as the obvious answer occurred to her. "I was unconscious, wasn't I? Did you *do anything* to me?"

"Shannon, for God's sake, I don't go around molesting delirious women. I brought you here because I was afraid to leave you alone. You were sicker than hell. I'd have called some of your family to take care of you if I'd known where to reach them. But I didn't, so I decided to do it myself.''

"I don't have any family." Her eyes narrowed to slits as she studied him.

"It's happened before, hasn't it?"

"Once or twice." She turned her back on him, started down the hall in the wrong direction.

"How often?"

She shrugged. "What's it to you, anyway?" She stopped a few yards away, turned and came back, apparently deciding to go the other way.

When she passed him, he took her arm, walked beside her. "Nothing," he reminded himself. "Absolutely nothing. The phone is downstairs, but you don't need it. I'll drive you anywhere you want to go."

She blinked up at him, pausing in their trek toward the stairway, which was now in sight. "You will? I mean . . . you're not going to try to . . ." Her gaze fell to the floor and she shook her head.

"What did you think—that I was holding you prisoner?"

She met his gaze, her own flashing again. "You locked me in."

"There was a reason." He started down the stairs, led her through the narrower hall to the second staircase and then down that. When they finally emerged on the first level, he guided her into his oval library, waved her toward a leather sofa.

She stiffened, remaining in the doorway. "What is this? I said I wanted out."

"Shannon, when you broke in here and asked for ten minutes, I gave it to you. I'm only asking you to return the favor."

Her head tilted to one side, a wary animal sizing up its chances with a predator. She didn't trust him. She had good instincts.

"You can leave whenever you want to. I won't stop you. There's a phone on the desk over there." He pointed. She looked, licked her lips, nodded.

"All right. Okay. Ten minutes. No more."

No more. Unfortunately for both of them, there was going to be more. A lot more. And he'd keep her with him by force if he had to. But first he'd try to talk her around to his way of thinking.

And he'd pray he wasn't worthy of all her fear.

Why the hell did she agree to sit here and listen to him? The guy could talk her into buying swampland in the desert if he applied himself. There was something about him . . .

She walked into the library, took a look around. The room's shape came as no surprise. The curving walls were lined with books, most of them old-looking, with that wonderful, slightly musty smell that old books always have. The sofa and chairs were rich brown leather. New. Their aroma mingled with that of the books, and that more subtle scent that was distinctly Damien.

She glanced over her shoulder at him. He stood right where he'd been before, watching her intently. It was his eyes—that's what it was. They were so huge and deep and expressive. So dark. Combined with the tenor song of his mellow voice, they were compelling.

"So, talk," she said, trying to sound callous, wishing she felt that way. She didn't want to think maybe she'd been wrong about him. She didn't want to let her defenses down. And she sure as hell wasn't going to trust the man. She didn't trust anyone. She and Tawny...they'd trusted no one but each other.

"What was that?" His sable brows rose slightly, and his jet eyes probed. He came toward her, then stopped.

"What?"

"You looked..." He licked his lips, shook his head. "Nothing. Never mind. It's none of my business."

"Probably not." She turned and ran her fingers over the dusty spines, glanced at titles. *Sumerian Mythology, The Gods of the Ancients, The Epic of Gilgamesh...*

"I know you think I killed your friend. But since I know myself better than you do, I'm inclined to disagree."

He came up behind her as he spoke. Too close. She felt his nearness like static electricity, raising the fine hairs on the back of her neck. She tried to focus on the titles instead of on the physical effects of being so close to him. A newer volume about Gilgamesh. And another. He had several versions of the same story.

"That in mind, I have to assume someone else is responsible for her murder. If I'm right, then you're at risk."

"*If you're right?* Sounds like *you're* not even convinced you're innocent." She turned in time to see him blink when she said it, as if she'd poked a raw spot.

"I thought you might be in danger. That's why I followed you home last night. That's why I brought you here when I saw that you were too sick to defend yourself. I was only trying to protect you."

She met his gaze, fighting to keep her own hard, not let it soften the way her heart had begun to do at those last few words. She swallowed hard. In all her life no one had ever thought to protect her. No one had cared enough to. She'd had no shelter against the cruel realities of life. She'd had to face them all, head-on, and her only protection had been her own strength. "Yeah? Why should I believe that? You barely know me, why would you want to protect me?"

"What was the alternative, Shannon? Stay here and let you die? Read about your body being found in the headlines of tonight's paper?"

"Tonight's, tomorrow night's...what's the difference?" *Someone* would be finding her body one of these days. After this last attack, she figured it wouldn't be much longer.

He frowned, his gaze probing so deeply she had to turn away. "What do you—"

"Look, I have to go. Is there anything else you want to say before I do?"

"If you go, and there *is* a killer stalking you, you'll be defenseless."

"I've been called a lot of things, Damien. Never defenseless, though."

"Shannon—"

"If I stay here, he won't try anything." She squared her shoulders, lifted her chin. "If he doesn't try anything, I won't be able to take him out. You get it?"

He blinked twice, understanding dawning in his black eyes. His hands went to her shoulders. Strong hands. Hard and warm and urgent. The urge to lean closer whispered across her mind. Stupid. She must still be slightly off kilter from last night.

"You *want* him to attack you."

"You're damned right I do."

"That's insane. You'll get yourself killed." He appeared shaken by the idea.

"It's perfectly sane from my point of view. And so what if I do? I'll take the bastard with me."

"You're risking your life—"

"It's not so much to risk. Let go of me."

He looked down at his hands, as if he hadn't been aware of the way they'd been holding her shoulders, the way they'd begun to pull her just a little closer. The way that scared the hell out of her, because she'd been thinking about getting closer to him. Wondering what would happen if she slipped her arms around his muscled neck and leaned against his broad chest. Would he hold her closer, harder? Push her away? Murder her?

His hands fell to his sides. He lifted his ebony gaze to hers. "What do you mean by that? That it's not much to risk?"

Fears crept up on her. She battled them away. She wouldn't talk about it. She wouldn't think about it. And she damned well wouldn't cry about it. Her eyes burned, but she blinked them cool again. What was so bad about death? *Life* hadn't exactly been a walk in the park. "I'm leaving now. You said you'd let me go. So let me go."

"I'm sorry, Shannon. But I can't."

The rush of anger was a welcome relief after the other things she'd been feeling. "I *knew* I couldn't believe a word you said!" She brought her fist into his middle clean and fast and hard, smiling smugly when he staggered backward, doubling over. She turned and ran toward the doors.

"Stay put, damn you!" The doors thundered shut as if a gale force wind had driven them. She felt her eyes bulge, the shivering up the back of her neck, the tensing of her spine.

She turned very slowly. He was just unbending himself, one hand pressed to the spot where she'd hit him. He looked angry. "How did you—"

"I'm a magician, remember?" He grunted, standing straight again.

"The—the house is rigged?"

"Something like that."

"You can't keep me here."

"I'm not going to let you get yourself killed. Believe me, Shannon, I don't like this any more than you do. But until this threat is removed, I'm your shadow. Whither thou goest and where thou lodgest and all that. I'll be there." He shook his head slowly, as if he'd just reached a decision and wasn't at all pleased about it.

"That's bull. You're up to something. You want something from me. Might as well put it on the table, Damien. I'm not buying what you're selling."

He licked his lips and the action drew her gaze, sent hot images sizzling into her mind. His kisses. God, what would they feel like? The thought seared her from the inside out.

"I need to see her body," he said at last.

She blinked, and dragged her attention away from his mouth. "You what?"

"I want to see your friend."

Shannon's stomach clenched like a fist. "For God's sake, why?"

He averted his eyes, paced back and forth in front of the bookshelves. "I have to see for myself how she died."

She blinked again, a cold foreboding settling in her heart. "What do you think you can tell by seeing her? Do you have any knowledge of forensic pathology? Have you ever studied death, Damien?"

His head came up, eyes level with hers, and she thought there couldn't have been more pain in them if she'd shot him through the heart. "All my life," he whispered.

"I must be insane." Her voice was near his ear, a harsh rasp as they crouched in the shrubbery near the rear entrance of Arista's medical examiner's office. "I've been calling every day to try and get her body released for burial. They keep putting me off, saying there are still more tests to be run. They wouldn't even let me see her." She parted a tangle of branches and peered through.

Damien snagged her waist with his arm and pulled her down beside him again. She was noisy and in constant motion. Clandestine surveillance could never have been one of her strengths as a private investigator. "Sit still," he warned.

But then he had trouble following his own advice. His arm remained around her tiny waist, despite his mind's commands that it move away. Her right side pressed tight to his left one. He could feel the softness of her breast, the curve of her hip, the firmness of her thigh against his. This was insanity.

"I didn't think anyone would be here so late," she said, as if their closeness had no effect on her at all. "What are they doing?"

A shiny black hearse with a government emblem on the sides, and the letters "DPI" in bright yellow paint, backed up to the door. The driver emerged, walked around the vehicle and opened the back. Shannon stiffened beside Damien. "They're moving her!"

He tightened his hold on her. "It could be anyone, Shannon."

She shook her head hard, meeting his gaze, her own tortured. Then her head swung forward again, as the office door opened. Two men pushed a gurney out into the night, stopping behind the hearse.

"That's the ME." Shannon nodded toward the shorter, pudgy one who wore the white lab coat. The other man was taller, elegant in his movements, solidly built and darkly attractive. He wore an expensive gray suit and a long black wool coat.

"You'll rule it a suicide," he told the medical examiner. His voice carried the ring of authority.

"There's still the PI that found that body—"

"We'll be in touch with her. Don't worry. We've dealt with situations like this before." The driver and the ME collapsed the gurney and lifted the vinyl-encased body up into the hearse, while the tall man stood with his hands thrust into his coat pockets, watching. His breath made little steam clouds that hid his face. He exuded confidence.

The ME walked back inside, shaking his head and muttering, as the driver slammed the doors. Then the two got into the front seat and the vehicle moved away.

Shannon was shaking all over. "Where are they taking her? They can't just take her away like this. Dammit, Damien, let go of me!"

He held her tighter. She kept struggling until the hearse rolled out of sight, and then it was as if the fight went out of her. She felt limp. Her head lowered to his chest and her hot tears dampened his skin. She clung to him with one hand and rained painless blows on his shoulder with the other. "You should have let me stop them."

He threaded his fingers in her hair, moved his palms over it again and again. He knew this pain. He knew just what she felt right now, what she'd felt since her friend's death. Too well. Maybe that was another reason for this closeness he had to keep fighting. The grief. The shared pain.

He held her for a long time while she cried. He hadn't had a chance to look at the body, but he'd been close enough. He'd lowered the walls around his mind for an instant, just long enough to focus on the dead woman. He needed to practice more, to hone his mind better. But he had managed to understand one thing. Tawny Keller's death had been brought about by a vampire.

Damien still wasn't certain if that vampire was him.

Shannon straightened, swiped her eyes so hard it must have hurt her. "Something's going on, Damien. Those men were feds or something—the ME wouldn't lie about a cause of death unless he had no choice. I know that. He's a suit, but an honest one."

Damien nodded his agreement, but was as baffled as Shannon. "I don't understand this any more than you do...unless..."

Her head came up sharply. "Unless what?"

He shook his head. "I was going to say, unless they actually believe in the existence of vampires, but that's unlikely, isn't it?"

She shrugged and looked away. But Damien wondered. If he hadn't kept himself so closed off from others of his kind, he might know more. Was the federal government aware of their existence? What in hell was this DPI?

Shannon touched his arm. "I want to go home. Take me home now."

He saw her clearly in the darkness, her red, swollen eyes, the track of each and every tear she'd shed, burned into her pale ivory flesh. "You'd be safer at my house, I think."

She shook her head so hard her hair flew. "I can take care of myself. Take me to my place or I'll go somewhere and call a cab. It's up to you." She sniffed loudly.

He helped her to her feet, encircled her shoulders with his arm and walked with her around the building to the sidewalk, toward where he'd parked his car. The chilly October breeze whisked over them, and he hoped it cooled her burning cheeks.

"If you insist, I'll take you to your apartment. But you still might be in danger, Shannon. I'll just have to park myself outside the building and try to watch over you from there."

"Sure you will. And pigs will fly, too." She went to the passenger door of his gleaming black car. One of his indulgences. A Jaguar. He liked it, liked driving it fast, liked the new smell of it. When that smell wore off, he'd immediately buy another. He had few enough pleasures in this life.

She opened the door and stood there, staring over the car at him. "So are you gonna drive me, or not?"

"I'm gonna drive you."

CHAPTER FIVE

Damien sat in the car near the front of her apartment building. It wasn't much of a building. Tall, narrow. Too few windows, and fire escapes with huge sections missing. The ugly red bricks looked ready to crumble. The security was nonexistent. It wasn't a slum, but he didn't like the idea of her living here.

She came onto the balcony twice, glancing down at his black car. He shivered a little when she leaned on the iron rail. The damned thing probably wasn't in any better shape than the rest of the place. After that he saw her part the curtains a few times, and he knew she was looking, checking to see if he was still there. Almost as if she expected him to leave.

Maybe she'd be better off if he did.

Damien couldn't bring himself to believe he'd killed those other women, but he couldn't ignore the possibility, either. He didn't know whether this change in his hunger was normal, something every immortal felt with age. He didn't know if others had killed without even being aware of it. Was something like that possible?

He thumped his fist on the steering wheel as the questions tormented him. Traffic and people passed by. Lights in buildings blinked off one by one as this less-than-elite section of Arista went to sleep.

He wished now that he hadn't avoided all contact with others of his kind, wished there were someone he could ask about these things, and about this DPI, whatever it was, and the murder of Tawny Keller. *Damien* ought to know. As far as he was aware, he was the oldest of any of them. He ought to have the answers, but dammit he didn't.

He thought of the letters he'd received from the one who called himself a scientist, Eric Marquand. If anyone could shed some light on all of this it might very well be that young, curious man. Damien grimaced at the idea of asking for help. The very thought of contacting Marquand made him squirm with unease. He'd existed alone, in a vacuum for so long now. His only emotional ties were the safe ones he felt with his crowds of fans. When they stood and cheered for him it was almost as if time melted away, almost as if he were an adored ruler again, a beloved king, basking in the unconditional love and loyalty of his people. It was the adoration of those crowds that had driven him to perform all these years. A man could only do without love, connections, for so long. The audiences gave him enough to sustain him. It was the only love allowed into his solitary life, and it was enough. It had to be enough.

He shook his head slowly. No, he'd try to solve this thing on his own. He'd only use Eric Marquand and his studies of the undead as a last resort. And in the meantime he'd watch over Shannon, keep any harm from coming to her.

A job that would be a lot easier if only he could listen to her mind. The idea of trying it again sent a bolt of phantom pain throbbing through his temples. Still, it was one of the benefits of being who he was. He ought to use every tool he had to solve this puzzle, to keep her safe.

He braced himself, and very slowly, began to lower his defenses to allow the myriad vibrations outside to filter into his mind. He consciously kept a thin veil in place and focused all his energy on her, putting her image firmly in his mind's eye. He tried to attune his senses to hers, to feel what she felt.

For an instant the rush of sensations surrounded him, but he forced himself to bear it. He grated his teeth against the bombardment and concentrated harder. Gradually, the intensity eased, quieted, lightened. He sifted, searched, sent his mind out in search of hers.

She wasn't in the apartment.

He stiffened in his seat as he felt her thoughts. Anger. Alarm. Urgency. Something about her car. She was running...a rear exit. A parking lot.

Damien was out of his car like a shot and speeding around the building. He saw her there, her feet and legs bare and cold in the autumn chill. She wore a short blue nightgown that shimmered like silk, but wasn't, and her hair was pulled up into a bushy blond ponytail that bounced wildly as she ran over the pavement.

He looked in the direction she ran, and saw two young men crouched at the door of a primer brown Corvette that had to be as old as Shannon was. One of the men turned as Shannon approached, and he laughed. She never slowed her pace. The thief started toward her and lifted his hand. Damien saw the tire iron he held. He lunged forward, knowing as he did that he couldn't reach her in time. Already the two stood close, and the man's hand swung down, no doubt about to crush her skull.

But Shannon's small hand shot up and gripped the man's wrist, stopping the tire iron's descent. Her knee jammed hard into his groin, and the man grunted loud, doubled over. The tire iron clanked to the broken pavement. Damien froze for a shocked instant as Shannon spun backward, smacking her heel across the man's chin and laying him flat on his back. It happened in two clicks of a second hand.

The second man turned toward her, pulling a gun from his tattered jeans. Before he leveled its sights on her, she kicked it out of his hand, sending it sailing in an arc and then skittering across the pavement. He swung a fist at her, but she ducked, and when she straightened, she brandished the tire iron the other one had dropped.

He held his hands up in front of him, backing away. "Okay, lady. Okay, you win." As Damien hurried forward, the thug helped his partner to his feet, and the two ran into the darkness. He heard their rubber soles slapping. They didn't go far, though.

He gripped Shannon's arm, still dazed by what he'd seen. "Are you all right?"

She nodded, but didn't say anything, still trying to catch her breath. Damien turned to look at the unpainted car and shook his head. He was going to blast her for risking her life over a hunk of scrap metal, when he heard the unmistakable click of a hammer being pulled back. His head went up, and his piercing night vision showed him one of the two thugs, holding the gun, pointing it at Shannon.

Damien whirled toward her, propelling himself forward just as the blast shattered the night. He felt Shannon hit the ground hard underneath him. And he felt a searing pain burn through him.

Anthar watched as he always watched—witness to every breath the pagan drew—and smiled slowly to himself. The bastard. The insolent, blasphemous bastard. Damien the Eternal. Whatever he called himself now, it didn't matter. He'd be gone, vanquished, destroyed by his own hand. Conquered by his own emotions. And soon.

The thugs whose small minds Anthar had implanted with the notion of stealing the woman's car were bumbling fools, yes. But at least one of them had fired his weapon at her. And the heathen had thrown himself in front of the bullet.

Finally, after endless millennia, the bastard cared for another living soul. Anthar had waited so long, tried so often to hurt him this way. But Damien kept to himself, cared for no one. Not even the women he took on occasion, while Anthar watched from the shadows, his presence so carefully cloaked even Damien couldn't sense him there. Damien drank from those women so gently, so careful not to harm them. Sickening, gutless worm! So tenderly he would use them that Anthar would become convinced there must be some feeling there. But alas, none ever came. When those women had died, Damien the Eternal hadn't even been aware of their passing.

Damn him to everlasting torment!

Ah, but this time would be different. This time there *was* something more. Just the something Anthar needed to hurt him in the most devastating way possible.

But he must proceed with caution.

Damn, but it wouldn't do to take the bitch too soon. He had to test Damien's feelings yet again. He had to be sure the oldest immortal alive would feel the ultimate pain, shame, remorse. . . . He had to be sure.

Another test was in order.

They were gone. He heard them run and then nothing. Damien's body lay heavily on top of Shannon's. She was on her back. He was angled across her chest, his head near her left shoulder.

"They're gone," she said, and shoved at him. "You can get off me now, Damien. I don't know why you came rushing out here like some knight on a charger, anyway. I can take care of my—" She'd pressed her hands to his shoulders to move him off her, and touched the warm dampness seeping through his shirt. He felt the shock that passed through her body. She sucked in a coarse breath. "Damien?"

He moved, but slowly. It hurt to do it. He sat up, and she jumped to her feet, bending over him. His white shirt was stained crimson. He pressed one hand to the front of his shoulder and tried to stand.

Shannon bent to help him, sliding an arm around his waist and holding him firm. "Damn you straight to hell, Damien, you've gone and got yourself shot. What's the matter with you, jumping on me like that?" She walked toward the building's back entrance, pulling him along with her.

He glanced down at her, almost giddy with relief that he'd knocked her out of the way in time. "That gun was pointing toward your head. Was I supposed to stand there and let them shoot you?"

"Yes!" She reached out to open the door, then held it with her hip while she helped him through. "Dammit, you're probably going to bleed to death."

He was not going to bleed to death. Actually, the wound was minor except for the excruciating pain it caused. Debilitating, momentarily paralyzing pain. His shoulder still screamed with it. But he'd expected that. One of the few things he did know about his kind was that sensitivity to pain—to any physical stimulus—increased with age, just as the strength and psychic powers did. As for the tendency to bleed dry, it didn't concern him too much. He could keep pressure on the wound until dawn. It wasn't bleeding all that badly. It would heal with the regenerative sleep. Any injury would.

What did concern him, besides the pain in his shoulder, was the feel of her small arm anchored around his waist. The way she held him tight to her side as they entered the elevator, the urgency in her eyes when she looked up at him. Her smell. Her warmth.

"You're pale. Did it bleed much?"

"I'm always pale. And no, it's nothing."

She narrowed her eyes and stared at the spot where he pressed his hand to the wound. "It's not nothing—it's a bullet. We'll call an ambulance from the apartment."

He shook his head, but studied her determined face, noting the strength in it. "Why did you rush out there in your nightgown, Shannon? Why risk your life, when calling the police would have been just as good?"

"What're you, kidding me? My car would have been long gone by the time the cops got here. Do you know how long and hard I work just to keep up the payments on that car?"

"Corvettes don't come cheap." Not even primer-coated ones whose rust spots had been sanded off, he supposed.

The doors slid open. She tightened her grip on him and started into the hall. "Not just a Corvette. A 1962 Stingray, mag wheels, four barrel carb and an engine that would blow your black Jag's doors off."

He smiled. He couldn't help it, and the pain didn't stop it. "Your dream car?"

"Abso-freaking-lutely. *Nobody* messes with my car."

"I'll keep that in mind."

She stopped outside her apartment door and pushed it open. She hadn't locked it and that bothered him almost as much as the hole in his shoulder, but he refrained from commenting on it. He'd seen firsthand why she kept insisting she could take care of herself. She hadn't done half-badly at it.

She pulled him inside, kicked the door closed, and didn't let go of him until she'd eased him onto the sofa. And when she did, he felt the absence of her touch like another wound in his flesh. She hurried back to the door, locked it. So she wasn't completely careless with her own well-being. Then she knelt in front of him and reached up to tear the sleeve away from his shirt. She tried to push his hand aside so she could look at the wound.

"It's barely a scratch." He kept his hand where it was.

"That's a lot of blood for a scratch, Damien."

"I'm a heavy bleeder. I'll be fine."

She scowled at him. "Hey, you jumped in front of a bullet for me. The least I can do is take a look at it." She reached for the shoulder again.

He ducked her hand. "Oh? Then you're admitting that I probably just saved your life?"

She straightened, propping her fists on her hips. "Yeah, for what it's worth, you probably did."

"At no small risk to my own?" He prompted. She said nothing, but tilted her head to one side. "Well?"

"All right. Okay, I'll give you that much. So what's your point?"

"That I'm not planning your murder, for starters." He got to his feet, not waiting for her reply, and walked to the bathroom. He was a bit weaker than usual, a response to the amount of blood he'd lost. Good thing he'd had the presence of mind to put the pressure on right away. It wouldn't take much to incapacitate an immortal as old as he was.

He closed the door behind him. One place he did not want to spar with Shannon Mallory was in her bathroom, where mirrors abounded. But he felt her presence there, even though he'd locked her out. It was in the still-damp towel slung over the shower-curtain rod. And in the clothes she'd been wearing earlier, in a little heap on the floor. And in the scent she favored. Subtle. Not floral or fruity. More enticing than that. Herbal. Like exotic incense or some rare spice. It clung to everything, even the air was tinged with it.

He opened the cabinet and tried to put her out of his mind and focus on the matter at hand, namely applying something to the wound to staunch the blood flow until dawn. He'd sit with his hand on it for the next few hours if necessary, but he'd prefer not to.

There. A roll of gauze. Some adhesive tape. A hairbrush with a few honey gold strands catching the light and glowing at him. It was like a halo around her, that hair of hers. Like something unreal. "Angel hair," Netty had called it.

Dammit, stop thinking about her!

He peeled the shirt away from his chest, tearing it so he didn't have to ease the pressure on the wound. He tossed the ragged, blood-spattered white garment into her wastebasket. One-handed, he wrestled the little cardboard box open and dumped a pile of gauze pads into the sink.

She thumped the door. "Are you all right?"

"Fine, Shannon. Relax."

"Let me in. I want to help."

"I'll be out in a minute."

"Damn you, Damien—"

"You're repeating yourself, Shannon." He didn't think the gauze pads would be enough, and glanced around for something more substantial to pack the wound. "Tell me something, will you? Why didn't you bring your gun out there with you?"

"Because I'd have killed the little bastards if I had." She pounded on the door again, jarring it. "Open the damn door."

"No."

"Fine, see to yourself. There's a little brown tin in the cabinet. Pine tar. It's made from the sap of pine trees. An old folk remedy. If you're too pigheaded to see a doctor, then at least use some of it. It'll stop the bleeding better than Super Glue."

He frowned. There was a slight trembling in her voice, one that belied the careless way she tried to throw her words at him. He spotted the tin, flipped the top off and sniffed suspiciously at the dark brown goop it held. Piny. Okay, it was worth a try.

"Did you find it?"

He thought she'd walked away, left him to fend for himself. She was still standing on the other side of the door, waiting. "Yes. It looks disgusting."

"Smear it on."

He nodded, dipping two fingers into the stuff, then removing his hand from the wound just a little. The bleeding began again immediately, but he was able to spot the edges of the graze, and pinched them together. Then he smeared the thick, tarlike substance over the wound.

It was almost instant. The blood flow stopped. Cautiously, he eased the pressure of his fingers. But the flesh didn't pull apart. The tar held it sealed tight. He shook his head in wonder.

"Damien? You okay?"

For such an obstinate thing, she was certainly worried about his health. "I'm okay. Your concoction works wonders." He pressed a gauze pad to the wound, wrapped a strip around it and taped it in place. Then he ran a little water in the basin and washed the blood from his chest, his arm, his shoulder, his hands. Only when he'd rinsed every trace of the pinkened water down the drain did he open the door. And when he did, she was still standing there. He couldn't have missed the way her stiff stance relaxed slightly when he stepped out.

Her gaze flew over his face, to his shoulder, back to his face again. He saw her worry, her fear for him, and it touched him in spite of himself. Then her eyes moved downward, over his unclothed chest, lower, to the snap of his pants. Her cheeks colored, and he smiled a little, wishing he had the energy to try to read her thoughts again right now.

"Stupid jerk."

Damien blinked. "Excuse me?"

"You're a jerk, locking yourself in like that. What if you'd passed out in there? Huh? What am I going to do—kick the door in?"

He laughed. She got angrier, so he forced himself not to laugh anymore. "You have a very strange way of showing gratitude, Shannon."

"*Gratitude?* You think I'm *grateful* to you for almost getting yourself killed on my behalf? What're you—dense? You pull any more crap like that and I'll—" She blinked fast, and turned her back on him. Not before he'd seen the moisture gathering in her eyes, though.

Something in his throat expanded, cutting off his airway. He lifted one hand, and without intending to, settled it on her shoulder. Her hair brushed his knuckles and he shivered. "Shannon—"

She stepped away from his touch, paced to the center of the room, turned, her face expressionless. "I don't think the attempt on my car was related to this other business. Do you?"

He stared at her, wishing he knew why it bothered her so much that he'd helped her. Why it was so hard for her to accept that he wanted to protect her. "I'm inclined to think not" was all he said. "They only shot at you because you charged at them like the cavalry."

"Yeah, well, if I hadn't they'd have had my wheels."

"How did you know?" She'd turned again, walked to the sofa, sank onto it as if she were exhausted.

"I have a remote car alarm. Someone tries to get into the 'Vette, this little device in my purse sounds a warning." She pushed her hair away from her face with one hand, then paused in the act. "How did *you* know?"

"I..." He glanced away from her narrow, piercing gaze. "I was walking around the building, just checking for anything unusual. I heard them, but by the time I realized what was happening, you were..." He turned to her again, trying to see more than just what her delicate face revealed. "You were kicking the hell out of them. Where did you learn to fight like that?"

"Trial and error, mostly." She looked past him, and he wondered what she was seeing. "Tawny and I used to practice on each other. Usually ended up a pair of walking wounded, but you have to be able to take care of yourself when you're a kid on the streets. She's as good as I am . . . I mean, she was. That's why I can't understand why—"

She broke off, met his gaze again, licked her lips. Damien knew what she would have said. Why didn't Tawny fight off her attacker? Why did she submit? The answer was all too simple, really. A vampire doesn't have to attack his victims or struggle with them. He seduces them. They offer themselves, willingly, even eagerly, to his promise of ecstasy.

Guilt reared up inside him, and he couldn't hold her stare. Some immortal had rewarded that willingness, that childlike trust, with murder. Some immortal. But who?

Not me. It wasn't me . . .

"It *wasn't* you, was it?"

He shook himself free of the instant notion that she'd read his mind, or that he'd spoken the thought aloud. Coincidence. She rose and stepped closer to him, staring up into his face, her eyes narrow, darkening to the color of cinnamon.

"You wouldn't risk your life to save a stranger if you were cold-blooded enough to kill another one. Would you?"

"Of course not."

But what if I did? What if I killed that innocent girl, and what if this one is next in line? The next time the thirst becomes unbearable, the next time it overpowers my will . . . Inanna, save me, but already the scent of her, the warmth of her skin, the pinkness of it, is getting to me. I can hear the sweet river of blood running in her veins. I can smell it. And she's so soft, so beautiful... I want her. I want all of her....

"You stayed. I really didn't think you would."

"What?" He shook free of the voices in his mind.

"When you said you'd come here, watch out for me, I didn't believe you. You surprised me." She frowned, and paced slowly away from him, head tilting to one side as she walked. She stopped a few yards away, turned toward him once more. "So if you're not going to kill me, then what *are* you after?"

He looked at the floor, shook his head deliberately. "I should go."

"Why?"

He was turning toward the door, when she asked the question. He stood where he was, his back to her. When her body heat warmed his bare flesh as she moved to stand behind him, he went rigid.

"You agreed with me that the car thieves were probably not related to the murder. So the killer might still try, right? I mean, I'm in as much danger now as I was earlier, right?"

He closed his eyes as her scent assaulted him. "At least. Maybe more."

"Then stay."

Oh, but this wasn't right, this roar inside him, urging him to turn around and crush her to his chest. To take her mouth until she gasped for breath and to— It just wasn't right. It hadn't been long enough for the thirst to bring on this need. And it wasn't thirst alone this time, burning through him. It was desire, too. Not the desire that coupled with the hunger, but one born of itself. Or born of her.

Her hand touched his uninjured shoulder. Her small fingers squeezed his flesh. "Look, Damien, you saved my life. Much as I hate to owe anything to anyone, I can't overlook something this big. Last night, when I was sick, you took care of me. I just want to return the favor."

He shook his head, tore the door open. "You'll be safe by day."

"*By day?* What—"

"I'll keep watch until then, but not here. From the car. And if you come down there, Shannon, I can't guarantee anything. So stay put."

"But I—"

"Good night." He stepped into the hall, closed the door behind him, and with a burst of speed, managed to be halfway down the stairs before she'd yanked the door open again.

Okay, so she'd misjudged the guy. Badly. All right, she'd flat out accused him of murder. He'd pretty much convinced her she'd been wrong. Twice he'd appeared out of nowhere right at the moment she'd needed help. So far he hadn't asked a thing in return.

Of course, she wasn't stupid. He wanted something; he just hadn't gotten around to asking for it yet. Nobody helped anybody without a damn good reason. She'd learned that the hard way. Oh, the lovely foster family that had taken her in had seemed hunky-dory at first. All that bull about how they loved children, couldn't have any of their own, wanted to help a down-on-her-luck teenage orphan who had just about run out of hope of ever being adopted.

Right.

Tawny had been with them a month before Shannon moved in. She'd come from another institution, but Shannon had been in most of them by then. They'd never met— a small miracle, since their paths must have crossed a hundred times as they both went through the system. They'd hated each other's guts at first. At first. But then the insanity began. Mr. Grayson had some pretty sick ideas. And his wife knew all about it, but was too much of a mouse to let him know she knew.

Anyone who thought two sixteen-year-old girls couldn't fend for themselves on the mean streets ought to try living with that kind of threat looming for a while. The streets are a breeze after that.

God, to think she and Tawny had toughed it out through hell and high water, only to come to this. Tawny dead. Shannon not far behind her. Why the hell had they bothered surviving at all?

But that thinking was borderline self-pity, so she swiped her mind clean like a blackboard under a damp sponge and started over. Damien. Yes, she'd been thinking about Damien, and whatever it was he wanted from her.

For a second there, she could have sworn it was sex. Something about the way his body went all tight when she touched his bare skin.

But she dismissed that idea almost as soon as she thought it. The guy was an idol. He could have any woman he wanted, just by snapping his magic fingers. Why the hell would he be interested in her?

So there had to be something else. And it would be only a matter of time until she found out what.

Meanwhile, she needed to concentrate on something else. What in God's name had he meant when he said she'd be safe in the daytime?

CHAPTER SIX

She stopped in at the office for the first time in three days. The legwork had kept her out, tracing Tawny's steps in the week before she'd died, trying to find out who'd killed her, why and how on earth they'd done it in such a macabre manner.

The only lead she'd found was Damien, and she was no longer sure the guy was anything other than an eccentric, world-renowned magician who valued his privacy and went to great lengths to preserve the mystique of his alter ego. She'd tried her damnedest to check his background, but had come up empty. Before exploding onto the scene as the world's most beloved magician, he had, it seemed, no past at all.

"Shannon. Hey, where you been? I was starting to think you'd gone outta business."

She smiled at Sal, standing in the doorway of the pizzeria, with his clean white apron covering his rounded middle. She hadn't told him, or anyone, that Tawny's murder would be her last case. "Hey, Sal. Not out of business, just busy. What's new?"

"Rent's going up next month."

"What—again?" It didn't matter. She wouldn't be here next month.

Sal nodded, rolling his eyes. "Probably a letter waitin' for you. Got mine yesterday."

"This place isn't worth what we're paying now," she grumbled. She unlocked the door beside Sal's, swung it open, mounted the steep stairway.

Sal came to the bottom and called up to her. "You could afford the rent if you didn't drive such a fancy car, you know."

"So you keep telling me. It'll be fancier as soon as I save up enough for a paint job." She'd get that done. She promised herself she'd get that done before she went down for the count.

"That's baloney. You don't look good, Shannon. You eatin' right?"

"I will be today." She reached the top of the stairs and unlocked her office door, then paused to look down at Sal. "Two slices for lunch, with the works."

"Everything but anchovies. I know how you like it."

She smiled, swung her door open and stepped inside. The man sitting in a chair in front of her desk rose, set the file folder he'd been perusing aside, parted his lips to say something, and then thought better of it. His gaze dropped to the revolver she was pointing at his chest. She'd jerked the gun from her waistband in a split second, before he'd even turned fully. He stood very still.

"Who are you, and what the hell are you doing in my office?"

He licked his lips, a quick, nervous little dart of his tongue. And then she recognized him. He was the one who'd taken Tawny's body out of the ME's office last night.

"Take it easy with that thing. I have ID. May I?"

She nodded, a little shiver dancing up her neck. "You pull anything other than a wallet out of that fancy jacket you're wearing and it's gonna have a big hole in the front."

His hand dipped into the jacket, came out with a small leather folder. He handed it to her, and she took it, never moving her gaze from him. She flipped it open, glimpsed a photo ID from the corner of her eye. She took a quick look, her gaze darting back to him every other millisecond or so. Stephen Bachman. Then she read a little further and blinked.

"CIA?"

"One of its subdivisions."

"Which one?"

"That's not important."

She narrowed her eyes, scanning the card more carefully, trying to see whether it was genuine or a fraud. She had no way of knowing. She gazed at him again. Tall, broad-shouldered. He had an athletic build to him, and his dark hair curled a little at the ends. Gray suit, spotless white shirt. Telltale bulge beneath the left arm.

She wiggled the gun barrel. "Put your weapon on the desk, Mr. Bachman. Slowly."

He nodded, removed his gun, a shiny nickel-plated 9 mm Ruger, and set it on the desk. She stepped forward and picked it up, tucked it into the back of her jeans. "How'd you get in here?"

He smiled a little. "I told you. I'm CIA."

She held his gaze, nodding, and then took the file folder he'd been reading. It contained her notes on Tawny's death. She frowned hard. "Why is the CIA involved in a murder investigation?"

"Oh, come on, Ms. Mallory. We both know this is no ordinary murder. May I sit now, or do I have to be standing in order for you to shoot me?"

She nodded, moving behind her desk as he sat. She took her own seat. "Just what the hell is going on?"

The man stared hard at her. "You're the one who found her. Why don't you tell me?"

"What do you want from me, Bachman?"

"You're going to tell me all about Tawny Keller. And all about yourself. And everything you think you know about this case."

She smiled slowly. "Why would I do that?"

He shrugged, pursed his lips. "Because we both want the same thing. To catch her killer. And because if you don't, I'll have your private investigator's license pulled before noon."

"Sure do know how to sweet-talk a girl, don't you? Tell you what. I'll tell you everything I know, if you'll answer me one or two questions first." She *wasn't* going to tell him a damned thing. For all she knew, he could be a fraud. Then again, maybe not. He certainly had clout with the ME's office.

His eyes narrowed. "If I can. What do you want to know?"

"Why I can't get Tawny's body released to me. I want to give her a funeral." She knew he had the answer to that question. She waited.

That tongue darted out again. "Settle for a memorial service. Buy a marker, if you want. You won't get the body."

"Why?"

"It's now the property of the federal government. That's all you need to know."

He might as well have slapped her. "What the hell have you done with her, Bachman? I know she's been moved. Where is she?"

"Good little private snoop, aren't you? How'd you know we moved her?"

She bit her lower lip. She wouldn't show weakness, turmoil, nothing. Not to this suit. "ME's been giving me the royal runaround. I had a suspicion. You just confirmed it."

He nodded. "Not bad. But I can't tell you where she is. Sorry."

He glanced at his watch. "You want to move on to the next question? I don't have all day."

She fought with her temper and won. Voice level, cold, she asked him, "How did she really die?"

"Blood loss."

"I know that. I mean . . . how?"

He stared hard at her. "Damned if I know."

It was such a blatant lie he might as well have been wearing a sign. He made sure she knew he was lying. So smug. The bastard.

"My turn, Ms. Mallory. You've been seeing a doctor—four times in the past month. What's the problem?"

She felt her brows lift. "There *isn't* any problem."

His head tilted sideways. "I thought you were going to cooperate."

"I am. I didn't feel well, got checked out. There was no problem."

"I can verify this more easily that you'd believe."

"Why am I not surprised?"

He studied her for a long time. He wasn't sure if she was being flippant or blatantly honest, she could tell. Good, let him wonder.

"You've seen a lot of Damien Namtar in the past couple of days."

She blinked, then stopped herself from registering her surprise in any other way. "Have I been under surveillance?"

"Not yet."

"Him, then?"

His lips thinned. "I need to know why you've been seeing him."

So the CIA was watching Damien. She wondered if he knew it. "I'm a fan," she told Bachman. "Is there something I should know about Mr. Namtar?"

"I'm not altogether sure you don't already know."

The puzzled expression she felt twist her brows was genuine. What the hell was that supposed to mean? "Do you think he had something to do with the murder?"

"Anything's possible."

Bachman was talking, but he wasn't saying a damned thing. The briefcase he held caught her gaze. "Maybe I should watch myself, then."

"Maybe you should stay away from him altogether."

Was that a warning? What did this bastard know?

"I'm already familiar with your background, and the victim's—"

"Tawny. Her name was Tawny. Use it."

He snapped open the briefcase on his lap, flipped open a notebook. "Whatever. You were wards of the state, assigned to a foster home in Flatbush. Then both ran away. It's what went on between then and now that's tough to document. She was obviously a whore. How did you survive? Same game?"

She pulled the man's own gun from the back of her jeans, worked the action and pointed it right at his nose. "Your time's up, Bachman. Get out."

"I'm not finished." He closed the notebook, then the case.

"You'll be more than finished if you don't leave—now."

He nodded. "Fine. There are other ways to find out what I need to know." He reached for the folder on her desk. She squeezed the trigger. The bullet shattered an ashtray two inches from Bachman's hand. He froze, turning to stare at her. It was anger not fear she saw in his eyes. "I could have you in jail for that."

"I could blow your brains out and say I mistook you for an intruder. Leave the file here, and go."

His eyes darkened, but his hand fell to his side. He stepped toward her. She opened the door and moved aside. In the doorway, he turned to face her. "You keep quiet about your friend's death, Ms. Mallory. It's going down as suicide and the first time you say differently, you might just disappear yourself.''

"If you think I'll let it die, you're wrong."

"You have no choice in the matter. And I mean what I say. You don't know what you're dealing with here." He glanced down at the Ruger she still held and opened his hand. "My gun?"

"Not anymore." She slammed the door in his face.

It took her all of five seconds to decide to follow him when he left, and as she did, she racked her brain for answers. Bachman must be legit. The ME wouldn't have cooperated otherwise. So why was the government so interested in the murder of a prostitute? The *way* she'd died. It had to be. But *how had* Tawny died, exactly? How had someone put those marks on her throat, drained her blood? And why?

She had a feeling Bachman knew. But the son of a gun wasn't talking.

Damien pored over the pages of the newest translation, searching...always searching. But for what? No matter how many stone tablets were uncovered in the sands of Iraq, no matter how many cuneiform symbols told the story of Gilgamesh the hero, Gilgamesh the king, there would never be one recording the true end to the tale.

He slammed the book closed, tossed it to the floor. His eyes burned, but he blinked them clear again. Rereading the stories never failed to reignite the pain. Stupid. It was long gone now. Netty cleared her throat, drawing his attention.

"You have a guest."

At Netty's side in the library doorway, Shannon stood staring at him. She shifted the backpack that hung over her shoulder, glanced past him to the book he'd just thrown. "If it's a bad time—"

He shook his head quickly and got to his feet. "No. Pet peeve, that's all."

"She looks so much better tonight, doesn't she now, sir? More color to her cheeks." Netty patted Shannon's arm. "I'll bring ya a hot toddy. Just the thing for this chilly autumn night. Warm your bones."

"That's really not—" Shannon broke off. Netty was already hurrying away with those abbreviated, high-speed steps of hers. Shannon shook her head, smiling a little.

Damien couldn't take his eyes off her. But when her gaze met his again it was troubled. "What's wrong?"

She licked her lips. "Look, I don't know why the hell I'm even here. Except maybe I owe you. That and that I've got good instincts. I had to have, the way I grew up. Not so much who to trust and who not to trust. More like who'd slit your throat and who'd just rob you blind."

He frowned. She was rambling. Nervous. "You don't trust anyone."

"Right."

"You said you and Tawny learned to fight on the streets. I meant to ask—"

She shook her head, stopping him. "It doesn't matter."

"Yes, it does." He stared at her; those huge amber eyes seemed to reach out to him. "Where was your family?"

She looked at the floor. "My mother dumped me when I was a baby. I don't even remember her."

"Then you were adopted?"

Her lips twitched a little. "They tell me I was a sickly kid. Skinny, asthmatic. I grew up a ward of the state, saw lots of institutions, a few foster homes. I met Tawny in one of them." She turned a little away from him, fingered the strap that was anchored over her shoulder.

"And then?" He wanted to know. He didn't stop to tell himself that he shouldn't. It wouldn't have mattered if he had.

"Things got rough. We decided we could do better on our own. And we did."

He considered reading her mind. "How old were you?"

"Sixteen. And that's all I'm going to say about it. I came here, Damien, despite the fact that I still don't really trust you, because right now I distrust you a little less than the other guy."

She'd changed the subject so firmly that he knew she wouldn't reveal any more of her past to him. So he took the bait. "What other guy?"

She paced the room, shoving her hands into the deep pockets of her brown suede jacket. She moved toward the fire. Stood near it, as though she were absorbing its warmth. "On the streets, when someone does you dirty, you do them right back. But it works the same the other way. I guess I've never gotten that damned unwritten code out of my head. You helped me out, so here I am. Maybe I'm an idiot, but here I am."

He moved closer, wishing he could see her face, read whatever was in her eyes. He understood her pain over losing Tawny a little better now. They'd been together since they were just kids. They must have been like sisters. "Shannon, I don't have a clue what you're talking about."

She whirled around, standing so close he could feel her agitated breaths on his face. Her eyes were wide, dark gold.

"I think you're in trouble, Damien. I think maybe we both are."

But the urgency in her eyes faded when she glanced past him. Frowning, he turned to see Netty just beyond the doorway, a steaming mug in her hand. She stepped forward, beaming a smile as she brought the toddy to Shannon.

"Thanks, Netty." Shannon sipped. "Mmm, wonderful. Aren't you having one?" Her gaze probed Damien's.

"Ah, he never eats a thing, this one. Surprised he don't waste away before my eyes."

"That's all for today, Netty. Go on home to your grand-children."

She nodded, blew Shannon a kiss, then waved as she trotted away in search of her coat. Shannon sipped her drink and walked to the book lying on its bent pages. She set the mug down and bent to pick the heavy volume up.

"Oh. Gilgamesh again. You read about him a lot, don't you?"

"Hobby of mine."

He heard the back door close, though he knew the sound would never reach mortal ears. Soon afterward, the car started up and Netty drove away.

"Not a pleasant one," she said. "You weren't too happy with whatever you read in here."

"It's what I *didn't* read in there. But that's off the sub-ject, isn't it?"

"Can I take it home? I'd like to read it."

He nodded. "It'll bore you to tears. Moldy old stories that don't matter anymore. You said you were in trouble, Shannon."

She set the book carefully on the desk. "I said *we.*"

She shrugged the backpack off, let it thump to the floor. The thing was heavy. She knelt, unzipped it and pulled out a stack of papers. Then another. File folders, notebooks, photographs, manila envelopes. "I thought you ought to see these."

"What are they?"

She fished in the bottom of the bag, making sure she'd removed everything, then shifted her position, curling her legs beneath her for comfort. "Don't know for sure—haven't gone through it yet." She glanced up at him, her eyes slightly shiny. She was excited, maybe still afraid, but wound up, as well. "Damien, did you know the CIA had you under surveillance?"

"The CIA?" He almost laughed. Then he saw her frown, and knew she was serious. He shook his head slowly and sat down across from her. "Shannon, what's going on?"

"This suit broke into my office today. It was the same man we saw last night, with the ME. When I got there he was going through my files. Flashed some fancy ID card and said he was CIA. 'One of its subdivisions' were his exact words. This DPI—if it's for real—must be it. He wanted to know all about Tawny and me, and then he started asking about you. Threatened to have my investigator's license pulled unless I talked."

Damien felt a slow anger begin to simmer. "He threatened you?"

"Don't worry—I didn't tell him anything. But he knew I'd been with you lately, and he more or less said you were being watched." She shook her head, glancing down at the pile of documents in front of her. "Do you have any idea why they'd be interested in you?"

He shook his head. There was only one reason he could think of, and that was impossible. No government agency would take the existence of his race seriously enough to investigate it. The murder, then. It must have to do with the murder. "You said they asked about Tawny?"

Shannon's glimmering amber eyes clouded just before her lashes lowered, hiding the emotion in their depths. "They aren't going to bring her back, Damien. He wouldn't tell me where they took her or why, just that her body belongs to the government now, and I...I can't even bury her." When she looked up her eyes swam with tears. "He knows how she died—I'm sure of it. But he won't say. I have to know, Damien. Can you understand that? I have to know what happened, who put those holes in her throat, what she went through, whether she suffered or was afraid..."

She was hurting, this pixie with the leather-tough heart. She was hurting because her best friend had died. And he knew that pain so well that he hurt, too. He reached up, cradled her head in his hands and drew it downward to rest on his chest, with the mound of papers on the floor between them. He stroked her silky hair, wishing he could do more. "I'm sorry, Shannon. I know how much it hurts to lose someone you loved. There's no other pain like it. I know." It wouldn't ease her pain to know how Tawny had died. She'd never believe it if he told her it really had been a vampire. So he didn't.

She let him hold her there a moment longer, then she straightened, blinked for a moment and stared hard into his eyes. "Who did you lose?"

Enkidu's face hovered in his mind's eye, his laughter filled Damien's ears. Just as if no time at all had passed. "A friend," he told her. "He was like a brother, like the other half of me. My weaknesses were his strengths, and his were mine. We did everything together...." Damien swallowed the lump in his throat, searched her face. What was it about her that had him talking about Enkidu this way? He hadn't voiced that old anguish in ages.

"And then he died," she whispered. "And now you're a recluse." She tipped her head to one side. "Is that why? Are you afraid to have any more friends, because they might leave you someday?"

"It isn't a question of 'might.' Death is certain, guaranteed to every mortal on the planet."

"I'm all too aware of that. But life's too short to waste it alone."

He smiled in an attempt to break the tension. "You're one to talk. I haven't seen hordes of companions beating paths to your door."

"No, but not because I avoid making friends. I don't shut myself away from the world, Damien, the way you do. I just don't make attachments easily."

She looked up as she spoke, and the fire's light glowed its reflection in her eyes, made her golden hair gleam. Did she want an attachment now? With him? The gods had better help him if she did. She really was beautiful. So fragile looking, skin as delicate as lily petals. The hardness, the calluses on her heart, didn't show.

Damien shook himself when he realized how he was staring. He looked away quickly, glancing down at the papers. "You haven't finished telling me how you got these."

"Oh." She blinked, seeming to gather her thoughts. "Well, I threw the guy out on his ear and then I followed him. Some spook. He didn't even notice. He's staying at the Hilton over on Tenth. I lurked around until he went out again, then just went to his room and helped myself."

Damien's head came up fast. "You—"

"It's kid's stuff, getting into a hotel room. I used to clean them, you know, to put myself through school and help pay the rent. I just gave the clerk the creep's room number and said I'd lost my key." One hand dipped into her jacket pocket and she pulled out a key card. "He was more than happy to give me another. Figured I'd hang on to it, in case we need it again."

"Shannon, the man's going to know these papers are missing."

"Yeah, and if he has half a brain, he'll know who took them. I imagine my license is as good as gone. Doesn't matter, though. He would've pulled it anyway. He was pretty ticked off when I shot at him with his own gun." She smiled, appearing more like a mischievous teenager than a wounded, wary adult. "Don't look like that—I was only trying to make a point. I didn't hurt the guy."

"It isn't him I'm worried about."

Her brows went up and down expressively. "Well, it oughtta be. He really ticked me off."

Damien felt his lips pull into a reluctant smile as she got to her feet and walked back toward the table where she'd left her drink. He scanned the folders while she sipped. She moved closer to the fire again, her back to him.

"I was planning to close the office soon anyway. Already quit working on everything except Tawny's murder. Sent most of my clients to other agencies."

A manila folder had her name on its tab. Frowning, Damien opened it and saw medical notes, test results. The file was thick. He closed it, glancing up at her back, and slid it under a sofa cushion just as she turned again.

"Looks like we'll have to pull an all-nighter. You up for it?"

"If you are," he said. He was more than a little bit worried about letting her see whatever was in the reports on him. But he couldn't think of a way to get around it. He still couldn't believe this Bachman man knew . . . No. It was impossible. But if Bachman *wasn't* investigating the undead, then just what *was* his interest in this case and in Damien?

Shannon squeaked and jumped backward, sloshing her drink. A brown field mouse raced past her feet and stopped in a corner. Shannon set the glass on the mantel and grabbed the brass poker, turning toward the creature.

"Wait." Damien stepped forward, closed his hand around hers and took the poker away. He replaced it in the holder.

"What're you, nuts?" She certainly looked at him as if he was. "You let one in, you'll be infested before you know it."

He shook his head, pointed. "Look at it, Shannon." She turned her head, staring at the tiny, white-bellied mouse. Its brown eyes bulged and its body trembled. "Just stand still," he told her. Damien moved forward slowly, his eyes sending silent messages to the creature. When he was close enough he crouched down, cupped his hands and scooped the mouse into them.

"There. See how harmless he is? You scared him half to death." He closed one hand around the body, careful not to crush it.

"I scared him?"

With one forefinger he rubbed the tiny head. He glanced up at Shannon. "He's just looking for a few crumbs and a warm place to spend the winter. Want to pet him?"

He held the mouse out, and she backed away. "No, thanks."

He shrugged and walked toward the doorway.

"What are you going to do with it?" She trotted behind him. "Damien, if you put it outside it's just going to come back in."

"There's a rickety little woodshed out back. I'll turn him loose in there. Mice love woodsheds."

By the time she finished reading, Shannon was feeling more than a little bit uneasy. She'd found herself looking up at Damien over and over again while she'd read the notes, noticing the lack of a single gray hair. Not a wrinkle on his smooth face. Damn, the man had to be old enough to have accumulated a few crow's-feet. Then she'd laugh at herself, realizing how ridiculous it was to be thinking what she was thinking. Then she'd read some more, and feel a little uneasy all over again. Line after line of reasons to believe Damien Namtar was a vampire. A *vampire,* for crying out loud. The so-called evidence was lined up like a grocery list. Times of Damien's comings and goings, side by side with the times the sun rose and set on the day in question. Where he'd been seen, and when and with whom.

He read steadily, never glancing up. He looked puzzled, and then worried, and then angry.

Finally, she stood up and stretched the kinks out of her muscles. She forced herself to dismiss every bit of what she'd read as nothing more than the rantings of a nut. "Well, I guess that settles it. The guy's not CIA, or if he's is, he's suffering from burnout. God, he thinks he's the latest version of Kolchek."

"Who?" She glanced down and smiled, but the tension remained on Damien's face, in his black eyes.

"Kolchek. You remember, the old TV series with the vampire hunter.... Damien, don't look so devastated, the guy's insane."

He rose, head down, and paced toward the fire to toss another log onto the dwindling flames.

"Either that, or you're really a vampire."

He spun to face her, eyes wide.

"Hey, I was kidding. Take it easy, will you?"

"I can't take it easy, Shannon. The man's been recording my every move for days. I don't like it."

"Well, of course you don't. Who would?"

She returned to her spot on the floor and snatched up the last sheet he'd read, wanting to know what had upset him so much. He lunged toward her, reaching for the paper, but she ducked away and scanned the lines.

Then the blood rushed to her feet and her breath froze in her lungs. "My God..." Her gaze shot to Damien's. He stood motionless, looking devastated. "You didn't want me to see this, did you?"

"Do you blame me?"

She licked her lips, and reread the lines. Tawny's body was the second that had been found. The first, another young woman, had died of identical wounds to the throat. And there was a note that she, too, had volunteered to be Damien's assistant onstage. Rosalie Mason. The woman Shannon had tried to find.

She shook her head, staring at Damien in disbelief.

"That's why I didn't want you to see it, Shannon. That look that's on your face right now. I know what you're thinking."

"That's bull, because right now, *I* don't even know what I'm thinking." She got up again, walked to where she'd dropped her backpack and picked it up. "I'm going now. I'm overtired, and if I don't get some sleep soon, I'll be bunking in your shed with that mouse."

"You can use the guest room—"

"No." She softened her tone. She didn't really believe any of this, did she? Of course she didn't. "No, I really can't. Not tonight."

"You're afraid of me."

She chewed her lower lip, blinked twice. "I'm not. Maybe that's what worries me." She took a single step, then turned back and picked up the new book on Gilgamesh, the one he'd been reading when she'd arrived. "You, uh, you said it was okay to borrow this, didn't you?"

Damien nodded. Shannon slipped it into her pack, then slung the bundle over her shoulder and started for the door. Damien followed, touched her shoulder, stopping her before she went out.

"I know you don't trust me, Shannon, but I have to follow you home. It's still dark, and—"

She spun around, blinking up at him. "That's right, it is. And that reminds me to ask you why it is you're so sure I'm safe during the day, but in danger at night."

"Vampires only hunt at night."

A little chill ran over her nape at those words. She ignored it. "Get real, Damien."

"I'm serious." He sighed hard, pushed a hand through his hair and stepped away from her.

"There's no such thing." But when she said it, her words were barely more than a whisper.

He turned and met her eyes. "Then let's say the killer wants it to look like a vampire. Can you buy that?"

She nodded, still wary.

"He'll hardly change his tactics now and strike by day."

She felt the tension in her spine ease. "For a minute there I thought you were going to say you believed in this stuff. Had me worried." She was still worried. She just wasn't sure what about. Not that he was a blood-sucking night stalker. Not that.

CHAPTER SEVEN

The final test. It would be definitive. After this there would be no question as to Damien's fondness for the delicate mortal woman.

Anthar had allowed himself no contact with her. He'd kept his mind utterly isolated from her, just as he knew his nemesis had wished to do. It would never do for Anthar to develop a soft spot for her. She was a pawn. Her purpose was to mete out punishment, and nothing more. Anthar felt no hint of the instinctive urge to protect her. And if he had, he'd have ignored it. The fuel that powered his actions was more powerful than anything else could be. The need for vengeance. He'd been obsessed with the downfall of this onetime king for too long to allow anything to interfere.

And the test he'd devised this time would tell him all he needed to know. He'd use an element that could spell destruction for any immortal. Damien the Eternal would have to risk more than the passing pain of a bullet to save his mortal pet. He'd risk his very existence this time, or watch her die. If he should try and fail to save her, well, that would only add to his torment. If he should not try at all, then Anthar would know he hadn't cared.

It was all so simple to arrange. But not now—dawn was too close. Tonight, with the first layer of darkness on the autumn sky. He'd begin by making her sleep...very soundly.

The story was riveting.

She hadn't wanted interruption. She'd turned on the answering machine and refused to answer the door, even when the man thumping impatiently on the other side had most likely been an angry CIA spook by the name of Bachman. She had no idea why he didn't just break in. Maybe he really believed she wasn't here.

Didn't matter. She had no time to talk to him. No. She needed to spend today trying to decide whether Damien Namtar could possibly, in her wildest dreams, be a cold-blooded murderer. Or maybe he was just completely insane. Multiple personalities, perhaps, and maybe one of those personalities was a vampire.

After he'd left, she'd tried to sleep, couldn't. Countless scenarios popped into her mind, and kept her tossing and turning well into the morning. The result being that when she finally did sleep, she hadn't awoken until noon. She was beginning to keep some pretty vampiric hours herself.

When she did finally rouse herself, he was on her mind again, from the second she opened her eyes. The only conclusion she'd reached was that she just didn't know enough about the man to make a judgment call. And she'd decided then and there to read this book, cover to cover. To try to see what was in here that moved him so deeply, and maybe find a clue to what made him tick.

And now she knew, and it moved her, too.

Sad, tragic story. All about a great king and the man who became his closest friend—more than a friend, really. Gilgamesh had been a bit of a tyrant at first. A strong man, fierce in combat, abundant in wisdom. So much so he was thought of as half man, half god. But he'd forgotten how to feel compassion for his people.

Enkidu was raised on the steppe, among the wild things. People thought of *him* as half man, half animal. But he came into the ancient city of Uruk one day and deliberately stood right in Gilgamesh's path. A public challenge. The two fought, and the description of the battle was more poetic than anything Shannon thought she'd ever read:

> They fell like wolves
> at each other's throats,
> like bulls bellowing,
> and horses gasping for breath . . .
> crushing the gate they fell against.
> The dry dust billowed in the marketplace
> and people shrieked. The dogs raced
> in and out between their legs.
> A child screamed at their feet
> that danced the dance of life
> which hovers close to death.
> And quiet suddenly fell on them
> when Gilgamesh stood still
> exhausted. He turned to Enkidu, who leaned
> against his shoulder and looked into his eyes
> And saw himself in the other, just as Enkidu saw
> himself in Gilgamesh.
> In the silence of the people they began to laugh
> And clutched each other in their breathless exaltation.

A lump formed in her throat as she read on. The two had been inseparable from then on, and the book told of their adventures together, how they were two parts of a single whole. And how, finally, Enkidu had slowly died as his friend looked on, helpless to save him.

The verse narrative was moving, and that surprised her. She hadn't expected writers from something earlier than 4000 B.C. to be so expressive. She blinked back tears as she read another passage, aloud, just to savor the beauty of it as it described Gilgamesh's crippling grief.

''The word *Enkidu*
roamed through every thought
like a hungry animal through empty lairs
in search of food. The only nourishment
he knew was grief, endless in its hidden source.

Shannon stood very still, knowing exactly how the man
had felt. She'd felt that kind of grief when Tawny had died.
She still felt it. She had to wait a few minutes before she
could read further. Her tears blurred her vision, but she had
to finish.

Engrossed, she read on. Gilgamesh, no longer a great
ruler but an ordinary man who'd lost his way, wandered in
the desert, perhaps a little insane, in search of the secret to
eternal life. He became obsessed with the idea of becoming
immortal and of carrying that secret home with him, to
bring Enkidu back to life. A mission that was doomed to
fail.

By the time Shannon closed the book, there were small,
spasmodic sobs pulling at her breastbone. She brushed her
eyes dry, shook her head and tried to focus on her reason for
reading this heartbreaking tale in the first place. To understand Damien.

Of course. He said he'd lost his best friend. God, he'd
even described their closeness in a way that mirrored the
closeness of Gilgamesh and Enkidu in the ancient tale. No
wonder he identified with it. And with her. It was as though
some triangle of endless mourning connected the three of
them.

But what did that mean to her?

She set the book down, absently caressing the cover, and
paced the length of her living room, then back again. Could
Damien be a killer? A man who was moved to tears by a
story thousands of years old? A man who obviously felt

things more deeply than any man she'd ever met? He couldn't even let her kill a little field mouse, for God's sake.

All her life she'd been taught, over and over again, not to trust anyone. Not anyone. So why did she so stubbornly persist in wanting to trust him?

All right, maybe it was time she took a good long look at her motivations here. She did just that, over a long steamy soak in a scented bath.

She'd never been with a man, had never wanted to be.

Until lately. Lately, she'd caught herself thinking about it more than once. Wondering if there was a chance it could actually be as wonderful as Tawny used to always tell her it could be. And she had to be brutally honest and admit that it was Damien who was inspiring these kinds of thoughts. No wonder, really. He was such a sexual creature.

It was getting dark outside. He'd be here soon, to stand guard over her for the night. She really ought to get out of the water and dress. What would he do, she wondered, if she kissed him?

Didn't matter. She wasn't going to find out.

Was she?

She felt a peculiar lethargy stealing over her body as she soaked. An unnatural kind of exhaustion, as if she'd popped a sleeping pill or something. She sponged her skin and fought it.

She thought maybe she'd like to find out after all. Hell, she had nothing to lose, and why not experience everything she was curious about before her life ended?

God, she was tired. Her eyes drooped and her body sank a little lower in the water. She dragged herself out of the tub and pulled on a robe. Was it this damned illness making her so sleepy? She'd already dozed half the day. Whatever, it was irresistible. She shuffled to bed, wet hair and all.

It wasn't the smoke that woke her—it was the alarm. Shrieking at her, breaking the night with its whistling pitch.

She was half-dressed before she smelled the smoke, creeping in and surrounding her senses, little by little, so she wasn't certain for a moment. It might be her imagination. The alarm might be malfunctioning, and...

She pulled on the jeans she'd left on the floor, since they were within reach. She was hopping into the living room as she tugged them up, snapped them, yanked on the zipper. She was headed for the door, but stopped in her tracks when she saw the wispy gray fingers reaching toward her from beneath it.

They grew longer, floating upward, spreading. She took another step and felt a deep terror twist to life in her soul. She pressed her palms to the door, only to suck air through her teeth and yank them away from the heat.

"God! Oh, God!" Panic beat a message across her heart. She fought it, tried to use her mind. She whirled in a circle, then dashed across the room, yanking a blanket from the back of the sofa, heading for the bathroom. She jerked at the tub's faucet and dumped the blanket in. She jumped in on top of it, stomping on it up and down until it was soaked, then hauled it out, dripping and cold, and carried it back to the door.

The smoke seeped steadily beneath it now, and she dumped the wet blanket to the floor, kicking it tight to the crack under the door. Then she watched. The smoke stopped.

A sigh of relief that she knew wasn't called for escaped her lips anyway. She ran to the phone, picked it up and jiggled the cutoff. Dead. Her throat went dry. She licked her lips, standing in the room's center, turning slowly in a full circle. What could she do? She was twenty-three stories up and her only way out was through a door she knew better than to open. What in the name of God could she possibly do?

She went to the bedroom to stare out the window. Flames lit the night. She saw their orange glow dancing upward from the stories below her. She saw the flashing lights of rescue vehicles bathing the crowd that had gathered below. She saw people in their nightclothes, wandering like bugs. God, how had she slept through all of this? And she saw the huge gap where the fire escape ought to be. She would be down there soon, being led around by those fire fighters like the bug people were. Just as soon as they put the fire out and came for her. She would. She only needed to keep her head.

She went to the closet, opened it and picked up her worn-out baseball bat. She hurried back to the bedroom, and the window shattered with the first impact. She hoped the people below were far enough away to avoid the flying glass. She imagined they were. They'd expect windows to be smashed by the ones still trapped.

Trapped.

She bit her lip, and tore her gaze away from the people below and the flame's color on the night sky. She went back to the living room and glanced longingly at the balcony. But red tongues of flame leapt up around it, attacking from the one below. She couldn't go out there. No haven there.

She returned to the bathroom, stoppered the tub and let more water rush into it. Cool water. And then she filled a dishpan, carried it into the living room and hurled the water at the hot door. The paint on the inside was blistering now. The smoke was finding its way around the blanket. The next dishpanful hit, spattered, splashed back on her face.

She threw another blanket into the water, this one to wrap herself in should she need it.

What else? What else?

Her heartbeat escalated when she realized she was sweating. The temperature of the room was increasing. The floors...God, the bottoms of her bare feet felt the heat seeping up through the floors.

Calm. Calm, don't panic. Go to the window again. Let them know you're here. A signal.

She tied several sheets together, taking her time, trying to keep her hands from shaking so hard, knowing there was nothing to do but wait. When she glanced up, she saw a layer of smoke suspended at waist level, and she got down from the bed to sit on the hot floor. She tied the end of her sheet banner to the bedpost and tossed the rest out the window.

They'd see the white flag in the night. They'd come for her.

Her eyes burned. The inside of her nose stung. Her chest hurt.

It's the smoke. The smoke is the enemy. Have to stop breathing so much of it.

She went to the bathroom again, to the overflowing tub, but she didn't turn the water off. She took a clean washcloth, wet it and held it to her face. She swiped at her burning eyes, but when she opened them again, it was dark.

The power had gone. The tub spluttered to a stop. She held the cloth over her nose and mouth to filter the air, but she choked anyway. She pawed for the tub, dragged the wet blanket from it. That thick, acrid stench coated her mouth and tongue. She dropped to her knees and crawled from the bathroom, pulling the sodden weight behind her.

The explosion came from nowhere and from everywhere. Burning brands rained on her like shrapnel, and a blinding wall of flame stood where the door used to be. She crawled faster, on knees only, coughing, clutching the washcloth to her face with one hand and pulling the soaked blanket with the other. She found her way to the bedroom door by the light of the inferno spreading like a pool through her apartment. She hurled herself through, then closed it and pushed the blanket to the bottom.

The coughing racked her now, and with each bout she spasmodically inhaled more of the smoke that was choking her. Killing her. She sat on the floor, turning herself slowly, blinking her watering eyes in pitch-darkness to get her bearings. The window—she wanted to get back to the window. She choked again, dragging in more of the acrid stench. Her finger screamed in white-hot pain, and she suddenly realized the ring she wore was burning a brand into it. She yanked it off, threw it away. Her hair was soaked in sweat, her skin sizzling with the heat.

And then she found the window. She found it by the glow of the sheets she'd hung out, which were burning now, like everything else. Flames climbed the sheet like a rope and leapt the windowsill to invade. She lurched to her feet, to the bed. She fumbled with the knot she'd made, but a fit of choking caught her, held her in a merciless grip. She had to stand long enough to undo the knot on the bedpost. When she finally got it free, and sent the sheets sailing to the ground below, she dropped to the floor again.

Only this time it wasn't volitional, and she didn't get up.

He had never intended to use the power of the psychic bond between her kind and his. But he was increasingly glad he'd begun to relearn the ways of doing it. As soon as dusk fell and he came fully awake, he homed in on Shannon. He'd go to her, take up his nightly vigil, just as soon as he'd showered and dressed. And until then he'd keep track of her with his mind.

He ignored the cravings of his body. He shouldn't feel such an urgent need yet. It hadn't been that long. And the damned hunger that kept dancing in his mind shouldn't be wearing Shannon's face. Damn, what was happening to him?

He tried distracting himself from this irrational need for her by thinking of new and amazing feats to perform for the crowds while he took a record-fast shower. He thought about escape tricks, and reminded himself to go through that book on Houdini that he'd bought last month, while he threw on his clothes. But all the time, in one corner of his mind, he was feeling her thoughts, experiencing what she did, smelling and tasting and hearing along with her. The old talent had come back to him with a little practice, more powerful than he'd remembered it.

She'd been silent, so deeply asleep she hadn't even dreamed.

Then there was an abrupt shift. Every one of her senses went rigidly alert. Damien smelled smoke, felt it, thick and stinging, clawing at his nostrils, scratching his eyes. Heat like a lead blanket tried to smother him. He felt her fear. Stark terror. All so fast, it had happened.

Fire. And he knew, dammit, that his skin would go up like gasoline if he touched the flame.

Didn't matter, though. He had to get her out. If not, he'd have to experience her death. Feel the gradual ebb of her life force, see what she saw in her mind as she battled the final enemy. Anyone but her, he thought in sudden panic, and the real possibility of it hit him. She couldn't die, not Shannon. It would kill him this time.

He'd done it, then, hadn't he? He'd let himself start caring about her.

Damien stepped out of his house, lifted his arms. Seconds later he soared, a shadow in the night sky, a streak of darkness there and gone so suddenly no mortal eye would see him. He soared toward her, and he felt her heartbeat slow.

Damn you, you won't win. Not this time!

He sped through the starry sky, piercing clouds like an arrow. He felt the cool, crisp air on his skin, and then the searing heat on Shannon's. He smelled the biting autumn air and then the stench of smoke. And then he was there. The conflagration raged like a tower of pure hell, and he dove, swooping through the broken glass of her bedroom window.

He thudded to the floor of a smoke-filled room, and even with his night vision, he could barely see. The heat was intense, and here and there tongues of vicious flame broke the inky blackness. He avoided them, focusing only on Shannon, and he found her, dropped to his knees beside her just as her labored, raspy struggles for breath stopped altogether.

She lay still, eyes closed, a limp angel. He scooped her into his arms, cupping her head with one hand and held her face to his. He blew his breath into her lungs. Once, twice, again.

She coughed, drew a strangled breath, only filling her lungs with more smoke. Her arms came weakly around his neck, and her face pressed to his throat. She choked his name before she lost consciousness again.

Cradling her to his chest, a burden so light he barely noticed the added weight, he leapt through the window again, speeding through the night too rapidly to be seen, like one more wisp of sooty smoke that appeared, then vanished in the blink of an eye.

He came down away from the lights and the crowd, in a darkened alley between the next two buildings. The street just beyond was a chaos of sirens. Red and white flashes bathed Shannon with color. Vehicles moved back and forth, horns blasting, voices shouting.

She stirred in his arms, drew a wheezing breath and then exploded in a seizure of coughing that he thought would tear her body apart. He held her to his chest until the paroxysm passed, then searched her soot-streaked face. "Shannon?"

She blinked him into focus with red eyes, frowned, then glanced beyond him to the burning hulk. Red-orange tongues of fire lapped at the night sky, as if they'd consume it, as well. "How—"

Her question was cut off by her coughing. He carried her out of the shadows, into the crowd. He shoved his way through until he reached an ambulance, then snatched the oxygen mask from its hook on a tank.

"Hold on, mister. I'll handle it." The young man turned a valve, held the mask to Shannon's face and waved an arm toward the ground. "Lay her down here."

"A stretcher." He bit the two words out and glared at the man in white.

"Sorry, but they're all in use. Just give her to me—" As the medic spoke he reached for Shannon, but a sweep of Damien's arm sent him stumbling aside. "Hey—" Damien shut him up with one glance before he looked for a soft place where she could rest. He spotted an empty police car and carried her toward it. The man swore under his breath, but came along, carrying the oxygen tank. Damien yanked open the rear door of the cruiser and lay her down across the back seat. She was coughing again, pushing the mask away, trying to sit up.

"Damien—"

"It's all right, Shannon. You'll be fine now."

"You got—" A fit of coughing took her and she was weak when it let her go. She sat up anyway, her arm along the back of the seat to brace her. She held the clear plastic mask to her face, head bowed as she sucked a few breaths of oxygen, but her eyes never left his. Her head came up, slowly, as if it weighed too much for her neck to support. "You got me out."

He nodded. "Rest. You need to—"

"How?"

He said nothing, just watched her. She turned her head to stare at the blazing building. She drew two more breaths, then moved the mask aside. "You went in there, didn't you? You walked into that..." Her brows drew together and she returned to her scrutiny of his face. She coughed again, drew herself straighter, searching his eyes.

An ambulance pulled up beside the police car. Two paramedics jumped out, yanked a gurney from the back and rolled it to a stop behind Damien. The one with the oxygen tank tapped the roof. "We've got an ambulance available now. We can transport her."

She shook her head. "No, I'm fine."

"We're taking you to a hospital, miss. You inhaled a lot of smoke—"

"I *said* I'm fine." She got her feet to the pavement again, shoving Damien aside so she could stand up, then closing a hand on his shoulder for support. She glanced just once more at the building, then met Damien's eyes, her own shooting sparks that were just a bit duller than usual. "Why?"

He wasn't sure just then that the smoke she'd inhaled hadn't damaged her brain. "You need see a doctor, Shannon. Lie down on this gurney and—"

"Stop talking to me like I'm two years old and spill it, Damien." She paused to cough, wheeze, gasp, pressing the palm of one hand to her chest, bending almost double. The young man held the mask she'd discarded to her face. She took one gulp of oxygen and pushed it aside, lifting her head with an obvious effort. "Why did you risk your neck for me like that? Again? You have a death wish or what?"

He frowned at her. "You know you and your lousy attitude are beginning to get to me. I went to a lot of trouble to snatch you, kicking and screaming as usual, from death's door. I don't expect a thank-you at this point, but you'd better believe you are going to see a doctor if I have to throw you over my shoulder and carry you there myself."

She sucked at the oxygen, eyes narrowing on his face.

He cocked his eyebrows. "Don't get that suspicious look, Shannon Mallory. This wasn't a plot to get you to stop suspecting me of heinous crimes. If that was all I wanted to accomplish I could have left you in there."

The mask moved away. "I never said—"

Her glare faltered, and she began coughing hard enough to tear her lungs to shreds, he thought.

He picked her up. "I'm tired of arguing with you, dammit." He held her hard and climbed into the back of the ambulance. He sat on a seat, with her on his lap, and sent the attendant a nod.

The youth clambered in with them, bringing the oxygen along, bending over to affix the mask once more to Shannon's face. Damien could see the medic wanted to suggest Damien follow in a car, meet them at the hospital. He even opened his mouth to do it, but he changed his mind. The other man closed the double rear doors and went around to the front. The vehicle lurched, jarring her against his chest. Her arms encircled Damien's shoulders and she let her head relax against him. He closed his eyes. In seconds they were under way, siren blasting.

They hadn't gone far, when she lifted her head, reached up to yank the mask from her face, but Damien caught her hand in his, held it, stared down into her eyes. He could will her to be still. But he found himself wanting to convince her, instead. He liked her spirit, irritating though it was.

"Shannon, there is nothing in this for me. That's what you're wondering about, isn't it? What my angle is, what I'm after? Nothing at all."

She twisted her hand from his and yanked the mask away. "I didn't ask for you to jump into the middle of my life." She drew a slow, careful breath. "I don't need a hero."

"I didn't claim to be one."

"Ha! You ran into that burning building like some kind of comic-book superstar! There was no earthly reason for you to—" Her accusatory comment was cut off by another bout of coughing, and Damien pressed the mask to her face again.

When she'd calmed and faced him again, he lifted the mask. She looked at him in silence for a long time. Her gaze fell to somewhere in the vicinity of his chin. "There was no reason for you to risk your life like that." She spoke more softly, he thought, so she wouldn't instigate a return of her choking and gasping.

"There was every reason," he told her. He pushed her hair away from her face.

Her eyes narrowed, shooting amber sparks at him. He wiped some of the soot from her face. She tried to sit up, and he let her. She slid from his lap to settle on the edge of the gurney. She didn't look him in the eye. She stared downward, and her golden hair fell over one side of her face. "I thought...I really thought it was all over, in there."

"I'm glad you were wrong."

She nodded. "I owe you, Damien...again." The ambulance turned and slowed. Then came to a stop. The rear doors opened, and she got to the ground by herself, refusing his help as well as the medics'. The young man reached out to take Shannon's arm, but she jerked it away. "I can walk perfectly well by myself. God, you'd think I was... was..." She stood, wavering slightly, glanced at Damien, blinked. She lifted one hand toward him.

He caught her when she began sinking. Stubborn woman! He carried her through the double Emergency Room doors that opened on their own at his approach. He walked into chrome-and-white chaos, the smell of Lysol, the squeak of rubber soles on spotless floor tiles and the clatter of wobbling wheels on gurneys as they were pushed along. She muttered that she was fine and didn't need to be carried. He was ushered to an examining room, where he laid her carefully down on a table that was covered in immaculate white paper. She smudged it with soot.

Damien evaporated as soon as the first nurse appeared with a stack of forms to be filled out. Shannon sat on the edge of the bed and filled in the blanks, wondering if they handed this same stack to cardiac-arrest victims before administering CPR.

A nurse came in with a soft, damp cloth and a basin of warm water and proceeded to wipe the soot from Shannon's face. Okay, she thought. They were sweethearts. She was just thinking bitchy thoughts because she was in a bitchy mood. Damn, she'd lost just about everything she had.

"The doctor will be right in, Ms...." The blond woman glanced at the forms. "Mallory. You just relax and let me get your vitals, okay?"

Shannon nodded as a thermometer was popped into her mouth.

As it turned out, that nurse spent a good half hour with her. The doc was in and out in five minutes flat, pronouncing her well enough to go home, and then the nurse was back, wondering what she was going to wear.

Shannon hadn't thought of that. And when she did, she thought of other things, things she'd never see again. Her Sting CDs, her brown suede jacket...

Her eyes flew wide, she clutched her middle and groaned in real pain.

The nurse grabbed her shoulder. Damien burst into the room. "What's wrong? What's happening?"

Shannon moaned again, louder. It *really* hurt. "My car. Oh, my car, my car, my car." She covered her face with her hands when Damien and the nurse exchanged looks. "After those thugs tried to steal it, I parked it in that damned sinkhole they call an underground garage. Oh, damn, don't you get it? My car..." She groaned. They didn't understand. They couldn't. "Just get out and leave me alone," she muttered into her hands.

She heard the door close, thought she might be by herself, looked up. Damien set a big shopping bag on the floor and came toward her. "You're crying." His magic fingers rose and wiped the tears from her cheeks.

"You think it's stupid, crying for a car." She sniffed and tried to stop, but more tears flowed. She gave up, closed her eyes and let them come.

His hands slipped over her shoulders, around to her back. He pulled her head to his chest, and he rocked her slightly back and forth. "I don't think it's stupid."

"Tawny... used to collect them."

"Cars?"

She sniffed and nodded, pushing her face closer to his chest. That white shirt of his still held the smell of smoke, but his scent was there, too, and it crept into her brain and rubbed her sore spots with a healing touch. "Matchbox cars," she told him. "The Corvette was her favorite. But it was my favorite, too. We'd always fight over that one. Little, candy-apple red Stingray with the doors that really opened and closed. She'd put it on her dresser, and I'd snatch it and put it on mine. We were too old for toys, but hell, we didn't have much to call our own in those days." She cried a little harder, ashamed of herself, but needing to do it. "And... and my birthday came, with no party or presents, just like always. And she—she wrapped that stupid little car up in a page of comics and gave it to me. It was her favorite, and she gave it to me. She swore someday we'd have a real one, and we'd ride around together...."

His arms tightened around her. "So that's why your car means so much to you, hmm?"

She nodded again.

"It might be okay, you know. They have the fire pretty much contained, according to the radio, and it didn't look to me like the lower floors were too badly damaged."

She lifted her head, gazing wide-eyed at his face. "You think?"

"It's possible. I'll check on it for you just as soon as we get you settled in."

She felt her brows draw together. "Settled i—"

"I went to a department store a few blocks away while you were being examined, picked you up a few necessities."

"You—"

"You're coming home with me, Shannon. And I don't want to hear any arguments about it." He stood in front of her, searched her face.

She was quiet for a long time, searching his right back. His dark eyes, his raven hair, the face that made her want to trace each strong feature with her fingertips. He'd saved her life . . . twice now. He certainly wasn't going to hurt her.

"Damien . . ." She hesitated, hating to voice her fears, but forcing herself to go on. "Do you think the fire—"

"They're saying it looks like arson, but they won't be certain for a day or two."

She gnawed her lips. "It's all connected, isn't it? Someone doesn't want me digging into Tawny's murder."

"There's no proof—"

"It might even have been Bachman. He said he could make me disappear." She eyed Damien, wishing she knew the truth.

"I just don't know. It might have been an attempt on your life. It might have been a coincidence. Either way, you'll be safer with me. I don't want you alone anymore, Shannon."

She didn't *want* to be alone anymore, either. She simply nodded. "Okay."

CHAPTER EIGHT

He scooped her up in his arms again and strode through the emergency room over the protests of the nurse, who kept talking about hospital regulations and wheelchairs. There was a part of Shannon that rebelled against the coddling. That little suspicious voice in her mind that insisted he must have a motive, whispered constant warnings in her ear: *You don't need anyone to take care of you. You can take care of yourself—you always have. Don't get used to this. It's not gonna last, and we both know it, don't we? It'll just make you weak. Yell at him. Tell him to put you down.*

But she didn't. Because there was another part, a part that seemed to be growing bigger all the time, that liked the way it felt to be cradled in his strength. The hard arms that held her, the solid chest she leaned against, were feeling less like invaders of her independence and more like her own solid fortress, her refuge. It felt *good* to be held this way, dammit. And who the hell ever said she didn't have the right to feel good once in a while?

She put her arms around his neck, mentally thumbing her nose at that cynical voice. He stepped outside, into the hospital parking lot, and she thought there had never been an autumn night that tasted as crisp and clean as this one. There was a second, as he carried her toward the black Jag that crouched like the cat it was named for, when she wondered how he'd got the car here so fast. Someone, probably a cop or a fire fighter, must have brought it over. It didn't matter, really.

He settled her on the seat, pulled the safety belt around her, fastened it. Then he looked at her, just looked at her for a long time. She could see his eyes moving minutely, as if he had to see every part of her face. Their focus shifted, from her forehead to her nose to her jaw. Her lips, her eyes.

She lifted a hand, thinking she might still have soot smeared on her skin. But he caught it, stopping it, holding it in his. She met his ebony gaze. His lips moved just a little, the barest whisper of a smile. He stepped back and closed her door, still staring at her face. After a moment she offered a small smile in return. Finally, he dragged his gaze away, went to his side of the car and got in. And then he drove.

When they reached the house, he carried her again. "You'll want to shower. Your robe is still in the bedroom you used before." This he said as they mounted the broad, curving staircase.

The cynic was getting louder. "Damien put me down. I'm not too helpless to walk up a flight of stairs."

"I'm not as sure of that as you are." He kept walking.

She didn't argue anymore, sensing it wouldn't do much good anyway. Besides, they were already heading up the second flight. He'd put her down soon. Now, why wasn't she as relieved by that thought as she'd expected to be? He held her crushingly tight, as if he were afraid he might drop her. She let her head rest on his shoulder, and then felt the oddest certainty that he'd bent his head to brush his lips over her hair.

Silly. Just her imagination overworking itself again.

He flung the bedroom door open, stepped through it and lowered her to the floor. His hand clasped her waist for longer than it had to, just to steady her. He looked so concerned that it made her uncomfortable, and she took a step away from him. "I think you're right. I want a shower. Get that damned smoky reek out of my hair before I choke on it.''

He nodded, but didn't leave. He opened the closet and set the shopping bag he still carried on the top shelf, then turned to her again. "Can you manage by yourself?"

That made her smile a little. He really must think she was a wimp. "What are you gonna do, Damien, bathe me personally, just in case I'm not strong enough to lift a bar of soap?"

The worried expression in his black eyes changed. They darkened or intensified or something. For a long time, she couldn't look away. And when she finally did, she felt shaken, a little weak-kneed, and not from smoke inhalation.

"I'll be back to check on you in a few minutes." His voice wasn't even or calm, as it had been before. He turned and left her there, and she got the impression he was in a hurry.

When the door closed she stared at it, licked her lips. "Yeah," she whispered. "And then what?"

She scrubbed. She shampooed her hair again and again, and stood under the shower spray until she wondered if his supply of hot water was endless. As she lingered in the shower, she thought of Damien. The great magician. The man. What made him want to perform for a living? she wondered. And what had he done before? And . . . and was he thinking about her as often as she'd been thinking about him lately?

She shook her head and told herself to get a grip. When she thought she'd finally rid herself of that clinging smoky odor, she toweled dry and reached for the clothes he'd just bought for her, the ones she'd worn to leave the hospital. But she smelled the smoke again. Well, no wonder. She'd been coated in that scent when she'd put them on, and now the clothes were infected. It figured, didn't it?

She wrapped up in a towel and went in search of the robe she'd left here. She found it in the closet, pulled it on. But as she did, she glanced up at that shopping bag on the top shelf. It still bulged. He had said he'd bought the stuff for her, hadn't he? She wondered if there was anything more substantial in there to put on. She stretched out an arm, but the shelf was too high to reach that way.

Biting her lip and glancing around, she spotted a chair and quickly pulled it over to the closet. She climbed up, and the bedroom door opened, and Damien stood there, arms crossed, looking at her the way he might look at a little girl hanging upside down from a set of monkey bars.

He'd showered, changed. He wore a pair of black jeans that fit him way too well and a wine-colored button-down shirt, with the sleeves rolled up to just below his elbows, so her eyes were instantly drawn to the fine dark mist of hair on his forearms. When she met his gaze again, he was smiling.

She ignored his amused expression and reached for the bag.

"Watch out!"

His yell came just as she felt the chair slide sideways and begin to tilt. She toppled. The bag flew out of her hands as she plummeted. She groped for a hold. The next thing she knew, she was slamming into his chest so hard his back smacked into the wall. Her arms automatically clung to his neck as he held her upright against him with her feet dangling a few inches above the floor. His arms were tight around her waist, crossed at the small of her back. Her face was above his, and only a fraction of an inch away. She caught her breath. He didn't let her go. He was staring. She didn't know what part of her so fascinated him, because her own gaze was fixed to his mouth.

It wasn't the first time she'd caught herself looking at those full lips of his and wondering what kind of a kisser he was. Would he be gentle, well mannered, neat? Or hard and hot and messy? Probably the latter, she figured, narrowing her eyes as she thought about it. Yes. Definitely the latter.

He closed his eyes and thumped the back of his head to the wall, as though trying to clear it or something. His arms loosened on her waist so she could slide down, but as her body moved over his, she felt the rigid arousal behind his zipper, and she knew her heart skipped a beat.

She turned him on? Good grief, she hadn't realized that. Well, all right, she'd suspected it once or twice, but . . .

Her toes touched the floor. She unlaced her arms from around his neck and lowered her heels until her feet were flat. He opened his eyes. She hadn't noticed before how thick and glossy his lashes were, or how the irises themselves were smooth as black satin. She took a step away from him, but her eyes remained mated to his.

His big hands rested just above her hips now, and she felt his fingers knead her flesh there, but she wasn't sure if it was a voluntary movement or something he did unconsciously. She thought about the magic in those hands, the ease with which he moved them onstage, the way things would appear in them as if from thin air, the way the very elements seemed to respond to their commands, to obey their every wave or even a snap of those long fingers. What kind of magic could hands like that work on a woman? And she thought about the hard length of him, stirred to life just by the touch of her body against his. And for just a second, she wondered what it would be like to let a man like this one make love to her. Probably beyond anything she could imagine.

He pushed her away, and he turned abruptly, as if he'd pound the front of his head against the wall this time. He didn't, but his magic hands were clenched into trembling fists at his sides and his shoulders were stiff and the muscled cords in his neck stood out.

Oh, come on. He couldn't possibly want her *that* much. Maybe, if she were some swimsuit model or cover girl, but not *her.* So what was this?

"I, uh, didn't hurt you, did I?"

His head fell until she figured his chin was touching his chest. He made a sound that was half snort, half laugh. His voice was very soft and kind of raspy when he said, "No, Shannon. You didn't hurt me."

She shrugged. "I didn't think so." She turned away from him, just in case he should look at her. She didn't want him to see how much he confused her. Sheesh, if he was that hot for her, why didn't he just say so? He couldn't possibly be afraid she'd turn him down. It wasn't as if a guy like this one probably got turned down often. Maybe not ever. He wanted her. So why didn't he do something about it?

She bit her lips hard, and waited.

"You ought to eat something," he said, and she wanted to scream in frustration. "Come downstairs."

In the circular room that was his favorite, a roaring fire awaited them. He wanted to be sure Shannon was really all right before he rested at dawn. She'd nearly died. He still couldn't quite believe she hadn't.

But she was alive, more alive than anyone he'd ever known. He watched her spoon down the chicken soup he'd warmed for her. He hadn't dared to try anything more complicated. It had been a long time since he'd worried about food, though there was always plenty in the kitchen. Netty had to eat while she was here, and bare cupboards might have made her wonder.

Shannon had finished her soup. Now she meandered around the room, examining things with the fierce curiosity of a child. She picked up the shiny black box that made things disappear onstage. She opened it, examined the mirrors inside, closed it again, turned it over. He watched her, seeing the life, the rampant vitality of her, her spirit. She'd nearly died. He couldn't get rid of that thought.

The robe was too short, and he really should have insisted she find something more to wear. There were other things in the shopping bag, but they both seemed to forget about that after she'd fallen into his arms. He'd forgotten everything for a few minutes. How to breathe. How to think. She'd wanted him to kiss her. He knew it with a certainty that made his head spin.

Yes, he really ought to go back upstairs for that shopping bag right now. Her legs were too shapely, too smooth-skinned and firm. It was too easy to envision them wrapped around him.

Why in hell had he brought her here? Was he completely insane? Did he really think he could keep her here with him, spend every waking moment this close to her, alone with her, and not lose control, not reveal himself? Maybe he *was* insane. How many centuries could sanity last, anyway? Was *it* immortal, as well? Hell, maybe he'd never *been* sane in the first place.

She approached the huge marble fireplace, whiskey-colored eyes catching its glow. Her gaze moved over the framed charcoal drawings of the ancient world. One depicted the Euphrates, cutting a path through the desert. She glanced at the artifacts in their clear glass cubes. Frowning, she bent closer to the marble figurine under the glass.

"What is it?"

"An ancient goddess of love and fertility. The Sumerians called her Inanna, the Babylonians, Ishtar. Queen of Heaven."

"She's beautiful. It looks old."

"Almost five thousand years old."

Her amber eyes widened, and she lifted the glass cube that covered the piece, then glanced at him. "May I?"

He nodded, watching as she held the small sculpture, ran her fingers delicately over it. "I can't believe I'm touching something that people thousands of years ago might have touched, something this old."

He wanted her to touch him that way. He was that old. Older.

She shook her head in wonder and replaced the glass. Then pointed to the piece beside it. "And this one? What is it, a goat?"

"Yes. It's newer, made around 2600 B.C. The blue in the horns and beard is lapis lazuli. The rest is gold."

"You collect this stuff?"

He nodded, watching her gaze move over his face as if its shape fascinated her. Then she turned to the last piece on the mantel. "This one's kind of ugly."

"It's not art."

"What *is it?*"

"A piece of a story." He moved forward to stand beside her. She squinted at the carvings that covered every inch of the stone's face.

"This is writing?"

"Man's earliest form of writing. Cuneiform script. This piece was done around 4000 B.C., in Sumer."

She studied it more closely, as if trying to absorb its meaning. "Does anyone know what it says?"

Damien nodded. "It's part of the story of Gilgamesh."

She looked up quickly, and he saw regret in her eyes.

"Gilgamesh. Oh, God, Damien, your book . . . the fire—"

"It's all right."

"But I—"

"Shannon, it's just a book. The latest translation. I have dozens of others with the same story in them. You've seen them yourself—"

"But it's precious to you."

It was. They all were. But how could she know that? "I can get another one."

"*I'll* get you another one. And a copy for myself while I'm at it." She sighed, her hand resting feather-light on the glass. "It was a wonderful, terrible story. I'm glad I read it before the book burned."

He frowned at her, trying not to see that in the firelight her skin resembled fine silk, trying not to hear the sincerity in her voice. "You did?"

She nodded absently, her gaze going back to the uneven chunk of stone. "Tell me what it says."

He closed his eyes. "You don't really want to hear—"

"I do. That story touched me, Damien. I think I understand the pain that drove Gilgamesh into the desert. I lost a best friend, too, you know."

"I know." And he did. "This is a recounting of Enkidu's death. Gilgamesh was at his side, clutching his hand. Enkidu looked at Gilgamesh and spoke to him. This is what he said."

Damien turned his eyes to the stone. "'You will be left alone, unable to understand in a world where nothing lives anymore...'" He tried not to feel the pain of that horrible day again. It had changed over the centuries, even altered its form, but never dulled. He still felt it like a freshly whetted blade slicing his soul. His voice thickened as he read on.

"'You'll be alone and wander, looking for that life that's gone, or some eternal life you have to find. Your eyes have changed. You are crying. You never cried before. It's not like you. Why am I to die, you to wander alone? Is that the way it is with friends?' Gilgamesh sat hushed as his friend's eyes stilled. In his silence he reached out to touch the friend whom he had lost."

Damien stopped with one hand braced against the mantel and stared into the flames. He only brought himself up out of the well of pain when he heard her sniff. He lifted his head, glanced at her, and saw tears in her amber eyes.

"It's so sad. And you read it with such emotion." She sniffed once more and ran the back of one hand over her eyes. "You should have been an actor."

"I am."

She nodded, biting her lip, turning toward him again. "You told me that you'd lost a friend, too. That's why you feel so strongly about this epic, isn't it?" He nodded, not trusting his voice just then to speak. "You've read so much about Gilgamesh. Was there more?"

"More?"

"To the story." She looked at him with so much hope in her eyes. "It's so sad to believe that's all there was. There ought to be more. Did he ever find the secret? Did he manage to bring his friend back?"

Damien sighed, shifting his gaze back to the stone. "He found immortality, but it didn't make him a god, the way he'd thought it would. It didn't give him the power to bring Enkidu back. It made him a demon. The people who'd adored him hated him and called him a monster. They didn't even believe he was Gilgamesh anymore, but some evil imposter. Their king was dead. His foolish search for eternal life condemned him to an endless existence, where he was forced to witness over and over again the triumph of the one enemy he'd hoped to defeat. Death."

She turned again to the stone. "It *says* all that?"

"No, Shannon. That part of the story hasn't been uncovered yet. It's just my own theory."

She stared at him for a moment, her jaw slack. Then she blinked her shock away and lightly punched his shoulder. "Cheerful SOB. Aren't you? Couldn't you come up with a better theory? Something with a 'happily ever after' at the end?"

"I wish I could."

She smiled, but her lips trembled just a little. She reached down to the stack of logs, picked one up and tossed it into the fireplace. A shower of sparks rained out, and Damien jumped out of the way. He thought his heart skipped a beat. But none made contact, and he hastily replaced the glass screen in front of the flames.

Shannon didn't seem to notice. She was settling down on the floor, amid the pillows on the Turkish rug. She crossed her legs and patted a spot beside her. "I could discuss Gilgamesh all night. He fascinates me, but I'm hereby tabling the creation of a happy ending for him until another time. There's something a little more immediate we need to talk about."

"Like what?"

"Like how we're going to catch Tawny's killer. We haven't made a hell of a lot of progress so far, in case you haven't noticed."

He lifted his eyebrows. "Does that mean you've finally decided I didn't do it?"

"Do you think I'd be here if I hadn't?"

It wasn't really an answer. Actually, he thought she just might be here either way. She had a little too much courage sometimes. "You have an idea where to begin? Because I certainly don't." He crossed his legs and sat down beside her.

"As a matter of fact, I do."

His head came up quick at the tone in her voice. Why did the way she said those words, that slight lifting of her chin and that hint of stubbornness in her eyes, send a chill up the back of his neck?

"Tell me, then."

She tilted her head to one side, eyes sparkling again. "You're not going to like it."

"Why am I not surprised?"

She smiled, and he knew he'd made a mistake by sitting down here with her. She was too close, and her scent twined into his mind, tying it up in knots. His gaze moved over her face, such an exquisite face, high cheekbones, mouth like a plump bow, small turned-up nose. He'd like to see that face twisted in an ecstasy so sweet it was painful. He could give her that.

Problem was, he was afraid he might kill her in the process.

Her brows drew together, her hand lifted to touch his face. "You all right?"

Her touch on his skin was agony. He turned away, and her hand fell. "Fine. What's this idea I'm not going to like?"

She seemed a little hurt by his action, but she went on anyway. "The killer is only striking the women who've volunteered to assist you. At least, that's the way it looks so far. I thought he might try for me when I became your latest volunteer, but he didn't. So we have to rebait the trap. I'll be your one-and-only, full-time, exclusive assistant from now on."

"Absolutely—"

"Starting tomorrow night."

"Not."

"I knew you wouldn't like it." She held his gaze, and in the bright challenge shining from her eyes he could almost see her daring him to dish up his best arguments.

"You'd be risking your life."

"Moot point. I might already be on his hit list."

"And you might not."

"You can't keep using audience volunteers, Damien. It isn't fair to make them targets—"

He stood, paced away and turned to face her again. "I won't use them anymore."

"Then he's liable to start preying on your paid assistants." She rose, too, and came toward him. "At least with me, it's an informed decision. Those other women have no idea what they're letting themselves in for."

He pushed one hand through his hair, hating that she made sense. "I'd rather close the show, cancel the rest of the performances."

"You'd be sued."

"I don't care."

She lifted her chin, standing close to him and practically on tiptoe, trying to look him levelly in the eye. "We'll never catch him unless he tries again. This is important to me, Damien. The risk is nothing. I've got nothing to lose. All I care about right now is catching this bastard and making sure he pays for what he did to Tawny."

"Shannon—"

"And I'm willing to make a concession." He waited. "I'll stay here with you, make it easier for you to continue in this role you've taken on as my protector, much as I don't need one. If you say no, then I'm out the door, right now, tonight."

"Where would you go?"

"I still have my office. I could bunk on the couch there."

Stubborn, beautiful witch. "I could camp on your doorstep and watch over you anyway."

"But I'm safer here. This place is like a fort."

He lowered his eyes, knowing defeat when it was staring up at him from a pair of honey golden eyes. "All right. All right, I give up. You win."

Her arms snaked around his neck, and she squeezed him hard. "Thank you, Damien. You won't regret this."

Oh, but he already did.

It was nearly dawn when she finally noticed the time and said good-night. And while he hated using mind control on her, he did invade her psyche just a little, instructing her to sleep the day through. He couldn't have her snooping around the mansion during the day, or taking off on her own and getting into trouble when he couldn't help her. She was just spirited enough to do either. Probably both. He was endlessly thankful that fire at her place had occurred at night. Otherwise, she'd be gone already.

Gone. The thought put a lump in his throat. He tried not to let it keep occurring to him over and over again after she'd gone up to bed, but it persisted anyway. He swallowed hard, and walked up the stairs to peer in at her. Some stupid need to see her once more, just to confirm that she really was alive and here with him.

He cracked the bedroom door. Naked longing, hunger, bloodlust welled up within him when he did. She lay there, amid the pile of covers she'd kicked away. Sound asleep. Her robe was a small soft puddle on the floor. If he were an artist, he'd paint her, just like this. Naked, relaxed, alive. Beautiful. One corner of the sheet clutched in her fist, held between her breasts. With everything in him he wanted to go to her, touch her, run his trembling hands over her flesh, explore her moist recesses with his fingers, his lips, his painfully erect arousal.

He pulled her door closed, pressed his back to the wall and drew a tormented, openmouthed breath, expanding his lungs until he thought they'd burst.

The thirst raged. The need. The hunger. And if she was going to be safe in this house, he had to find a way to assuage it. He knew, too well, that if he resisted, if he denied his savage nature too long, the craving would build and build until he was out of control. Until *it* took over.

That was the way it had been with the two dead women. He'd thought it would be all right. It had always been before. He'd only taken what they'd offered, sating his endless thirst in the process, feeding at their tender throats, quieting the monster within that demanded sustenance.

And for a few insane seconds in their arms, he might have taken leave of his senses. It was possible. Maybe he only regained his grip on sanity when he was home again, lying still, feeling their warm blood rushing through his veins.

No, dammit! He was certain he'd left them alive. He'd only sipped. He'd never be the instrument of a living being's death. Never. Anyone, a newborn baby, would be more likely to commit murder than Damien.

He tore himself away from the wall and stalked through the wide hallway, down the winding staircase. Now the hunger called again. This time, he wouldn't be stupid enough to deny its power over him. He wouldn't try to fight it or put it off. He couldn't let it grow until it reached the point of madness. Not again. Not with Shannon in the house. So near. So sweet.

She'd be succulent.

"No!"

Damien stopped in the center of the foyer, closed his eyes and focused on her mind, her soul. It took only a second to be sure she was still asleep. Before he left, he armed the security system. What he had in mind would take just a few minutes. No one could get to her in that amount of time. She'd be safe.

Damien slipped out into the night, whirled until he became only a gray blur to human eyes. And then he flew, a dark streak across the sky.

CHAPTER NINE

Shannon opened her eyes to see Damien standing at the foot of the bed, staring at her. His black eyes blazed. His jaw was tight, his stance rigid. He said nothing, just watched her.

She sat up, let the covers fall away from her body, and realized she was naked beneath them. She drew a gasp and jerked the covers up to her neck again. Then lifted her gaze to his. It hadn't wavered. She knew he'd seen her breasts for just an instant. She felt heat moving up through her face, a rush of embarrassment, and she couldn't keep looking at him. Her chin lowered until she saw only her fist, clutching the blankets to her throat.

She felt a tug. Then another. She glanced up fast. Damien held the bedclothes in his hands, just below her feet. He pulled them toward him. Slowly but steadily, the covers slipped away. She wanted to jerk them back . . . or at least part of her did, but she couldn't seem to move. Her arms were numb, heavy, useless.

Her breasts were visible now, and the blankets and sheets still kept slinking lower. Satin whispered over her hips, her thighs, her knees. She shivered, but it wasn't cold. Her ankles were exposed now. Her feet. Damien held the rumpled bundle of covers to one side and let it fall to the floor.

She couldn't roll away from those probing eyes, or lift her arms to cover herself. She sat still, immobilized by some force she didn't understand, as Damien's hot gaze explored every inch of her body. She saw the bulge at the juncture of his thighs beneath those tight black jeans he wore. She knew what was going to happen. She wasn't afraid. No. It was time. She wanted this. He took a single step toward the bed.

"Damien," she whispered.

"Let me love you, Shannon."

She couldn't catch her breath to answer, so she only nodded. He reached out to touch her—

Her eyes fluttered open, and she was alone in the room. Alone in the bed, under the soft weight of blankets and a comforter. She lifted the covers and peeked underneath. She'd slept in the buff for lack of a nightgown or any clothing at all except the loose-fitting robe, which tended to tangle around her legs. No wonder she'd had erotic dreams. The feel of satin sheets against her skin had been the inspiration, not the strange man of illusions. That was all it was. Just because he'd been invading her waking thoughts lately didn't mean he'd been the cause of her dream.

But she knew better than that, didn't she?

She grated her teeth and punched the pillow. She'd had a hell of a time getting to sleep. In some ridiculous part of her mind she'd been waiting for, even *expecting,* him to come to her. But he hadn't. Of course he hadn't.

She looked around for her robe, belatedly realizing it was dim in the room. Night already? She glanced at the little wind-up clock on the nightstand—7:15. Dusk. God, she never slept this long at once. Then again, she'd never had dreams like the one she'd just had, either. She sat up in bed, ran one hand across her forehead, and found it damp with sweat.

The knock came at her door and she jumped. Her gaze flew to the wood as his deep voice floated through.

"Shannon? Are you awake?"

She bit her lip. Her dreams had been accurate, if farfetched. They'd reproduced that satin touch of his voice on her senses. And the warmth of his breath, dampness of his lips as he'd whispered against her skin.

Not him, she reminded herself. My dream.

"Shannon?"

"Just a minute." She hopped out of bed, hugging most of the covers around her, still frantically looking for her robe or the clothes she'd taken off the night before. Nothing was to be seen. She made it to the door, opened it a crack and peeked through at him.

He stood close to the door, as dark and mysterious as ever. Spotless white shirt, tight black pants with tapered legs. God, he was sexy.

"I brought you something to eat." He held a plate in one hand, but his gaze was fastened to her shoulders and her neck, and the fist with which she held sheets and blankets to her breastbone trembled. "Can I come in?"

She blinked. "I'm not exactly dressed—"

He shrugged and shouldered the door open, strolling in as though it were an everyday thing. "Shannon, I'm around half-dressed, beautiful women all the time. I can handle it, I promise." He sent her a smile as she clumsily adjusted her coverings under her arms. He set the plate on a nightstand.

"Yeah, maybe you can, but I can't." She crossed to the bathroom, blankets and sheets trailing behind her like Lady Di's bridal train. Tugging her tails in behind her, she closed the door. "Where are my clothes?"

"I asked Netty to get them cleaned for you. They're in the closet."

He sounded as if he stood right outside the bathroom door. She didn't hear him move away. "Well, would you kindly hand me something to put on?"

He chuckled, but a second later he knocked. She cracked the door and his hand poked through, clutching a pair of jeans and a sweatshirt, and fresh new underwear. "Those aren't mine."

"Netty did a little more shopping today. Can't have you wearing the same thing everyday, can we? Take them, Shannon. They won't bite."

She took the clothes and closed the door again, then quickly dressed.

"I don't know why you're bothering. You won't be in them long."

Shocked, she stared at the bathroom door. Finally, it seemed, he was ready to make a move. It wasn't at all what she'd envisioned. "That's the crudest proposition I've ever had." She opened the door and stood, hands on hips, facing him. Butterflies battled inside her stomach. She'd been right in reading the signs last night. He did want her. The moment of truth was here. "Can't you do any better?"

He touched her face, trailing warm fingertips over her cheek, until she fought the urge to close her eyes and lean against him. "I can do better. Don't doubt it. But that wasn't a proposition, Shannon. Just a statement of fact."

Her eyes popped open and she scowled. "You're taking this just a bit for granted, aren't you?" She hadn't even decided to say yes yet.

"You said you wanted to be my assistant until we caught the killer, didn't you?" She nodded mutely. "Well, you certainly can't do it dressed like that."

Embarrassment brought heat to her face, but she turned her head to hide it from his sharp gaze, and tried to convert the discomfort to something more constructive. "If you think I'm parading around onstage in one of those skimpy sarong skirts with a bikini top, the way your other assistants do, you're in for a surprise, Damien."

"You won't be parading. You'll be graceful, floating, dancing. And we only have about an hour to rehearse, so will you kindly eat this feast Netty cooked for you so we can get on with it?"

* * *

This was not right. He'd fed, just to be sure the hunger was assuaged, just to prevent himself from feeling this powerful lust for her. And he'd been sure he was perfectly in control when he'd come to the room. He'd marched in, with Shannon wearing nothing but a tangle of blankets, just to prove it to himself.

But all it had taken to convince him otherwise was a single glimpse of her smooth skin, bare shoulders and delicate neck, the outline of her collarbone under her skin, the shape of her jaw. The lust hit him again the second he'd set eyes on her, hit him as powerfully as it had before he'd fed. Something was wrong. This damned thirst must be getting stronger. He'd never felt the need again so soon. Never!

And it wasn't a temporary thing. The feelings grew more intense with every second he spent near her, until he was thinking of little else. He wanted to feel her warm flesh pressed to his own, to hear the sounds she made as he worked her body, drove her to madness, made her want the things he did.

But he couldn't make love to her. For all he knew he might kill her if he did. And even if he wasn't the one responsible for the deaths of those other women, he still had reason to keep a distance from Shannon. He didn't want to let his feelings for her get any stronger. It would kill him to care that much again. When she left—as she must—it would kill him.

What was wrong with him? There were so many things he ought to be focused on right now. The killer who stalked the streets of Arista, the person who might make Shannon his next target, for one. If he hadn't killed those two women himself, then he had to know who had, or the murders might go on and on. And this new power his nature seemed to be gaining. He needed to explore it, to find answers to the questions tormenting him. He should contact this Marquand. The man might have some answers.

And then there was Shannon and this mysterious illness he'd worried about since he'd first seen its effects. He had, he thought, the answers to that in his possession, in the supposed CIA man's files on her. But he hadn't had time to go over them yet, with her always so close. Or maybe it was the guilt he felt at blatantly invading her privacy that way. But he needed to do that, to find out what was wrong with her before it became worse. She'd admitted that attacks like that had happened before—

She whirled across his room, into his arms, and flipped backward in an apparent faint. He nearly dropped her, he'd been paying so little attention. Her body's jerking movements were proof she was fighting laughter, and her eyes popped open a second later.

"I don't know how I'm going to get through this without giggling, Damien. It's so dramatic. I'm not a dramatic person."

He couldn't help but smile at the sparkle in her eyes, the dimples in her face. "No, I'd call you more irreverent than dramatic." He lifted her upright again and took his arms from around her. Holding her like this was too much, even now.

Netty's clapping came from the doorway and she hustled forward. "'Course it seems absurd now, Shannon, wearing blue jeans and dancing in a living room. It'll all be different onstage, when you're in costume and the music is thrummin' in your ears and all that misty stuff is twirlin' around your legs. You'll see."

"You think so?"

Netty wiped her hands on her apron and sent Shannon a wink. "Oh, I know these things. Toured with the Somerset Theatre Troupe in London when I was in my prime. Played Eliza Doolittle. Knocked 'em dead, I did."

Damien frowned. "You never told me that, Netty."

"You never asked," she replied. "Truth be told—" she tilted her head, addressing Shannon "—he's always been such a cold fish, I was beginning to wonder if there beat a heart in that big chest of his. He's different now, though, since you been comin' round."

Damien opened his mouth to tell Netty she was overstepping, but she cut him off before he said a word.

"Got to get to it, if I'm going to get to the theater in time to see Shannon's debut. If there's nothing else . . . ?"

Damien shook his head.

"Thank you for the clothes, and the meal, and everything else you've done for me," Shannon said as Netty turned to go.

"Nothin' of it, child. You remind me of an orphan in need of motherin'. I like coddling you just a mite."

Shannon's eyes widened, but Netty was already on her way out the door. She glanced at Damien as if dumbfounded.

"What is it?"

"What she said, I . . ." She blinked twice, then shook her head. "Just a coincidence, I guess. Never mind."

A short time later, she tugged at the bottom of the leopard-print bikini top and nervously adjusted the knot in the side of the matching sarong skirt. Roxy, Damien's former assistant, had not been happy about the change. In fact, she'd thrown a fit, and Damien had been tossing out one excuse after another, until, fed up and wondering who the hell had a name like "Roxy" anyway, Shannon had stepped between them. "Look, toots, I'm a PI. Repeat it and you'll wish you hadn't. I'm taking your place because Damien's assistant is liable to end up as some lunatic's target. Repeat *that* and I'll break your jaw. If you think I can't, try me. Any questions?"

Roxy, tall and elegant, stared down at Shannon for a long moment, gaping. Finally, she glanced at Damien again. "This had better be legit, Namtar. I have a contract."

"You'll still be paid for every performance."

She nodded once, spared a parting glare at Shannon, then turned on her heel and left.

Shannon sighed, shaking off the memory of the nasty little confrontation and focusing instead on Damien's every move out there onstage. She struggled to remember everything he'd told her. Keep her head up, back straight. Be graceful, confident.

That she was beautiful, and would be terrific. That was the second time he'd called her "beautiful." She could learn to like it.

When he nodded toward where she stood, she braced her hands against the prop table-on-wheels and pushed it out onto the stage. Damien introduced her as his "delectable assistant, Shannon." She waved to the crowd as he'd told her to, and was surprised when they applauded her loudly. The rock music swelled, and the show got easier as she went along, handing Damien the props from the table, adding little flourishes of her own now and then. When the trick was finished and Damien gallantly kissed the back of her hand, she fanned herself and winked at the audience. They loved it, applauding wildly as she sauntered offstage, pushing the little cart. It wasn't nearly as tough as she'd expected it to be. And it was kind of fun. She could flirt with him as much as she wanted, and he'd just consider it all part of the act.

She was incredible. So full of mischief tonight, and her sense of mayhem and devilment spilled over. It was contagious. The crowd adored her.

But when the mist swirled around his legs, and the low, driving music began for the finale, he glanced offstage where she waited and saw the twinkle had faded from those eyes. She was serious. She knew there was no comedy in this part of the act. He took a moment to be thankful she had her mirthful streak under control. He held one hand out toward her, and she swirled to him as the volume swelled. He took her hand, and she stilled, facing the audience, just as they'd rehearsed.

With one fingertip on her chin, her turned her to face him. Then, with a flick of his wrist, his fingers fanned before her eyes. The music pumped louder. She let her eyes take on an entranced, blank sort of stare. Then he slipped one arm around her waist, feeling the warmth of her flesh burn his skin. His other hand cupped the back of her head and he bent her backward. Drawing a steadying breath, he lowered his head to her throat, parted his lips, caught her skin between them.

And the lust roared to life.

It wasn't supposed to happen this way. He'd told himself that it would fade as soon as he began his performance. He'd repeated this same act, sometimes while the hunger was paining him, but he'd never been so tempted to make it real. He was sated. He'd fed last night just to kill the rampant desire. Why was it convulsing in his brain?

Her skin was like satin, and salty against his lips. He kissed her throat, and couldn't stop his tongue from stroking a slow path over it. He felt her shudder in response to that, and he heard her whisper his name, for his ears alone, a plea barely audible in her voice. Her scent twisted into his nostrils. The soft thrum of her pulse seemed amplified in his ears. He could feel the rush of blood passing just beneath the skin. His teeth closed just a little, and he heard the startled breath she drew.

Shaking himself, he realized that her hands clutched the back of his head. Her fingers clenched and relaxed in his hair, again and again, as if on their own. Her head tipped back a little farther and the pressure on his head increased. Ever so slightly, she pressed her throat to his sucking mouth. Imploring. Offering. Submitting. His body began to shake. The need engulfed him. Sweat dampened his face.

With a deep growl he hadn't meant to emit, he released her, tugged her arms from around him and lowered her, quickly and roughly, to the floor.

The crowd roared, coming to its feet as one entity. Damien faced them, blinking. For a few brief seconds he'd forgotten their existence. There'd been nothing but Shannon, the taste of her, the desire that suddenly exploded inside him. He'd even forgotten the capsule of stage blood he was supposed to break open and apply to her neck.

She was lying there, motionless except for the rise and fall of her chest as she breathed far faster than she ought to. His gaze was caught for a moment, mesmerized by the subtle lifting of her scantily covered breasts. They were large and round and soft. The valley between them seemed like a magnet to his lips, his face.

He looked away, sweeping the hair that had fallen to stick to his damp forehead with one hand. Without waiting for the curtain to fall and lift again, he swept the satin cloak over his face and whirled.

It was a raven that emerged from the fallen folds of his cloak tonight. It swooped out over the crowd before returning to the stage and then diving off stage right. The curtain came down to thunderous applause.

Ah, yes, this was going so well. Anthar watched, having only slipped into the theater in time for the finale. He was convinced Damien had been so engrossed in his pretty assistant that he hadn't even detected the presence of another ancient one. Of course, he never had. Anthar was good at veiling his presence from others. Still, he'd never been this close. Always before, he'd observed from a great distance, shadowed Damien's steps, witnessed his nights with those other two. But Damien had never sensed him there, and he didn't seem to have noticed Anthar's presence tonight, either. That was good. The fool was obviously enamored of the girl, obviously fighting with himself to keep his lust from sating itself on her. It was only a matter of time, then. Just as soon as Damien's will dissolved and he took the beauty to his bed, as soon as he ravaged her body and drank from her throat, Anthar would know. He was never far from Damien, always watching. He'd know when it happened, and then Anthar would move in.

It would be nothing to finish the job, to drain her dry. And he'd leave her in the bed where Damien had taken her, and he'd let that bastard find her there, let him believe her death belonged to him. Let him think he'd killed the one he loved.

Ah, the torment, the agony he'd feel then! It would be sheer beauty to see. And then the once-great king would take his own life. Anthar had no doubt of it at all. Gilgamesh the Great would be no more. His punishment, Anthar's vengeance, was at hand.

Anthar rubbed his hands together with glee and made his way out of the theater.

"You really are wonderful, Damien. They love you. Listen to them—they're still cheering."

Damien tried to take in her words without hearing the soft silken sounds of her voice. Erotic the way it stroked his ears, the way he could conjure it whimpering, sighing, crying out his name in the heights of pleasure.

Focus on something else, you idiot. Anything. The crowd, focus on the crowd.

He opened his mind, hoping the sensations of others would drown out his own. He'd feel their adoration, their love. It would be enough. It had always been enough. The only connection in his life, the only emotion he allowed himself. The love of the crowds. He deliberately ignored the voice of Shannon's thoughts, concentrating on those still cheering in the theater. And then his head came up sharply, and he grated his teeth.

Another, like him, was here tonight. Another vampire. God, he'd thought of this explanation for the murders, even tried to convince himself of it. But he hadn't really believed. Not fully. There'd been a big part of him that still believed he was the killer, and there wasn't another one like him for hundreds of miles. But one was here, tonight.

And the bastard was getting closer.

Damien leapt to his feet just as the door to his dressing room swung open. He gripped Shannon's arm, ignoring her questions, pulling her to stand behind him.

The man stood motionless in the doorway, staring at Damien. His eyes were black, his hair as raven as Damien's was. He smiled just a little and nodded, his gaze slipping past Damien to where Shannon stood behind him.

"I enjoyed the performance," he said slowly, carefully, and there was a slight accent to his words, maybe French. "You're talented, Miss Mallory."

"Thank—"

"Don't talk to her. Don't even look at her, or I'll tear you apart, right here." Damien was breathing too rapidly, and the rage that infused him was surprising.

One of the man's dark brows arched upward, as if he were puzzled. "There's no reason to be so hostile, Damien. I only came to talk to you."

"Then we'll talk alone."

"I assure you, I can be discreet, if that's what concerns you." He gave his head a small shake. "Perhaps this was a bad idea. Since you refused to answer my letters, I thought to see a performance, try to get a word with you in person.

I ought to have respected your privacy." He took a step backward.

"What letters? What are you talking about?" Damien demanded.

Shannon wrenched herself free of his restraining hand, thanks to his momentary distraction, and stepped around him. "Don't go." She slanted Damien a sideways glance. "Honest to God, I've never seen you so rude. What's the matter?" As she spoke she extended a hand, and the stranger took it, brought it to his lips. But when he lifted his head he was frowning.

Damien gripped Shannon's other arm and pulled her away from the stranger. "Who are you, and what do you want?"

But the other man's eyes remained on Shannon, and they were darker than before. "You'd best lie down, Miss Mallory. You aren't well."

Damien glanced at her, noting for the first time the paleness in her face, the coolness of her skin where he held her wrist. He closed his fingers, and felt the rapid patter of her pulse. And she was beginning to tremble, just a bit.

"I'm fine. Just a little tired."

The stranger's eyes sought Damien's, and the man shook his head so slightly it was barely a movement at all, as if to say, "She is not fine. Not at all."

Shannon drew a deep breath, and Damien saw her stiffen her spine. "I would like to go home, though. This theater is cold as a meat locker. Maybe you and Damien could talk there, Mr...."

"Marquand," he said smoothly, his accent utterly charming and seeming to fit perfectly with his Old World way of speaking. "Eric Marquand, and I think that's a wonderful idea."

"Marquand," Damien repeated. He closed his eyes, realizing his mistake, then wondering about it. How long had this Marquand been in town? Long enough to have committed two murders?

Stop being a fool, Damien, and get this woman someplace she can rest. She's on the verge of collapse. Can't you sense it?

The voice, coming into his mind so clearly it was as if the other man had spoken, took Damien by surprise. He'd never used the telepathy, always kept his mind closed and rarely spoke to others, except to command his victims to remember his visits as a dream.

He shook off the surprise and looked at Shannon again, this time attuning his mind to hers, as well. He felt the queasiness swirling in her stomach, the unbalanced feeling in her head, the cold creeping into her bones. Inanna forbid, not another attack!

"Shannon?"

"Fine... I'm fine."

But her speech was slurred, and her cold skin began to warm under his hand. He scooped her up and shouldered past the stranger. His questions could be answered later. Now all that mattered was caring for her, seeing her through this episode. Damn, why hadn't he found the time to read those files? Why?

CHAPTER TEN

By the time Damien's Jaguar sped into the driveway, she was barely conscious, shaking violently, burning with fever. He hit the brakes in front of the mansion, skidding on the gravel. He threw the door open, jumped out and ran to her side. His heart was in his throat as he bent to pick her up. It was bad. Whatever the hell this thing was, he knew it was bad. And it scared him. Maybe he shouldn't have brought her here, though she'd insisted. He ought to have called the paramedics, someone.

He started for the front door at a run . . . then froze when he saw the man who stood there, waiting. Enough like Damien to be his brother. Apparently, this Eric Marquand was powerful enough to travel faster than Damien could with the car.

The man nodded, grim faced, and opened the door.

Damien strode through, straight into the circular room Shannon liked so well, and lowered her to the sofa. The bold bastard came right in behind him, and Damien whirled. "Get the hell out!"

"Do you want to help her or not?"

His voice was very smooth, very calm. His accent barely noticeable. Damien tried to scan the man's thoughts with his unpracticed mind. He sensed no malice there. "*Can* you help her?"

"I'm not certain."

"If you hurt her, I'll kill you."

One dark eyebrow arched higher than the other. "For one so ancient you're very uninformed about our kind, aren't you, Damien? I could no more harm one of the Chosen than you. None of us can. None that I know of, at least." He glanced once more to the sofa where she lay trembling violently. "Blankets. Heavy ones. Stoke the fire, as well."

Damien scowled at the man. He was torn between wanting to set himself between Shannon and anyone who might be a threat to her, and his desperate need to help her. She moaned helplessly, and the sound slashed a path right across his heart, laying it open, making it bleed. He hurried to her side, sat on the sofa beside her. For all he knew this stranger could be the murderer. He wasn't about to leave Marquand alone with her. Not for a second.

"You'll find blankets in the closet at the top of the stairs." Marquand nodded, started to move away. Damien focused the power of his mind on the hearth, and the flames blew higher, roaring and snapping like a torch. The other man stiffened and sent an awed glance Damien's way before he continued up the stairs.

It was an hour this time before she calmed, and then she slept as if comatose. The young vampire had been of some help after all, feeding her some brew he'd concocted to ease her pain, lower the fever, and help her rest. Now he paced before the roaring fire, looking grim and sober.

"Why did you come here?" Damien finally asked, when he could drag his gaze away from Shannon's pale face. She'd be all right now. She had to be.

"If you've read my letters, then you know. I'm something of a scientist among our kind." He looked at Shannon and shook his head slowly. "I'd been warned against approaching you, but I have so many questions. I'm hoping you can answer them."

"Nothing more than that?"

Eric glanced at Damien, frowning. "I only came to see your performance, Damien. I've been hearing incredible things about you. My curiosity won out over my caution. Then, naturally, when I sensed this one's distress, I had no choice but to try to be of help." He tilted his head as he studied Shannon. "Never have I come across one so fair. Golden haired. Most are dark, like us." His head whipped around then, and that one irritating brow shot up again. "No need for that rush of jealousy, friend. I have a mate of my own. I've no desire to seduce yours."

"She is not my...*mate,* as you so quaintly put it."

Marquand's lips thinned. "What are you going to do?"

"What *can I* do?" Damien's stomach twisted into a knot. "You can see for yourself how sick she is. But she refuses to let me take her to a hospital. Hell, I don't even know what's wrong."

Eric searched his face in apparent disbelief. "Have you never known one of the Chosen before, Damien?"

"Of course not!" Damien spun away from Shannon, shoving a hand roughly through his hair and pacing the room's length. "Dammit, Marquand, you think I *welcome* this attachment? This fierce need to protect and watch over her? What does it come to, except pain and loss? I hate feeling anything remotely like this." With his audiences, he could accept the love and still remain distant. Somehow, it wasn't enough anymore.

Eric only stood, unbearably calm, and stared into the flames. "You have much to learn, my friend."

"Don't call me that. I have no friends. I don't want to have any."

Eric shrugged. "As you say. Still, there is much you need to know. About her, for example. How old are you, anyway?"

"Almost six thousand years." He heard the man gasp. "You can see you're just a child in comparison."

Eric came forward, gripped Damien's arm. "Were you the first?"

The light in the man's eyes was nearly blinding when he asked the question. "Why are you so curious?"

Eric's hand fell away. "I don't know. I've spent my entire existence questioning, seeking answers, experimenting."

"And I've spent mine in seclusion—except for the performances. I want no closeness at all." He glanced at Shannon. "She had to come to the theater that night. I'm afraid she might be dying. God help me, what if she's dying?"

"She may well be." Damien shook his head in instant denial, but the stranger went on. "None of the Chosen live beyond their fortieth year. None I've known of, at least, and I've tracked many through their lifetimes. This medicine I've developed is specifically to ease their discomfort at the end."

Damien's gaze was drawn inexorably back to her still, pale form on the sofa. The only color in her face were twin cherry blotches on her cheeks, from the fever. "I didn't know..."

"All right, my questions can wait. Yours are obviously more important right now. As I told you, Damien, I'm a scientist. The brutal truth is that these symptoms are what all of the Chosen ones experience near the ends of their lives. She's younger than most. Then again, her coloring is unique, as well. I'm certain that unless she is transformed, she'll die."

Damien swallowed hard and battled the bitter tears that fought to the surface of his burning eyes. He wanted to scream. To rant, to curse the gods. But he'd done all that once, long ago. It hadn't done any more good then than it would now. "How long?"

"How often do the attacks come?"

"This is the second time in under a week."

Eric nodded. "She has little time left, then. Days. Perhaps less. An attack will come, and she'll sleep, as she's doing now. Only it won't be sleep. It will be coma. And she won't wake from it. There is nothing to be done. The medication will keep her relatively comfortable." He moved forward, placing a hand on Damien's shoulder, squeezing gently. "I'm sorry, Damien. She won't suffer, I promise you."

Damien shook off the hand and walked slowly toward her. He fell to his knees beside the sofa and caught her warm hand in both of his. "I can't do this again. I can't watch her die."

"Damien, there are few mortals in this world who'd be emotionally stable enough to live as we do. It's not an option to be taken lightly—"

"The alternative is to let her die."

Marquand came forward, his steps soundless, stopping just behind Damien. "Would she want this? Does she even know it is possible?"

Damien said nothing. He only let his eyes trace the exquisite bone structure of her face. The delicate line of her jaw. The cheekbones. The satiny skin that covered them. And those lips, so full and plump, and slightly parted now as she rested. He couldn't bear to see her robbed of life. Not her, not the most vital, the most utterly alive person he'd ever known.

"She won't die this time, Damien. She'll recover. You'll have time to explain this to her, give her a choice. She'll need time to accept it as a viable alternative, time to consider the implications. It has to be her decision." He shook his head slowly. "And it will have to be made soon."

Damien felt a burning dampness flood his eyes. "Tell me something, Marquand. I think I already know, but tell me anyway."

"Anything," he said gently.

"Did you kill two women in Arista?"

He was silent for a long moment. "You're right. You know the answer to that already. I don't kill, Damien."

Damien dropped her hand, stood and faced the young one. "No, I didn't think you did. I would've known, I think. So this—" he lifted his palms up "—this curse. It's not even an option I can offer her. Not really."

Eric Marquand shook his head quickly as if trying to clear it. "Why not?"

"You've got no idea, do you? No, of course not. You're so young, so innocent. Where do you get your sustenance, Marquand? Animals?"

"Blood banks, and what difference does it make?" He scowled at Damien. "Where do you get yours?"

Damien paced from the sofa, deliberately keeping his back to them both. "Humans. The need..." His jaw felt tight. He lowered his head, covered his eyes with one hand. "Dammit, it gets stronger, more powerful with age. It becomes a living thing, impossible to resist. And only living blood appeases." He heard the words thickening in his throat, his voice becoming hoarse. "I can't see her die, but I can't condemn her to live like this." He lifted his head, found himself facing the tiny figure of Inanna. Her half smile seemed smug, knowing. He removed the glass, clutched her figure in his fist, raised his hand. "Damn you. Damn the world and everyone in it!" His trembling fist clenched tighter and the figure he held crumbled to bits beneath the pressure. He felt his face contort, and he bowed his head, pressing his fist to his brow as the dust and bits sifted through his fingers.

Marquand came forward. "Get hold of yourself, Damien. You have to explain this to me. Please, for her sake if nothing else. Are you saying... you kill?"

He didn't seem as much repulsed as he was fascinated. He stood beside Damien near the fire, studying him intently.

Damien lowered his fist, flung the remnants of the statue into the fire. "I didn't think so." He thought of the two women who'd ended up dead, and his fear that he'd been responsible. But he wouldn't divulge his deepest terror to this stranger.

"You needn't tell me, Damien. I hear you clearly."

Damien started, then twisted his head to stare at this stranger. "Damn you, stay out of my head!" He wasn't at all used to being around other beings capable of reading his thoughts. He'd mastered the art of keeping others' thoughts and feelings out of his mind, but never of guarding his own. There'd been no need.

"No matter," Eric said lightly, and Damien knew he was glad to have changed the subject. "It's easily learned. I'll help you. Tell me now, when did the need become so powerful? At what age did it become necessary to take from the living?"

Damien shook his head, devastation racking his body. Why didn't this child take his questions and leave him to suffer alone? Suffer? It wasn't a strong enough word. This was Enkidu all over again! The grief would kill him this time.

"I only ask because I want to help you."

"No one can help me."

"Dammit, Damien, don't be so...Enkidu? Is that the name you just—"

Damien whirled to face him. "Stay out of my thoughts, fledgling, or you'll go up in a ball of white-hot flames."

To his utter shock, the young man smiled. "Rhiannon said you could do it. I wasn't sure I believed her."

"Who the hell is Rhiannon?"

"Rhianikki, princess of Egypt. Only around three thousand years younger than you. Until now she was the oldest vampire I knew. But she's never exhibited this lust you claim. I mean, she does occasionally sip from the living, but only because she so enjoys driving Roland to the edge of frustration. That's why I asked when this powerful thirst took over."

Damien looked up slowly. *Roland.* He recalled the name. He'd helped a vampire by that name a couple of years ago. Poor bastard had been drugged and left for the sun. And Damien had gone to him, despite his vow of solitude. But he'd gone in disguise.

"Damien?"

He started, recalling the question. "Certainly more than thirty centuries ago." He searched Eric's face.

"You see? If it hasn't affected her, then there must be a reason. Something she's done or been exposed to that you have not. Perhaps I can find out what it is."

Damien's eyes narrowed in suspicion. "What is it you want from me, Marquand?" Hell, he sounded like Shannon now, questioning Marquand's motives.

"I want you to talk to me. Tell me everything. How you were made, by whom, when. I want to know if it's true that you can alter your form, and that you've accomplished flight. I want to know how you do these things. I want—"

"And in return, you'll try to find the answer to my unquenchable thirst." Damien turned in a slow circle and finally sank into a chair. "It's getting worse since I met her, you know. All it takes is her scent to drive me insane."

Eric laughed. "Yes, well, that isn't exactly the same hunger, my—Damien. I feel that, as well, at a simple glance from Tamara. You know that the desire for sexual release and the bloodlust combine in us, each feeding from the other, until it's impossible to distinguish them."

Damien's brows lifted and he studied the man again. He really did have a lot of knowledge.

"It's true," Eric said. "And that kind of frenzied need is only at its worst when the object of it happens to be the woman you love."

"I don't love her!" Damien roared the denial, shooting to his feet. "And I'm damned well not going to." He paced in a small circle, trying to contain his rage, trying not to vent all his anguish on Marquand, who was only trying to help. "All right. I'll agree to tell you everything you want to know. But I don't believe you can find a way to solve my problem, so I want you to agree to do one other thing in return." He returned to his seat.

"Name it," Eric said quickly, settling into a chair opposite him.

Damien folded his hands to keep them from clenching into fists. "I need help to find the truth about the deaths of those two women. I need all the help you can give me. And if it turns out... if it turns out that I killed them..." He looked at Eric, at his honest, intense gaze. He was beginning to sense that he could trust this man. "Then I want you to destroy me."

He hadn't wanted to believe the things Eric Marquand, the intellectual, had told him. That she was dying. That there was nothing that could save her mortal life. But as Damien sat beside the bed where he'd moved her and scanned the files this CIA person had kept on Shannon, he found only confirmation of what Eric had said. The medical reports were inconclusive. Her red blood cells seemed to be dying, inexplicably. Transfusions hadn't helped. The new red cells died almost as soon as they were infused. And her rare blood type would have made transfusions an all-but-impossible treatment anyway.

The Belladonna antigen. Eric had explained all about it. The Chosen, as they were called by the undead, were humans with the Belladonna antigen in their blood, apparently handed down from a common ancestor. They were the only people genetically capable of being transformed. All the undead had shared the same rare blood type as mortals.

Their other traits were not so easily explained. The way they exuded something that alerted vampires of their presence. The way the undead felt compelled to watch over them, protect them. It was, Marquand theorized, a chemical reaction of some kind.

But as Damien stared at Shannon's pale face, her golden tresses spread over the pillows, he knew that what he felt for her was more than chemically induced. He had to find a way to save her.

The files were thorough, and he read them front to back. They told of her mother's abandonment. Her childhood of being pushed and shoved from one agency to another.

At sixteen, she'd arrived at the last of the foster homes, where she'd met Tawny. And a few months afterward, both girls had disappeared. There was a notation that the man who'd been her foster parent was later convicted of child molestation, diagnosed as a pedophile and institutionalized. He'd committed suicide a few months later.

The bastard. If he wasn't dead already, Damien would have hunted him down and done the job himself.

"What are you reading?"

He looked up quickly, then set the papers aside and leaned over the bed. It was no wonder she wore the crusty exterior all the time. She'd had to develop a shell to protect her from life. He held her hand in both of his, and his initial urge on seeing her eyes open and looking at him was to press his lips to her fingers, her knuckles. Instead he lowered her hand to the bed.

"How are you feeling?"

"Better. Fine, actually."

But she wasn't fine. She was lying to him about that. She was dying, and she knew it. She'd known it for some time. He felt incredible relief at seeing the color slowly returning to her skin, the sparkle to her eyes, but he didn't let that relief show. She wasn't comfortable with his relief. Or his concern. And it occurred to him that she didn't want him to care about her. She never had. Now he understood why.

He got up, fighting against an insistent lump in his throat that wanted to choke him. He couldn't let her know that he was aware of her condition. She'd probably never forgive him for prying. Besides, talking to her about it meant dealing with it himself, and he wasn't sure he could do that. Not yet.

He'd let himself care about her. He was going to lose her. It was going to hurt. At least now he knew. Maybe he could keep his feelings from growing any stronger than they already had. Maybe he could minimize the damage, keep his head. Find a way to help her.

He flung back her covers and held out a hand. "Come on, get up. You have any idea how long you've been lying around? All last night, all day today while Netty fussed over you. It's night again, and she refuses to go home until she sees you're feeling better. Come on downstairs or we'll never get rid of her."

She looked uncertain. And then she smiled and slipped her hand into his. He tightened his grip, just a little. "You strong enough, Shannon? Do you want me to carry you?"

Before she could answer, the bedroom door flung wide. Netty stood in the doorway, glanced at Shannon and screamed like a banshee. She ran across the room with staccato steps and folded Shannon in a powerful hug.

She released Shannon only long enough to turn to Damien. "Out with you. She's wantin' a bath and a change of clothes, and then some tea." She put an arm around Shannon and urged her toward the bathroom. "You're goin' to be just fine, my girl. Netty will see to that." But Shannon's eyes met Damien's and he felt the warmth in their message.

"Go on now. Your friend, Mr. Marquand, is waitin' downstairs. I'll bring her along when she's ready."

Damien gathered up the papers he'd been reading and left the room.

All the while she bathed and dressed, and sat quietly while sweet Netty pulled a brush through her hair, the knowledge was eating away at her guts. Damien ought to know the truth. He'd been so good to her, and he deserved to know the truth. If he let himself care about her, even a little bit, it would only lead to pain. And he did care, a little. Much as she'd hoped he never would, and much as he tried not to let it show, he couldn't hide the look in his eyes when she'd woken up just now.

He'd gone through the agony of losing a friend. So had she. So had the mighty Gilgamesh myriad years ago, and it had brought him to a grief that had devoured his soul. She knew now, since their conversation about the epic by the fire, that Damien's grief was a lot like Gilgamesh's. He'd survived a loss that should have crippled him. What would happen if history repeated itself? He couldn't get through it again—she was sure of that. So the only answer was to tell him now, before he let himself care too much.

Is that the way it is with friends?

Enkidu's dying words echoed in her ears. For a second she heard them, as if she'd been there when they were spoken, in a voice gone weak and gravelly with physical pain, instead of having heard them read with that same emotion by Damien, identical agony racking his voice.

Netty helped her down the stairs and left, wishing her good-night before grabbing her coat and leaving for the evening. Seemed every time she saw the woman, Netty was leaving. Of course, that was because she'd been keeping such odd hours since she'd come here. Up all night, sleeping all day while Netty bustled around the place.

Shannon moved toward the library, with her heart breaking. God, how much she would like to have one night with Damien, one night to explore this electric pull he seemed to emanate for her, to discover the secrets of passion. To let him teach her all of them. It wouldn't be fair to him, though. She couldn't allow herself to get close to him, not physically, not emotionally. She had to warn him of the grim future, and then let him go. Let him distance himself from the pain, avoid it.

She stopped near the library door, startled to see two dark heads leaning over the desk. Damien looked up, saw her and shot to his feet. In less than a second he'd crossed the room, and for an instant she was sure he would sweep her into his arms. He'd hold her tight to his chest, his trembling hands clenched in her hair, and she'd hear his ragged sigh, feel his muscles slowly relax.

He'd never held her that way before. Except by accident, when she'd fallen from the chair. Her response would be automatic and irresistible. Her arms would wind around his waist. Her face would press into the white shirt, and her eyes would fall closed. When she inhaled, his scent would fill her, and when she exhaled she'd feel the warmth of her breath spread through the material beneath her face.

The fantasy died when he reached her and stopped. He stood away from her, his hands on her shoulders as if she might fall without support. He was touching her, but it was impersonal. A matter of courtesy rather than passion. And since she was determined to keep her distance from him, she ought to be grateful for it.

"You all right?"

She swallowed hard, nodded. But she wasn't. And she had to tell him she wasn't. "Fine, now."

"You shouldn't be up, Shannon. You need to rest—"

"There'll be plenty of time to rest when I'm...later. I feel fine now, really." She glanced past Damien, noticing the man she'd met just before she'd collapsed sitting at the desk, watching the two of them. "Hello again. I'm afraid I don't remember—"

"Marquand. Eric to you. You look a good deal better than when I last saw you." He rose and came forward as he spoke in that odd, old-fashioned way of his. His trousers were knife pleated, his jacket cut short, and both were spotlessly black against his crisp white shirt. "I'm glad you're feeling better."

"Thank you." She glanced toward the desk, the papers that littered it, and frowning, hurried forward. "What's all this?" She fingered the sheets, reading the bold print. "DPI?" She looked quickly toward Damien, then back to Eric Marquand. "Then this government agency is for real?"

Eric nodded grimly. "The Division of Paranormal Investigations," he explained. "A subdivision of the CIA and, I believe, the employer of your acquaintance, Mr. Bachman."

She turned slowly, staring first at Eric and then Damien in blatant disbelief. "*Paranormal* investigations? As in ghosties and ghoulies and things that go bump in the night? Is this where my tax money is going? But I thought the guy was just burned out and—"

"It's a bunch of hogwash, Shannon." Damien came forward, scooping the outspread papers together into a neat stack and dropping them into a desk drawer.

"But why are they investigating you? And why me, for God's sake? There's nothing the least bit paranormal about me." Neither man spoke, though Shannon waited expectantly. Then she recalled the questions Bachman had asked. He'd been interested in Tawny's murder. He'd taken possession of her body. He'd...

"You're saying that what was in Bachman's files was true, not just a lunatic's ramblings. This agency really does believe in vampires. Not only that, but they think there's one on the loose in Arista."

Damien opened his mouth, but Eric beat him to the punch line. "Yes, they do."

She felt her jaw drop and her eyes widen. She turned to Damien. "They think it's you, don't they?"

"They use government funding to investigate seemingly paranormal events," Damien explained calmly, sending Eric Marquand a look that could have wilted fresh roses. The look Eric shot back was almost as bad. They obviously disagreed over how much to tell her. "I imagine their main goal is in uncovering hoaxes, Shannon. Maybe they'll be able to find out how Tawny's death was staged to appear so much like some vampire's handiwork."

She frowned, shaking her head. "Are you sure that's all it is?" Her gaze sought Eric's, but he averted his eyes, saying nothing at all. She shot Damien another, probing, stare. "Because, Damien, if this Bachman's opinion is representative of the whole agency, then these people are serious. Your image could be digging you into a bottomless pit. On the other hand, it ought to be fairly easy to humor them. I'm telling you, fanatics can be dangerous, and this crew would have to be pretty fanatical to believe . . ."

She turned from him, pacing the floor. "You could fix it, though. Stage a press conference in broad daylight. Offer to undergo a series of tests, blood work, whatever. Get a photo op on the arm of a priest, that type of—" She stopped midtirade, stood in one spot and gazed from one man to the other. "What? What's wrong with you two, why are you watching me like that?"

"I'm going to leave now," Eric said softly, and the look he sent Damien was filled with unspoken messages.

"Eric, why are you involved in this, anyway?"

He smiled at her. "I've had a few run-ins with DPI before. I thought I might be of some help." He turned, nodded to Damien and left.

She watched him go, frowning in bewilderment. What was going on between the two of them? They obviously knew something they hadn't let her in on. She turned back to Damien, puzzled, then saw the nervous way his eyes moved over her face, the anxiety there, and she sighed. He was still worried about her.

She licked her lips. "We, um . . . we need to talk."

He nodded, but didn't seem to be looking forward to a heart-to-heart.

Telling him the truth about her health could wait. There were secrets being kept and she didn't like it one bit.

Coward. You're jumping at any excuse to put it off, and you know it.

"I'd like to know what was going on down here."

He shrugged, turning his back long enough to stroll around the desk. "We were talking about the murder, just tossing ideas back and forth. Eric wants to help us get to the bottom of this thing."

She waited. He stood there and stuffed his hands into his deep pockets, as if he didn't know what else to do with them, as if he were nervous.

"And you were talking about Bachman and this DPI. How are you going to deal with him, Damien?"

"I haven't decided yet. But not by blowing an image I've worked years to perfect."

She threw her hands in the air, palms up. "Damien, if the man thinks you're a *vampire,* you have to do *something.*"

"No, I don't."

She narrowed her eyes, moving forward until she could lean over the desk and look him in the eye. "You're keeping something from me. Don't deny it. I can see it in those black eyes of yours. What is it, Damien?"

"Nothing that needs to concern you, Shannon."

She squinted, as if that would clarify whatever was hiding beneath his words. "If it concerns Tawny's murder, then it concerns me." She shook her head in anger, and paced away from him. "Don't you get it yet, Damien? I'm *living* to get this guy. There's nothing more important to me. Nothing."

When she turned to face him again, saw the intensity in his black eyes, she almost amended that. There was something as important, rapidly approaching *more important* to her. Him.

"And we will."

"How?"

"We've already put the wheels in motion by having you appear with me last night. Be patient. Give it some time."

"I can't be patient. And I don't *have* time." He closed his eyes when she said that, as though she'd poked him with a hot needle. She rushed on. "I mean, you only have one more show, Damien, and then it'll be over. If he doesn't make a move, we might never know who he is."

"We will," he insisted.

She rolled her eyes, flipped her head back and turned in a slow circle, sick to death of his vague assurances.

He caught her shoulders in his hands, stopping her. "I have a surprise for you. Why don't you forget about all of this for just little while. You've been sick. You deserve to relax."

She lowered her chin, searched his eyes. "A surprise?"

He nodded, gripped her hand and drew her out of the library, through the hall to the circular living room and then along the arched corridor to the front door. He opened it wide and waved one arm with a flourish. *"Voilà."*

The Stingray glistened beneath its freshly applied coat of candy-apple red paint. Even its tires gleamed like new. "Is that...*my* car?"

He was pulling her down the front steps, into the biting October wind. It tossed his dark hair in a way that made her want to push her fingers through it. He stopped by the car, opened the driver's door, then ran around to the passenger side and slid in. She was still standing by the open door, shaking her head.

"Come on, get in. It's freezing out there."

She couldn't speak. A brick or something equally huge and rough-edged was lodged in the back of her throat. She sat down in the driver's seat, reached for the key and paused, her eyes widening. "What is that?"

She glanced sideways at Damien. He reached forward and pushed a button. The Spin Doctors' latest hit blasted from the newly installed CD player, rattling the windows. She reached up and turned it down. When she looked at Damien again, she found herself battling tears. "Why?"

He shrugged. "You wanted it red. I had the money. Why not?"

It was so thoughtful, so sweet, that he'd remembered her story about the Matchbox car. Even down to the color. "And the CD player?"

"You seemed to like mine."

No one had done anything so nice for her, not since Tawny had given her that stupid little Matchbox car on her birthday. She didn't want him to care about her, dammit . . .

But, God, it felt good to know that he did. Good and sad and terrible all at once.

She reached a hand up, touched his face. His eyes darkened. She could barely see them through the veil of tears in her own. His lips trembled slightly.

And then he turned away. "It's no big deal, Shannon. Come on, start her up and get some heat in here. Let's take it for a drive." He reached up to turn the volume higher.

Shannon bit her lip. Then she started the car.

CHAPTER ELEVEN

She ejected the Doctors and slipped in the brand-new Sting CD. Damien had a boxful of CDs stashed in the glove compartment. The guy was full of surprises. She didn't know why it felt like some kind of exquisite torture having him do something so wonderful for her. She wasn't sure if it hurt or felt good. She didn't know whether to laugh or cry, to feel ecstatic or depressed. And feeling both was exhausting and confusing.

She knew only that the small car put them close to each other, and the sentimental words flowing from the speakers now in that husky voice filled what little space remained between them. She could smell Damien, feel his warmth. An odd zing of energy, one she only felt when they were close, whirred in her nerve endings. It was electricity and attraction and awareness, and something else. As they drove through the cool autumn night, with fallen leaves shooting up behind them as they passed, she found her gaze on Damien more often than the road. On his strong face, his deep, glittering onyx eyes and his sensual lips with their dramatic color. He didn't have flesh-colored lips like a lot of men. His lips looked like fruit that's ready to be picked. And she thought they'd taste the same way.

His hand shot out to jerk the wheel to the left. She swung her gaze back to the pavement, where it belonged, but knew it wouldn't remain there long. She pulled a U-turn at the first wide spot in the road and headed back toward his house.

If there was one thing she wanted before she died, it was to make love to this man. The only problem with that was that it would end up hurting him. She bit her lip, negating that thought inwardly. As deeply as Damien felt things, she might very well end up destroying him. She didn't want to do that, and it surprised her just how much the thought of causing him pain bothered her. She hadn't cared enough about anyone to give a damn if their feelings got hurt. No one but Tawny, at least.

And to think she'd believed he was a killer.

God, her feelings were all mixed up.

Okay, better to concentrate on her most important goal in life. Finding this killer. Driving around listening to *Ten Summoner's Tales* on a starry autumn night with this incredible man was wonderful, but it was getting her nowhere.

"You know, he's never going to make a move against me when I'm with you."

She glanced at him as she said it. She'd studiously avoided staring at him for the past few miles, but his eyes were on her, dark and deep and dreamy, when she met his gaze. He blinked, as though she'd distracted him from some deep thinking.

"What?"

"Our killer. He's not likely to attack me when you're at my side. You know that."

He averted his gaze. "Maybe I'm not in as big a hurry to see him try to murder you as you are."

"I'm in a hurry to catch him."

"I'm not going to let you walk around alone with a big bull's-eye painted on your forehead."

"Then you want to let him get away? Because that's what will happen, Damien."

He frowned, his wide sable brows touching. "We'll think of something."

"That's not good enough." She turned slowly into his winding driveway, and he used a remote control he had in his pocket to open the gate.

"After the next performance—"

"The *last* performance."

"Right. When it's over, we might stage something. Make it seem as if you're alone, when you really aren't. Try to trap him."

"I don't want to wait that long." Mostly because she doubted Damien would go through with it. He was way too protective of her. It should irritate the hell out of her instead of making her want to hug him.

"Shannon, it's risky. It's using you like chum to bait a killer shark. It ought to be a last resort. With any luck he'll tip his hand before then, and we won't have to risk it."

She shut the engine off. She had her own ideas about how much they could and couldn't risk here. To her way of thinking, the biggest risk was the one that the killer would get away. Her life was no risk at all. It was all but over anyway. Where the hell was the risk in that?

"You're tired." He touched her shoulder.

"Hell, Damien, I've slept thirty-six straight hours. How can I be?" She didn't say she wasn't. She was. Drained.

"You're still pale."

She laughed a little. "Maybe this Bachman nut will think I'm a vampire next."

He didn't laugh with her. In fact, he looked pained for a second. She opened her door. "So, you won't let me try my plan tonight. I'm not up to fighting with you about it." She got out and started for the front door, knowing he was right behind her. "So how about we spend the rest of the night going over those notes Eric Marquand brought you? All that stuff about these DPI crazies." She waited at the door while Damien unlocked it, swung it wide and let her walk in before him.

"I've already gone over all that. There's nothing that can be of any help." He closed the door, locked it.

Shannon strolled nonchalantly through the short hall into the round room she was beginning to love. She let herself collapse backward onto the chaise. He didn't want her examining those papers Eric had given him. He'd locked them in the desk as soon as she'd entered the library and started looking at them. Strange.

"So, maybe tomorrow we can visit Bachman at his hotel, try to get him to answer some questions. What do you think?"

Damien blinked quickly. "I have a few appointments tomorrow. Business stuff. I'll have to be away for most of the day."

"Oh." She hoped her disappointment didn't come through in her voice. She wasn't eager to spend the day alone...

...*although*, the idea *did* present her with the perfect opportunity to take a peek at the papers in that locked desk.

He crossed to the hearth, tossed a couple of logs onto coals that never quite died down, then took a seat on the floor, amid the cushions. "Are you tired? You want to rest?"

"I'll be able to rest all I want tomorrow, while you're gone."

"That's a good idea."

She sat up, drawing her knees around underneath her. "So does that thing work?"

He followed her gaze to the wide-screen television. "Yes. I don't use it much. Can't say I'm overly fond of television. Mostly I watch the news and tapes of other magicians. Helps me spot my own flaws."

"If you have any flaws, Damien, believe me, they're invisible to the human eye."

He looked a little startled. She couldn't believe she'd actually done that. Flirted with him. She was a selfish bitch.

"I have them, Shannon."

Oh, why were his eyes drawing her to him like giant supermagnets? Why didn't she have enough character to resist? Why in the name of God was she sliding off the chaise and onto the floor beside him, curling up amid the pillows as if she just wanted to get closer to the fire. She did, and the fire was Damien.

"What are they? Your flaws."

His dark eyes were burning zigzag paths over her hair. "You'd run screaming if I told you."

She shook her head, and she read amazement in his eyes when her hair flew out around her and settled back to cover her shoulders. "It takes a lot to scare me. I'm not afraid of you."

His hand rose, floated magically upward, and his fingertips touched her hair, hesitant, unsure. "Maybe you should be."

She swayed forward, her mind no longer having any noticeable influence over her body's actions. She closed her eyes, tipped her face up and pressed her lips to his. They trembled a little, nearly pulled away. She pressed harder, parting her mouth in gentle invitation.

His sigh filled her. She drank it, and his hand slid more deeply into her hair, cupping the back of her head, holding her face to his. His lips opened and his tongue slipped between hers to lick at her mouth's interior. She opened wider, giving him all the access he could want. Her arms encircled his neck, and she kissed him with everything in her.

But he pulled away. He got to his feet, turning his back to her. He kept pushing a hand through his hair, and he bowed his head, staring into the fire. The tremors she felt racking her body were mirrored in his unsteady stance, his labored breathing.

"I'm sorry, Shannon."

She stayed where she was. If she got up, she'd go to him, throw herself at him like some desperate, love-starved wanton. She wouldn't do that, to herself or to him. "I'm not." She smoothed her hair a little and fought with her racing heart rate. "I've never been kissed like that before."

"Then the men you've known have been fools."

He still didn't look at her. She smiled at the compliment. A warm flood of pleasure rushed through her veins. "Wouldn't have mattered. I never wanted any of *them.*"

She saw the way his spine stiffened. He couldn't have missed the implication. That she *did* want him. God, it was unfair of her to put him through this.

He turned slowly, looked at her. "Shannon, believe me, you don't want to waste yourself on me. Especially if you've never been with a man. That's something too precious to—"

"Be honest about it, at least." She got to her feet, frustrated and angry and hurt. She turned away.

He caught her shoulder, turned her around to face him. "Shannon, I'm sorry—"

"Don't be. I'll survive." She shook her head hard, so her hair flew over her face like a curtain. "I never thought I could ever want any man, Damien. Never believed it was possible. Ironic, isn't it, that when I finally do, it's a man who doesn't want me back?" What was wrong with her? Why was she acting this way?

His hands on her shoulders trembled as they tightened, and suddenly she was crushed to his chest. His arms surrounded her, strong and hard, and her breasts pressed against him. His mouth covered hers, captured it, and his tongue delved and drank and stroked. Faster, rougher, deeper. She slid her arms around his neck, threaded her fingers in his raven hair and licked at his tongue with her own. God, he tasted good. She wanted him so much it was a living force inside her. She felt his hips grind against her and she arched toward him in response. His arousal pressed into her belly, rock hard and insistent.

A little tremor raced through her, along with memories she'd rarely allowed her mind to access. Memories of other hands, drunken, clumsy ones. And of fear. He seemed to sense her hesitance, because he lifted his head. "Shannon?" A choked whisper. Gleaming black eyes probed hers.

"Just promise you won't...hurt me." It was the voice of the little girl she'd been. The innocence she hadn't felt in so long.

His eyes fell closed. He levered himself away from her, just a bit, and his arms fell from around her, then rose to stroke her hair. "I won't hurt you, Shannon. Not ever. And that's why this insanity isn't going to go any further."

"Insanity?"

He pushed her away, turned her toward the arched doorway into the big dining room, urged her through it and beyond, past the library doors, to the wide staircase. "Go to bed. Rest. And don't ever make the mistake of thinking that I don't want you, Shannon. I do. Too much."

She turned, searched his face, not understanding. He'd ignited a fire in her blood and she wanted him to put it out. Here, now. She'd go up in flames if he didn't.

He averted his face, closed his eyes. "Go on. Now." Cruel words. Angry tone. Or desperate.

She ran up the stairs, trying not to cry before she reached the bedroom. She didn't want him to see her cry, to hear her frustration. The door flew open at her touch, smashed into the wall behind it, marring the satiny wallpaper. Shannon slammed it closed behind her just as forcefully, and with her back pressed to the cool dark wood, she felt for the lock, turned it without looking. Her eyes squeezed tight against the pain of his rejection. Her teeth grated to hold it back, but the battle was useless. The tears came—bitter, loud, hot tears that blazed their paths into her skin.

He'd said he wanted her. He'd kissed her as if he wanted her. But if he wanted her, he could have had her tonight. She'd humiliated herself, acted like a whore, offered herself as freely as if she did it every day. He couldn't know how much it had taken for her to open herself up to him that way. He couldn't know how much it had cost her.

She sank to the floor, sobs tearing at her chest.

The vase hit the hearth and exploded into a thousand onyx shards, raining down on the marble tiles, the pillows, the Turkish rug nearest the fire. Damien clenched and unclenched his fists, fighting to resist the desire that threatened to overwhelm him. He'd never wanted anyone the way he wanted Shannon. She drove him insane with lust. Desire tore through his brain, roared in his ears like a living thing, like a dragon breathing fire to ignite his soul, to devour his mind.

Inanna herself could never inspire passion like this! Dammit, what Shannon did to him.

"Damien?"

He whirled, his face, he was certain, twisted in a fierce snarl that would frighten the life out of a god. Eric Marquand didn't seem frightened at all, though. He stood there, nodded as if in understanding. "Are you all right?"

"No, dammit, I'm not all right. Do I *look* all right to you?"

Marquand turned away, as if to warm his hands near the fire. Damien had a sneaking suspicion it was actually to keep his expression hidden. "Are you in love with her yet?"

Damien made a noise halfway between snort and sigh. "That's the stupidest question... Of course not. You think I'm an idiot?"

"I didn't call you an idiot, Damien." Marquand still didn't look at him. It sounded as if there might be a slight smile hiding in his voice.

"It's physical desire. Nothing more. It's only because I'm spending too much time with her." Damien stalked into the entry hall, stopped near the door and snatched a coat from a peg on the wall. "I need to take a walk in the cold air."

"It isn't simple desire, Damien." Marquand stood beside him. "And walking isn't going to make it go away."

He thrust his fists into the coat, jerking it around him. "Oh, no? What is, then?" He injected enough sarcasm in his voice not to have it missed.

"Making love with Shannon."

Damien went utterly still, his back to Marquand. When he spoke, his voice came out as a rasping whisper, hoarse with pain and frustration. "I can't do that. I'm afraid . . ." He couldn't finish the sentence.

"Afraid you might kill her. I know. A hell of a predicament, my friend."

"I told you not to call me that."

"Keep telling me. I might listen someday." Marquand pulled his own coat on and calmly fastened the buttons, one by one. "Damien, I don't believe you killed those women, and I don't believe you could hurt Shannon even if you wanted to, but I suppose it's best to restrain yourself until we're sure." He clapped a hand to Damien's shoulder. "For now we'll walk, if you think it will help."

Damien turned slowly, searched this stranger's face, and felt, for the first time, the unseen bond between them. They were brothers. Marquand was sincere in wanting to help him through this hellish torment. That knowledge shook him to the core. For so long, he'd managed to avoid any kind of closeness, the slightest hint of caring. He couldn't imagine how to act, what to say. He swallowed hard, shook his head. It was as if, after wandering in darkness, lost, alone, without hope, someone had joined him. Someone with a candle.

I don't want this. Dammit, I don't want to care for this man... or for Shannon.

"Too late," a voice whispered from somewhere. Had it come from his mind or Marquand's? He glanced at the other man for an answer. Eric only smiled vaguely, and opened the door.

She couldn't have slept even if she'd wanted to, but she feigned sleep when she heard Damien's key in her door just before dawn. She knew he'd come in to stand over her, stare down at her. She felt his fingertips gently smoothing her tearstained cheeks, pushing the tangled hair away from her face. She smelled him, felt his warmth, heard his breathing. She wanted to open her eyes, to reach up to him. God, she wanted to feel those strong arms around her again, crushing her so tightly against him. Making her feel he wanted to be closer, closer than any two people had ever been. She wanted to feel his heart racing in time with hers, but...

She slammed her mind tight against those thoughts, against *any* thoughts of him. She resisted the urge to move her face against his touch. She could almost imagine his thoughts trying to reach her, his mind telling her to rest today, to stay here until he came back for her, not to wake until he returned.

Strange, the things her mind conjured. She closed it to him, refused to hear the odd things she imagined he was telling her. Refused to think of him at all. A few moments later she felt the satin touch of his lips on her face. And then he was gone.

She stayed in the bed a long time, only rising when the soul of the house screamed its solitude, assuring her that she was alone. She showered, dressed and hurried down the stairs, calling out to Damien just in case. There was no answer.

She'd been a fool. She knew that now. The attraction she felt for the man had distracted her from her purpose, and she'd lost precious time. There was no chance for anything between them. God, she'd known it was wrong even to try. She ought to be glad he'd rejected her. It would save him heartache in the long run. She'd been selfish, thoughtless, to let him know she wanted him. She must have gone temporarily insane.

Not anymore, though. He was keeping things from her, things that had to do with Tawny's murder and with Bachman and this crazy organization, DPI. She had to find out what. How could she hope to track down a killer if she didn't have all the facts?

Shannon went to the library, glanced around the room once before closing the door. She circled the desk, stopping behind it to give the drawer an experimental tug. Locked, as she'd known it would be. She wasn't unprepared. It was nothing to break into a desk drawer. The letter opener on the blotter was all she needed, and the drawer slid open without any further encouragement.

The papers had been arranged neatly in a manila file folder. So he'd looked at them again. They were supposed to be nothing, a bunch of irrelevant information, so why had he felt the need to go through them one more time? And what was Eric Marquand doing with a packet of information on this strange government agency, anyway? He'd said he'd had run-ins with them in the past. What kind of run-ins? she wondered. She shook her head, grimacing. With his dark good looks and antiquated mannerisms, it wouldn't be surprising if the lunatics had accused Eric of being a vampire, too. Crazy.

She removed the folder from the drawer, closed it and carried it with her to the circular living room. It was a comfort room. Damien was right about that. There was something in its shape and the lighting, the warm colors, the odd furniture, even the artifacts lined up on the mantel, that seemed to hug you close, warm your soul.

Only red-orange coals glowed on the grate. Shannon arranged a pair of small logs on top and blew gently until flames licked to life. Resin seeped and snapped and flared, and for a second she remembered the fire in her apartment building, the feeling of being trapped, the fear. But this place was the opposite of that hell. This place was a haven from anything bad. Or maybe it was Damien she was beginning to think of as her haven.

She went to settle down amid the pillows on the floor, but a sharp glimmer reflected the firelight, stopping her. She knelt, and saw one broken piece, then several, of what had once been an onyx vase.

Frowning, she picked up the larger pieces, then gathered the tinier shards by rolling them up in the rug. Then she shook it outside the door. She checked all the pillows carefully, brushing all the glass away before she made herself comfortable on them.

She tried not to imagine how the vase had been broken. Tried not to wonder whether Damien had been angry or frustrated, or just nervous and clumsy. Either way, she had to be at least partly to blame. And she wondered for the first time if maybe he'd been telling the truth when he'd said that he wanted her. Maybe there was some other reason he'd turned her away. But what?

Enough already. She'd come to the conclusion that thinking about Damien only distracted her from her real purpose here, hadn't she? When would she get that through her head? She sank into the pillows, opened the file folder and began reading.

CHAPTER TWELVE

He awoke with the night in the lush third-floor bedroom beyond the hidden door. He opened his eyes, his senses gradually sharpening in response to the usual stimulants. The silken softness of the satin sheets caressed his naked flesh. The plump feather pillow cradled his head. The warmth from the fire in the hearth below radiated into the room through the brick chimney in its center. The beat of the music from the stereo he'd set to turn on at dusk, with the help of an automatic timer, filtered softly from the speakers. He'd chosen Elton John tonight. A song called "Mellow," with a sultry rhythm that lived up to the title. The electric air freshener spilled the scent of the ocean into the room. The lights came on, dim at first, but brightening gradually.

All of it designed to comfort him in an existence where there was little comfort. He took his pleasures where he could find them. In things instead of in people. He surrounded himself with modern technology, luxurious fabrics, pleasing scents and soothing sounds. As he came fully awake, he knew it wasn't enough. Not anymore. He wanted Shannon. Her heated skin against his, instead of the cool satin. Her erotic scent filling him, rather than the artificial aroma; her sighs of pleasure surrounding him, soothing him more than any music could.

He sat up slowly as his strength filtered into him. His mind cleared its dull haze and began to sharpen. And then he went stiff with the sense of emptiness in the house. She was gone.

He threw back the covers, leapt from the bed, tried the trick of opening his mind to hers, of homing in on her thoughts and feelings to tell where she was. But his mind refused to focus. His brain screamed for action, and he complied. He threw on his clothes and ran downstairs to search the house, already knowing she wasn't there.

Netty awaited him at the foot of the stairs. "She left you a note," she said, as if reading his thoughts. "In the library, on the desk."

He shot a worried glance over her careworn face, and then moved past her into the library. Netty hurried along in his wake.

"Were you here when she left?"

"No. I've been in and out today, did some shopping for her, took care of some bills. She was still in bed sleepin' last time I checked in."

Damien strode to the desk and snatched up the envelope with his name scrawled on the front. He removed the sheet of paper, unfolded it, and imagined he could still smell her scent in the ink, feel the warmth of her hands on the stationery.

"Damien." It was written at the top of the sheet in her small neat hand. He glanced over the paper at Netty, and she nodded once, then turned to leave the room, wringing her hands all the way.

When the door closed behind her, he read on.

I couldn't stay after last night. I don't know if I can face you again, with the way I acted. I'm sorry. It was wrong of me to put you in that position, and I don't want you to feel guilty or responsible, no matter what might happen down the road. You've done nothing but look out for me. You're the kindest man I've ever

known, Damien. Maybe that's what made me want
you.

Still, I hope you can understand now, why I need
some time alone. I'm going away for a few days,
somewhere warm. Going to laze in the sun and try to
get my head together. Please don't come looking for
me. I want to be by myself, and I hope you'll respect
that.

There was nothing more, just her name scrawled across
the bottom of the page. But as he'd read her words, he'd felt
what lay beneath them. Her hurt. Hurt he'd caused. She was
ashamed of her actions, ashamed of wanting him. Damn,
that was the last thing he wanted her to feel!

And something else, there was something else. Something in the lines about going away that rang utterly false in
his mind, and sounded a warning he couldn't ignore.

She hadn't gone anywhere. He was sure of it even before
Marquand arrived, breathless, agitated, waving a bit of paper in front of him.

"You have to get out of the house." He said it without
preamble, after barging in. "I mean it, Damien. You're not
safe here."

Damien ignored him, still trying to puzzle out the truth
hidden in Shannon's lies.

"Damien, are you listening to me? Bachman knows where
you rest. He'll try for you by day as you lie defenseless."

Finally Marquand's accented words penetrated the haze
of pain and loss. "Impossible. No one knows where I rest."

Marquand thrust the sheet of paper into Damien's hands.
Damien didn't have time for this, but he glanced down and
read the brief note. "Bachman, he rests in a hidden room on
the third floor. The entrance has to be through the second
guest room on the right, though I don't know where exactly."

There was no signature, and the words were typed. No way to judge the handwriting. Damien shook his head in disbelief. His gaze met Marquand's. "Netty?"

Marquand shrugged. "It's possible."

"I can't believe she would—"

"I can't figure how else the bastard could have come upon this information. But worry about that later, Damien. For now you'd do well to get yourself another resting place, one well away from this house." Marquand paced the room in a small square pattern.

Damien frowned, studying the sheet of paper in his hand. "How did *you* come upon it?"

Marquand quit his pacing and turned to face Damien. "I simply checked the messages left for Bachman at the front desk of his hotel." He tilted his head to one side. "Honestly, Damien, you must begin to use your powers more efficiently. It's an elementary matter to use our mental powers to influence the actions of humans. I caused the clerk to leave his station for a moment and retrieved the messages. Simple."

"If it's so simple, then where the hell is Shannon?"

One of Eric's dark brows quirked upward.

"I told her to rest until nightfall. Mentally. It's worked before. Only this time it didn't. She was gone when I woke up."

"Interesting."

"Interesting? It's dangerous."

"It's possible she closed her mind to yours. The trick can be learned, even by humans, though I've rarely seen it happen. Then again, she'd have no reason to do it, since she has no idea what you are." His gaze sharpened. "You didn't take my advice and tell her, did you?"

"Of course I didn't tell her."

Eric shrugged. "Then I can only assume she felt reason to close herself off from you. Have you angered her in some way?"

Damien felt like screaming at the man. He was so damned calm! "Look, the why and how doesn't matter. She's gone and I get the feeling she's in danger. The only thing we ought to be doing right now is looking for her."

"So, look. What's stopping you?"

Damien nodded sharply and reached for the door handle. He'd begin with the car. It would be easier to track down than the woman. A firm hand on his shoulder brought him up short in the hall. When he turned, it was to see Eric with a pained expression on his face as he rolled his eyes, shook his head.

"Sit down, Damien. Clear your mind. Open it, seek her out."

"But if she's closed herself off from me..."

"You won't be able to influence her, but you ought to sense her presence, feel her surroundings, discern whether she's safe."

Damien shook his head slowly. "I'm not sure I can do it. God, Eric, you don't understand. I've never used this psychic ability. Never wanted to." He glanced up as a thought occurred to him. "Why don't you do it?"

Another irritated sigh. "The Chosen connect most thoroughly with a single vampire, Damien. In case you haven't yet realized it, you are that one for Shannon. I might sense her dimly, especially if she's in peril. But for you the knowledge will come much more easily. Try, please."

Damien nodded, but doubted it would work. He walked back into the living room, lowered himself onto the chaise and tried to relax and let his mind go blank. He closed his eyes.

"All we need now is Rhiannon with her incense and candles," Eric muttered. Damien opened his eyes, lifted his brows. "Nothing, just talking to myself. Concentrate, Damien. Focus your mind on Shannon. Put a picture of her in front of your eyes. Bring her to life inside you until you can feel her touch, smell her scent."

Damien closed his eyes again, and found it remarkably easy to bring Shannon to mind. It only took recalling the way her mouth tasted, its warmth, its depth, its heat. He shifted uncomfortably, but kept his focus. The sense of danger increased with his every thought.

It was incredible, that's what it was. It was absolutely incredible. No sane person would take any of it seriously, because none of it could possibly be true.

But it *seemed* true. Shannon had read the notes on the organization known as DPI. The Division of Paranormal Investigations. It was a secretive organization, one whose purposes the taxpayers and most of the politicians in D.C. knew nothing about. And its sole reason for existence, according to Marquand's notes, was to seek out and destroy vampires, though they claimed it was to discover their secrets through research. Marquand held the organization responsible for murders, kidnappings, torture.

Of vampires.

He claimed his own wife—no, *mate,* that was the term he'd used—had been abducted by the ruthless scientists. That she'd been subjected to horrible experiments just because they knew of her association with him. And that was when she was still mortal. Before he'd transformed her.

Still mortal? He'd transformed her?

Shannon had been shaking all over by the time she'd finished reading and replaced the papers in the desk. Marquand must be as crazy as Bachman. He actually believed himself to be a vampire. He *actually believed* it. Shannon wondered if he really even had a wife, or if this beautiful

Tamara mentioned in the file was just a figment of his obviously sick imagination.

But Damien believed it, too. He must, or he wouldn't still be associating with the man. He'd have had the guy committed by now.

She had to stop thinking about it, had to stay alert. She'd left the mansion in her car, knowing how noticeable it was, and she'd driven slowly, for a couple of hours, all over town, hoping to attract the notice of the killer. Then she proceeded to her office, driving so she could easily be followed.

Once inside, with the lights blazing an invitation to all comers, she checked to be sure the gun was loaded and ready. And she sat down to wait.

The killer, *the perfectly human* killer, would come for her. At least, she hoped he would. She couldn't have made it much easier for him. He'd come tonight or not at all, and if he did, she'd be waiting. She'd deal with Damien and Marquand and Bachman and their misguided delusions later. Right now, she only wanted to stop a killer, avenge Tawny, and she sensed her time was running out.

Death was a dark shadow that had been stalking her for a long time now. But tonight it felt closer than ever before. She could feel its clammy breath chilling her nape, feel its gnarled claws reaching out to her.

She had to get the bastard tonight.

She didn't have to wait long before footsteps sounded on the stairs outside. She stood up, lifted the gun, watched the doorknob turn.

But it wasn't the killer that quietly walked into her office. It was Stephen Bachman.

She lifted the gun anyway, pointing it squarely and steadily at the left lapel of that gray tweed jacket. He ignored it, walked up to her desk and took a seat.

"You ready to come over to my side yet, Shannon Mallory? Or are you going to wait until they make you their next victim?"

She blinked. He studied her steadily, just waiting.

"At least I know you're not one of them. You were driving your fancy car all over, right under the blazing sun."

"And you were following me."

"Smart girl. So why'd you leave him? You finally have sense enough to get scared?"

"I don't know what you're talking about."

"I'm talking about monsters, Shannon. Not the kind that lurk under a little kid's bed, but real adult monsters. Beings that live by killing. Animals that feed on fear and death. You know about Damien now, what he really is. You wouldn't be here if you didn't. Humans mean nothing to him, to any of them. We're disposable, here only to fill their twisted cravings." He leaned back in the chair and tugged on his flawless cuff. "You're damned lucky you got out when you did."

"You're crazy if you think I believe any of this."

"Any of what?"

"You know what. That Eric Marquand and Damien are...vampires. There's no such thing and you're nuts if you think there is."

"I don't think. I *know*." He tilted his head. "So the newcomer *is* Marquand. I thought it was, but I'd never seen him up close. We've been watching him longer than any of them. Almost had him once. Damien, we didn't know about. Not until the murders. I've only had him under surveillance since I got the report on that first body."

She laughed, ignoring the ball of knowledge that thudded into her stomach. "You're certifiable."

He leaned closer, his dark eyes intense.

"Have you ever seen him in the daytime, Shannon? Have you ever seen him eat? Hmm? Is there a mirror anywhere in that entire place?"

"There's food in the house. I've eaten there—"

"But he hasn't."

She shook her head. "And his schedule is only to keep up the image. It's a mystique, for the fans. That's all."

"A vampire murdered your friend, Ms. Mallory. And if you're not careful, you'll suffer the same fate...or something worse."

She frowned at him, her hand clenching reflexively on the pistol butt. She still pointed the weapon at him, too jumpy and nervous to relax her stance. "What do you mean, worse?"

He shrugged, got up and paced to the window. "I have a notion *Damien the Eternal* would have killed you by now, if that's what he wanted. I think he has other plans." Bachman shoved his hands into his perfectly fitted trousers pockets and pretended to study the view.

"Spit it out, Bachman. What are you dancing around?"

He glanced over his shoulder at her. "I think he wants to make you one of them. Keep you for his own sick pleasures. Forever. Worse than hell, if you ask me. You'd be his prisoner for eternity."

"How did you ever get so screwed up, Bachman?" She paced toward the door, then to her seat again, clutching the back of it with one hand, clutching her gun in the other. She stared at the floor, let the barrel drop along with her gaze. "Suppose I bought this line of crap? Wouldn't turning me into a vampire negate the whole plan? Wouldn't I be as strong as him then? How could he keep me prisoner?"

"You know precious little about the subject. Powers increase with age in these creatures. And he's so old we don't even have a handle on his origins yet. Marquand, we know about. Comes from France, transformed during the Revolution.''

She knew her eyes widened as her head came up again, knew she gasped. It was stupid, because she didn't really believe any of it. ''You're telling me Eric is over two hundred years old?''

He looked at her as if she was an idiot. ''That's young for them. The oldest one we have a file on is from Ancient Egypt, daughter of a pharaoh. And we suspect your Damien is even older than her.''

''You're nuts.'' She strode over to where he stood, near the window. ''Look, just what do you think you're getting from this visit? Why are you bothering to tell me all of this?''

His lids lowered to half-mast. ''Why do you think?''

She frowned, took a single step backward. But his hands on her shoulders stopped her. ''I like you, Mallory. I like your spunk. I even like the way you took my damned sidearm. Not to mention you're probably the sexiest damned female I've ever laid eyes on.''

Lies. All lies, and so obvious it was child's play to see it. He wanted something from her, and it damned well wasn't her body. She watched his eyes. ''You don't even know me.''

''I know you're sick, dying maybe.''

Her eyes flew wide. Her chin went up. ''How do you know that?''

''Your medical records. But you knew I had them. They were in the files you stole from my hotel room.''

Her medical records were in those files? But she hadn't seen them. Had Damien? Had he known all along about her health, and kept it from her? Why?

''You're a rare specimen, Shannon. You have a blood antigen and line of descent that makes you one of the few people in the world who can become one of them. Unfortunately, it also makes you sure to die young. They all do.

But we're doing research at DPI, Shannon, research that might help you."

Research. She'd read about their research in Marquand's notes. Tamara, strapped to a table in a hidden lab and tortured, until Eric Marquand had come to get her out. And then he'd been captured, drugged, nearly killed.

Maybe it wasn't all fiction after all.

"If you'd come with me, put yourself in my hands, we might be able to find a way to keep you alive. We might even find a cure—"

She pulled from his rough embrace. "Come with you where?"

"The facility in White Plains. It's a research center."

White Plains. It was mentioned in Eric's file. God, could it all be true?

"You'd be safe there, Shannon, under constant guard. We have the best doctors and scientists in the field—"

"So, then I'd be *your* prisoner? Hell of a choice I'm left with, isn't it?"

"You wouldn't be a prisoner. You'd be protected. There's a difference."

She was afraid of him all of a sudden. Afraid that he wouldn't take no for an answer. "Look, I'm all too aware how little time I have left. But I don't intend to spend it as someone's pet guinea pig. And I don't believe any of this farfetched crap about vampires. All I want to do is find Tawny's killer, and no matter what you say, I don't believe it was Damien."

His gaze raked her face. "I'm sorry to hear that."

There was a warning in his words. "Why? What are you going to do?"

He shook his head slowly. "You'll come with me, in the end. One way or another."

She lifted the gun's muzzle. "You planning to try and force me?"

"Not yet. Not with those two still out there. I don't aspire to end up like some of our other researchers who've tried that tack. But I would advise you to stay away from him, Shannon." He stepped past her, toward the door. "He's going down. I have no choice in the matter. He's a killer. And when it's over, I'll be seeing you again." The hardness in his face eased just a little. "And no matter what you might think, Shannon, it's for your own good."

She shook her head fast, following him to the door. "This is crazy. Bachman, he's not what you say he is. I swear—"

"You don't know. *I do.*" He opened the door. "I'm taking him out. There's no other way."

She argued, but she was talking to an empty doorway. Bachman was gone, threats and all.

She blinked slowly, feeling as if she were immersed in a strange dream. She wanted to wake up, but couldn't. She didn't want to accept that all of this was real. Bachman really believed in it, along with an entire division of the U.S. government. So did Eric Marquand. And Damien? What did Damien believe?

He found her sitting on the floor of her shabby little office, facing the door, her gun in her hand. Her eyes were perfect ovals of confusion. And damp. The lump in Damien's throat couldn't be swallowed away.

"I thought we agreed you would wait until after the next performance to tempt fate, Shannon."

He stepped inside. She stood. "I didn't think you'd find me so soon. You're too smart for me, I guess."

Frowning at the paleness of her face, he took a step forward. His heart jelled when she took a step back. "You afraid of me now?" he asked softly. "What happened?"

She shook her head in denial, but he saw the fear in her eyes. "I'm not. I just want to be alone, that's all. Can't you just go? Please?"

Holding her jittery gaze with his own, Damien shook his head slowly. "I can't leave you here alone. You know that."

She turned her back on him, and her hair flew with the abrupt motion. He wanted to touch it, bury his face in it, inhale its sweet fragrance. "I'm sick of you making all my decisions for me."

"I haven't—"

"You have!" She paced away, still not facing him. "*You* decided I should stay with you after the fire. *You* decided how we should investigate the case. *You* decided to let me perform with you, but only to put me off. And now you're deciding not to let me take what amounts to my last chance at getting this bastard. Look, I've been too independent for too long to let someone take over now." She stopped on the opposite end of the room, as far away from him as she could possibly get. "My life is my own. I say what I do and where I go. Right now, I want to be here, and I want to be alone."

"Why?"

She shook her head and looked at the floor.

"Dammit, I'm not leaving here without an answer." He strode across the room, and she cringed, sending a bolt of pain through his chest. He gripped her wrists, holding them to her sides. They stood facing each other, the window their backdrop.

She refused to answer, but the fear in her eyes was all the answer he needed. When she looked away from him, that fear increased. Her eyes widened and her skin went milky white. "My God..."

"What?" He stopped speaking when his gaze followed hers to the perfect image of her, reflected in the darkened window as clearly as if the glass were a black mirror. Though he stood beside her, his image wasn't there.

She met his gaze again, blinking, fear making her lips turn bluish and tremble as if she were freezing to death. "B-Bachman told me, but I... didn't believe..."

"Bachman. I should have known. He's been here, then?"

She nodded. What sense was there in lying to him? She searched his face, the same handsome face she'd found so beautiful before. "God, Damien, tell me it isn't true. This is all crazy, isn't it? It's a fantasy. It's a fairy tale."

He hesitated. "Shannon..." He tried to form words, but none left his lips. What could he say?

"You can't even deny it?" Shock made her voice a whisper. "I'm having a breakdown, aren't I? This is only happening in my mind. You aren't even here—I'm all alone. Maybe you don't even exist, and I—"

"That's enough, Shannon!" He put one arm around her shoulders and turned her toward the door. "Come on, let's get out of here."

She stiffened, resisting him. "I'm not going anywhere with you."

"The hell you aren't."

She snatched the gun from her waistband as she danced away, then leveled it at him. In a lightning-fast move, he took it from her, then crushed it to a small metal lump. He let it thud to the floor.

She shook her head too fast and stepped backward. Her pupils dilated, until the amber of her eyes was only a thin ring around them. He'd terrified her. He shouldn't have done that.

"I'd never hurt you, Shannon. You know that. You have to know that. I couldn't if I wanted to." Still she stared, wide-eyed, pale. He could see the erratic pulse thudding in her neck. "I can't just leave you here for the murderer to find. And I damned well can't leave you to Bachman so he can fill your head with nightmares or, worse yet, take you off in chains to some maximum-security lab for what those bastards call research." He saw her blink when he said that, and wondered if Bachman had suggested it already. "I only know about it because Eric warned me. Shannon, come with me. I'll try to explain—''

She lunged for the door, but he caught her around the waist and jerked her back. She ended up crushed to him, her heart pounding, her cheeks flushed. Her breaths came in short little puffs. She stared up at him, her lips trembling, and shook her head from side to side.

Having her this close to him stirred his senses to full alert. His heart raced in time with hers, and he spread his fingers over the small of her back. "Shannon...it kills me to see you so afraid of me. Don't you know that I could never hurt you? Don't you know...?'' He whispered the words, and saw her eyes moisten. His head bent, and he took her mouth, took it with a frenzy that couldn't been tamed. His hands moved all over her, unable to touch enough of her at once. He traced her spine, kneaded her shoulders, sifted her hair, caressed the gentle curve of her neck.

Very slowly it dawned on him that she was not resisting. Her trembling hadn't stopped, but it had changed. Her hands rose, timidly, before locking around him. Her head tipped backward in response to the thrusting of his tongue, and she suckled him. His ardor flamed high. He pressed his hips forward, to show her, and her hand ran up over his shoulders and down again. When she arched against him, he cupped her round, firm buttocks, squeezed them, pulled her harder against him, and heard the soft moan she made.

Insane with wanting her, he moved her backward until she bumped the desk. With a sweep of his arm he cleared it, and then he lowered her onto its surface. Her breaths came fast and warm on his face. He ripped the front of her silk blouse open. Buttons flew. Her breasts hid behind the lacy fabric of a bra, but he tore that away, too, baring them to his hungry eyes. With a little growl, he bent to nurse at them, feeding a need that went beyond hunger, beyond lust. He sucked hard at one tight bud, feeling it stiffen and stand. He caught the peak between his white teeth, snapping them down on the crest again and again until she screamed his name and clutched his head in both hands. Then he repeated the torment on the other.

She was panting now, each inhale short and shallow, each exhale a whimper. He lifted his head, watching her face as his hands moved to her jeans, their button, their zipper. He shoved the denim down over her buttocks, running his palms over their smoothness as he did. He pushed them down her thighs and she kicked them from her feet.

Then he straightened, standing between her legs with an arousal so hard it was painful. He stared down at her, bared to him, and he told himself he couldn't do this. He shouldn't . . .

"If you stop this time, I *will* shoot you," she whispered. "I don't want to hear any more of this craziness. I just want you."

He knew it was wrong, knew she was as afraid as she was aroused. And yet he sank his fingers into the silken curls between her thighs. He parted her folds, and explored her tight, damp center. He found the tiny nub, and pinched it between his fingers. She closed her eyes and cried out.

"Shannon, I—"

"I don't care! What have I got to lose, Damien? Dammit, make love to me!"

He prayed she wouldn't regret that command, even as he unfastened his pants to free his throbbing erection. He saw her gaze fasten to that part of him; he felt the touch of her eyes burning him. Placing his palms to her inner thighs, he spread her wider, and stared at the delectable feminine morsel before him. Then her hand closed around him and pulled gently. She guided him up tight to her slick center, squeezed him hard and let him go. Her gaze held his as she lay back on the desk, hips arcing toward him, waiting.

He sank into her slowly, gradually, deeper and deeper until there was no more of him to offer. He pressed tight to her, and she sighed long and coarse. Her hands clutched his buttocks. His hands closed tight around her waist, better to hold her to him. That grip tightened as he withdrew, and this time, he was not gentle when he plunged into her. Again, he pulled back, holding her imprisoned between his strong hands as he thrust once more. Her muscles tightened around him, as if wanting to keep him there forever. She lifted her head and shoulders from the desk, reached for him with her mouth, and he responded, bending over her, kissing her. He made love to her mouth as hard and deep and as urgently as he was making love to her body.

And then she went still, her entire body stiffening, her hands clenching, her breaths stopping for an interminable moment. He felt the tightening around him. An instant later she screamed aloud, and her body spasmed its release in waves that forced him to respond in kind. He spilled his essence into her, feeling as if it were drained from his toes. And then he sank onto her beautiful body, and he held her in his arms.

Watching their frenzied coupling from the fire escape, Anthar swore viciously in Sumerian and then in Babylonian and finally in English. He'd waited, waited endlessly for Damien to give in to his lusts and take the woman. And he had; at long last, he had. But he'd failed to drink from her. Somehow he'd overcome the instinct as powerful as nature itself, and he'd refrained from even a sip. Dammit! If Damien had so much as *tasted* her nectar, Anthar might have found an opportunity to separate them, finish her off and leave her for Damien to find. He'd have believed himself the villain. He'd have gone insane with remorse and grief and self-loathing. Why the hell hadn't the bastard tasted her?

Now Anthar would have to wait for another opportunity. And judging by the girl's health there might not be one. He hadn't realized how close she was to her end. If she died, his opportunity for the perfect revenge would die with her. Damien had to be driven to suicide. It was the only way to ease the agony of Anthar's wrath.

After all, that was the way Siduri had died.

Siduri. Ah, how beautiful she'd been, and how he'd wanted her. He might have had her, too. Anthar had often visited her little cottage by the sea. But alas, the Great Gilgamesh had stopped there, half dead and half mad, filthy and exhausted and starving. He'd paused on his quest for immortality, just long enough to destroy the life of an innocent barmaid. And she'd taken him in. She'd fed him, clothed him and held him in her arms to ease his pain. And when he'd recovered, he'd left her, cold snake that he was. He'd never once looked back, never once paid heed to her pitiful begging of him to stay.

He didn't even know how much she'd loved him, never learned of how she'd died.

She'd just walked into the sea. Just kept walking until she could walk no more. Then she'd swum. And like him, she'd never looked back.

Only Anthar knew. For he had her words, engraved in the stone tablet, written in the script she'd been forbidden as a woman to learn. She'd learned anyway. She'd learned from Anthar himself. And many other things, as well.

So beautiful, so bright. Dead because of Gilgamesh, as surely as if he'd choked her life away with his own two hands.

Gilgamesh would pay. Yes, he would, by whatever means necessary. He would pay by losing what he most loved.

CHAPTER THIRTEEN

She curled into his arms, trembling and all but limp, as Damien struggled to put her clothes back into place. It wasn't easy. When he tried to rise away from her, she clamped her arms around his neck and fought not to let him go. When he gently removed them and stood back, righting his own apparel, he saw tears gliding silently down her cheeks.

"Ah, Shannon..." He gathered her up, standing her on her feet and holding her to his chest. But her legs seemed rubbery and weak. She sank once, then stiffened her knees as if by sheer will. She cupped his face between her hands, searched it through the pools in her eyes.

"It isn't true. I knew it. It's all just nonsense. Bachman's crazy." Her words tumbled over one another in their haste to break free. "You're no monster. No monster could make love to me the way you just did. Tell me, Damien. Say it." She kissed his mouth, his cheeks, his eyes. "I've never felt this way before. Not for anyone, Damien. Only you, so you have to tell me it's all a lie. A dream. Make-believe." Again she kissed him, his jaw, his neck. Desperation making her tremble. He caught her shoulders to stop the madness, but she rushed on. "Yes, make-believe. An illusion, just like in your act. That's all it is. Illusion. Say it, Damien..."

The trembling increased, and he felt her kisses heating. Not with passion, but with fever.

He caught her face, held her away from him just a little. Her skin glowed milky white, with those telltale apples beginning to shine in her cheeks. Her eyes already dulled and took on that unfocused quality.

"Dammit," he muttered. "Dammit, not again."

"Jus' hold me." Her whispered words slurred into one another. "I'll be all right...long's'you hold me." She melted against his chest.

He closed his arms around her, scooped her up into them. He stared down at her relaxed face, her hooded eyes, and he felt a pain beyond all endurance. Something cold and hot all at once, freezing and burning his heart until the organ split into a hundred bits. He couldn't stand to see this, to see her suffer this way, to watch her die.

He clenched his fists as he held her, and cried out loud in his agony, the words in the old language. One no living man could know. He cried her name, and Enkidu's, and he cursed the gods and the world and life and death and pain. And then he buried his face in her hair and he wept hot, bitter tears.

Her warm, satin palm rested softly on his cheek. "Don't cry. I didn't want this...didn't want...didn't mean to love you...."

He lifted his head, staring at her in shock. She smiled very slightly, "I wish...I didn't have to die...to leave you...like this." And then her amber eyes fell closed.

"Damien."

He turned slowly, but couldn't take his eyes from Shannon long enough to look at Eric Marquand.

"Damien, you must bring her away from here. There's danger."

"Look at her, Eric...." Damien shook his head fast, as if denying his own words. "It's different this time, darker. More insidious."

Eric stepped forward and bent close to Shannon. When he straightened again, his face was grim. "I'm sorry. Damnably sorry."

Damien looked up, brows lifted, the question he couldn't voice settling in his eyes.

"She'll slip into coma before this night is out. She won't wake, I fear. The end is close."

"No...." Damien's knees buckled. He fell onto them, clutching her limp form to him, bowing double as he held her, rocked her.

"Come, Damien. Bring her to the house I've rented. Bachman's been following you and Shannon, not me. I'm sure he knows nothing about the arrangements I've made tonight." Damien didn't move. "Come, at least we can make her comfortable, keep her warm."

Damien nodded, mute with pain, unable to speak.

Blasphemous bastard, it's less than you deserve!

He stopped in midstep, tilting his head and frowning toward Eric for silence. Pure rage filled his mind, the thoughts, bitter with hatred, rang clear in his brain. But from where, or whom?

Watch her die, you dog! Watch her die and wish for death yourself, for I'll bring it to you soon enough, Gilgamesh of Uruk.

Just as suddenly as it had come, the sensations flooding his mind vanished. Damien shook himself, then glanced at Eric. "Did you hear it?"

"Faintly. The message was directed to you."

"How many others...like us...are there here?" He hadn't believed there were any besides the two of them in Arista, until now. Now he wondered.

"None, Damien. We'd know if there were. They'd have no reason to hide their presence from us."

"But they could? If they wanted to, they could?"

One brow bunching lower than the other, Eric nodded.

"It was a vampire, Eric. I'm sure it was. One who knows me." Damien bolstered himself after being thoroughly shaken by feeling such a rush of pure hatred flashing through his consciousness. He focused instead on Shannon, and the pain overshadowed everything else. "I can't even take her home. Not with Bachman planning to raid the place in search of me."

"He won't come near until dawn. It's still early. We'll be secure enough for the night, at least. We can make other plans from there. Come."

Moments later, Damien tucked Shannon's pliable form onto the chaise in the circular room. He sensed she'd rather rest here, near the fire, than upstairs alone in the big bedroom. She liked this room. Eric bent to add logs to the fire, as Damien sat beside her and stroked her hair.

"Oh, my! What's happened to her?"

Damien glanced up, seeing Netty's worried face, forgetting her possible betrayal in his concern for Shannon. "She's sick, Netty. Very sick."

"She needs a doctor, she does." The woman hustled forward, quick steps bringing her beside the chaise. She reached for Shannon's hand and grasped it to her breast.

"There's nothing they can do for her." Damien's voice broke, and he let his head bow. His neck seemed too limp to hold it any longer.

"You mean, she's dying?"

He bit his trembling lips until he drew blood.

Eric turned away from the fire. "Netty, some blankets for her, if you will. We can only keep her warm and—"

Netty backed away slowly, her face a jumble of confused emotions. "No, sir. No, sir, this isn't right!" She shook her head fiercely. "He said she'd be all right. He said it was all on account of the spell you'd put on her—" She broke off, eyes going even wider. When Damien's head came up slowly, she searched his face. "But you didn't put this on her. I can see that now, you didn't. Oh, Lord, what have I done?"

Eric stepped forward, coming between Damien and Netty even as Damien rose to his feet. "You're talking about Bachman, aren't you?"

Netty nodded, her gaze meeting Damien's again. "He said no harm would come to you! He said it was all to save Shannon. He told me you were . . . you were . . ." She shuddered and looked at the floor. "Demon spawn. Said she'd die unless I helped him."

"And you told him about the secret room on the third floor." Damien could barely control his rage.

She bit her thick lower lip, tears coursing down her face now. "Bachman said she'd die if I didn't tell. I only wanted to help the girl!"

"I ought to tear your heart out—"

"Shut up, Damien!" Eric held one arm out to his side to keep Damien from walking past him. Not that he could have actually stopped him. "Netty, it's not too late to redeem yourself. I intercepted the note you left at the hotel—"

She groaned softly. "I phoned him later. He knows, he does."

"Tell us what Bachman is planning," Eric coaxed.

She nodded hard, still glancing every few seconds at Damien, fear mingling with the remorse in her eyes. "I was to let him in at first light. He wanted to look at the room where you sleep."

"What he *wants* is to murder me in my sleep, you foolish woman."

"I didn't know. I swear it!"

Damien glared at her, then turned again to resume his vigil over Shannon. "I can't think about this right now. I—" He broke off with a shake of his head.

"Is it true, then? What Bachman says you are?"

"Netty, what kind of idiot would believe such nonsense?" Eric asked, with a laugh in his voice. "Bachman is insane, a fan gone over the edge. Surely you've heard of this happening before, stalkers plaguing stars of all sorts." He paused, and Netty nodded, thoroughly engrossed. "So, Bachman has convinced himself that Damien's stage identity is the real thing, and cast himself in the role of vampire slayer." Eric stepped forward, touched Netty's arm. "He's *dangerous,* Netty. He really means to kill Damien."

"And I almost helped him do it!" she cried. She buried her face in her hands, sniffling loudly. "I'm sorry, Mr. Namtar."

He didn't care, didn't even acknowledge her apology. He was too enveloped in pain to feel anything else. "Just go. Go, both of you. Leave us alone."

Netty broke into tears and ran from the room.

Eric came and knelt beside him. "It won't be safe here beyond darkness. You know that."

"I'll take her out of here before then."

"And go where?"

Damien shrugged, staring hard at Shannon, thinking of the words she'd whispered to him before her eyes had closed. "I don't know. It doesn't matter, really."

"Shall I return for you—"

"No. You've done enough. Keep your distance now, Eric. I don't need an audience, let alone any help for this grief. It's an old, familiar companion."

Eric nodded once, and backed away.

So alive. He'd never known anyone to be as much alive as she'd been. The sparkle of mirth in her eyes. Her delighted laughter. Her ferocity when she felt cornered or bullied or threatened in any way.

It had been a very long time since Damien had shared laughter with anyone. He had with her, he realized dully. Over and over again, she'd made him smile. She'd filled his loneliness with her constant presence. She'd brought joy and tenderness back into his existence.

And now she was dying. Leaving him to walk alone, as Enkidu had done. Leaving him, just when it seemed their goal of finding her friend's murderer was within reach. Just when he'd learned of another, a fiercely angry, vampire in the city. One who hated him—

He blinked slowly as he realized the implication of what he'd just thought. Another vampire. One who hated Damien beyond all reason.

He'd been responsible for those deaths! And driven by his own demons had staged them to look like Damien's work. That had to be the answer.

A light flickered somewhere in the endless night of his soul. He *wasn't* a murderer. The thirst hadn't taken control of him. More proof of that lay in what had transpired between the two of them before she'd succumbed to this illness. He'd made love to her. Frenzied, passionate, obsessive love to her. But he hadn't tasted her life's blood. He'd remained in control, despite the lust for her that raged inside him.

His reason before for not transforming her had been simple. He'd been suffering with the thought that he might be a killer, and couldn't bear to see her suffer the same someday. That reason was gone now. His other reason had been a selfish one. He hadn't wanted to let himself love her. He hadn't wanted to risk the kind of hurt he'd known before.

But it was already too late to avoid that. And if she were immortal, maybe he wouldn't have to lose her at all.

He looked at her, stretched out on the chaise like an offering to a demon god. Would she want it? Would she have accepted the dark magic if he'd offered it to her while she'd been able? Could she bear a life without daylight, without the kiss of the sun? Could she abide the notion of her eternal soul bound forever to her eternal body?

He swore viciously and turned away. He couldn't make that decision for her. He couldn't! No matter how much he loved her, how it would tear him apart to see her die. He had no right.

Tears swam in his eyes. He didn't battle them. He buried his face in his hands and felt his shoulders quake with sobs. And then her hand rose, touched his back.

He turned, sliding onto his knees on the floor. He clutched her hand, kissed it, then bent to kiss her face.

"I'm...sorry," she whispered. "I should...have warned you."

"It wouldn't have changed anything, Shannon." He'd have loved her even if he'd known all along. He was certain of that.

She stared up into his eyes, her own damp, unfocused and glittering with the firelight's reflection. She blinked at the tears, but more quickly flooded to take their place. This time she let them come and her hand clutched his tighter. "I'm so afraid."

He didn't know what to say. What could he say to comfort her?

"I've denied it, you know. Held my chin up, pretended to be this big brave person, but I'm not." Tears flowed freely, leaving angry red streaks on her skin. Her lips pulled tight, her teeth bared. "I don't want to die, Damien. I don't want to be brave anymore. I don't give a damn about dignity."

He stilled, staring down at her face. "Do you mean that, Shannon?"

Her face relaxed. Her eyelids drooped, and he knew the end was close. Her breaths came so shallowly, and so randomly. No longer regular. "I'd...I'd give anything..." she whispered. "Anything...if I could just live..."

Her eyes fell closed.

He cupped her face between his hands, shook her gently. But she was beyond reach now. Sinking into the coma Eric had predicted. She wouldn't wake again. But she didn't need to, did she? Hadn't she just given him her decision?

Not really. She's feverish, sick. She didn't know what she was saying, didn't realize I could actually do it . . .

All true. But did it really matter? Could he really bear to let her die? Could anyone, mortal or immortal, sit idly by and watch someone he loved slip away, knowing he had the power to save her?

No. No, that was beyond endurance. No matter how he tried to tell himself it was wrong, that she should have been given the option while she was still cognizant enough to make an informed decision, he couldn't turn away. He didn't have that much strength in him. He couldn't face the madness again, and he knew it would come. He felt it descending on him as he sensed her heartbeat slowing, her breaths becoming less and less frequent. He couldn't do it, dammit! He couldn't go on without her. He couldn't sit here and watch her die, when she'd just all but begged him to save her.

He lifted her, his palms sliding up to her shoulder blades. Her head fell backward, hair like a golden silk curtain. Sweet Sleeping Beauty. He was about to give her the kiss that would wake her from death's slumber. He was no prince. She deserved better. He lowered his head, and as his lips touched her skin, he whispered, "Inanna, forgive me. Enkidu, help me. Shannon, sweet Shannon...stay with me."

Anthar roared his rage aloud, forgetting his need for anonymity. It mattered little, for the heathen was too enamored with his precious morsel to notice. He'd noticed earlier, though. He knew there was another, one who wished him dead. He knew, and he'd be on his guard now. So much the better. The bastard would know why he suffered before he died.

But damn! To be robbed of watching Gilgamesh grieve for her death was a blow! He'd planned, waited so long. Of course, he'd wished to arrange it differently, to kill her himself and let the great one believe he'd done it. Then to watch Gilgamesh consumed by despair unto the point of taking his own worthless life.

All his plans were ruined.

Ah, but he would not give up his quest for vengeance. Siduri deserved to be avenged, and she would be. Anthar would simply have to kill Gilgamesh himself, and the woman, too. Her first, to increase the eternal one's pain. Perhaps he'd make Gilgamesh watch while he took her. Yes. She'd give little resistance, even with her newfound strength, she'd be a weakling compared with him.

And Anthar feared Gilgamesh himself, but little. He was nearly as old, the difference being a matter of minutes.

Anthar had followed Gilgamesh into the wilderness after Siduri's suicide. Followed to exact his revenge then. He'd caught up in the midst of Gilgamesh's meeting with Utnapishtim, the Enlightened One. The ancient wise man, it was said, had been made immortal by the gods in order to save him when the great flood ravaged the world. But he'd been charged not to share the gift, lest it become a curse instead.

Yet something about Gilgamesh must have touched the old man, for after great thought and much tormented arguing, he'd granted Gilgamesh's wish. They'd exchanged blood, and the act left Utnapishtim weak, and Gilgamesh strengthened.

"You will live forever now, my young friend," the old one had whispered, before sending Gilgamesh away.

Anthar slipped in right after, and took advantage of the old man's weakened state to force him to repeat the ritual he'd just witnessed. If Gilgamesh lived, so must Anthar. He must live long enough to have his revenge.

And so he had.

And so he would.

Shannon had no idea how much time had passed, when she opened her eyes. She felt a little foggy at first, as if her head were stuffed full of wet cotton. She struggled to sit up, but her bones felt heavy and uncooperative.

Strong hands helped her, eased her up, and she looked around, frowning. They were not in Damien's house. She glanced up at him, then remembered the way they'd made love, and she smiled softly. "How long have I been asleep?" Her brows drew together. Her voice sounded strange to her, somehow deeper and more resonant than before. But that was silly.

"All of last night, and all through today."

"It's night again?"

He nodded. His eyes were troubled, worried about something, and she had no idea what it could be, unless he was suffering over her sickness. Yes, that must be it. She'd had another attack right after that incredible sex on the desk in her office.

On the desk!

She lifted a hand to touch his face. She'd have to tell him the truth, prepare him for the eventuality that was unavoidable.

A low-flying bat swooped between them and shot upward once more, drawing her gaze. She gave her head a little shake and looked again. She could see every inch of its small body in perfect detail, despite the darkness. She could count the bones delineated in the thin black skin of its wings. Her eyes seemed to be working at high speed, because she could see each and every flutter of those wings, though they beat too rapidly for that to be possible. They ought to look like a blur. Then she bit her lip and her eyes widened even farther. She could *hear* each flutter, as well, and the piercing squeals, and their echoes bouncing back like sonar blips to tell the creature what lay ahead. And she could smell it. She could *smell it.* It was musky and ripe. My God, she felt the air currents stirred by those wings, passing by her face.

She shook her head slowly. "That's not possible."

"What isn't?" Damien leaned forward, gripping her hand, and she could count the lines in his palm just by feeling them. She looked up into his face, and saw the unearthly gleam in his black eyes in a way she'd never seen it before. She saw the pale perfection of his skin, and she knew his scent, erotic and enticing though it was, could not be human. His hair was too perfectly raven, too silken, too soft, to be human.

Or maybe she'd succumbed to an overactive imagination because of a lunatic named Bachman. Maybe she was having a breakdown of some kind. She licked her lips. "Damien, why are we outside?"

"We had to leave the house. Bachman planned to come for us today, so I brought you here."

"Where, exactly, is here?"

He smiled and glanced around. "A cave I know of, deep in the woods outside the city. You remember? We passed these woods in your car the other night. No one can find us here. You're safe."

The wind blew a perfect harmony. She heard notes she'd never heard before. Every rustle of every leaf, every branch as it bowed. "This is so strange."

"Tell me."

She looked at him again, shocked once more that he appeared so different to her, so obviously different from any other man. And so afraid. What was he afraid of? She shook her head. "No. There's something more important I have to explain to you, Damien. About... about this illness of mine."

He lowered his eyes.

"I'm..." She licked her lips. "I'm dying, Damien."

Without looking at her, he replied, "No, Shannon. You are not."

She gave her head a shake. He hadn't seemed surprised at all. No shock, no questions. Just a simple denial. He lifted his head. His black gaze stabbing into hers, he added, "Not ever."

She blinked. "What do you mean?"

...he wants to make you one of them. You'd be his prisoner, forever...

She tried to blink away her memory of Bachman's words, but they wouldn't leave. She shrank back a little. "Damien, what are you saying? What are you going to...to do to me?"

"It's done."

"What's done?"

He reached out, fanned his fingers in her hair, spread them wide, as if to feel more of it. "Do you remember last night, when death was so close you could feel its cold breath on your nape? Do you remember crying, telling me you'd give anything, if only you could live? Don't you feel it, Shannon? Don't you *know?*"

Her breath caught in her throat. She remembered very little after their lovemaking on the desk. Too little. Hadn't she decided that all of this talk of vampires was craziness? Someone's insane fantasy? It couldn't be real. Hadn't she begged Damien to confirm that for her, right after they'd made love?

And hadn't he failed to do it?

There are no such things as vampires!

She stood up, feeling an unfamiliar strength seep into her. The fogginess in her brain had gone, leaving it sharp and alert. Her senses jangled with awareness, as though a zillion electrodes were pulsing tiny currents into her nerve endings. She felt energized, healthy, strong. More alive than she ever had.

She glanced down, opening and closing her hand and studying it as she did. Why did it feel so different? At last, she pressed that same palm to her throat, driven by some wild impulse, some impossible notion. And she felt the tiny indentations, two punctures, quickly healing over.

Her gaze flew to his. She shook her head in denial.

"It's all right, Shannon. There's nothing to be afraid of." He lifted a hand, took a step toward her. "You won't be sick anymore. You won't die. You'll never die."

"My God!" Another step away, and still he advanced. "My God, it's true, you are—"

"And so are you."

"No!" But even as she shrieked the word, she knew it had to be true. Why else were her perceptions so altered? She cupped her palm over the wounds on her throat, as if covering them could make them disappear. "How could you, Damien! How could you do this to me?" Tears crept into her voice. She choked on them, fought them down.

"Shannon, I had to. You were dying. I couldn't let you die when you kept telling me how much you wanted to live."

"You can't do this, dammit!"

He lowered his hands, stood where he was. He seemed to bear some silent devastation she was beyond caring about. "It's done." Like a judge handing down an irrefutable sentence. Two words with more meaning than any she'd ever heard.

"So, now what happens? You keep me with you forever? I turn to you for everything? Is that what you expect now, Damien? Because you know I can't exist this way on my own, don't you? You know I have no idea how to survive like this, what to do, where to turn. So I'm utterly dependent—is that the idea?"

She was terrified, *terrified* of what she was now. Alive or dead? Human or some other sort of creature? Natural or a freak? Immortal or damned?

He only shook his head, obviously confused. "Of course you can depend on me to—"

"The hell I will!" She shouted it, her voice too loud to be natural, so loud it hurt her own ears. She squeezed her eyes tight and forced herself to speak more softly. "What can kill us?"

"What?"

"What can kill us? Tell me, damn you."

He blinked slowly before answering. "Sunlight. The slightest touch of a live flame. Any injury that causes severe bleeding. We're like hemophiliacs in that way. If you can't get the bleeding stopped right away you..." His voice trailed off. "Shannon, why are you asking me this?"

"Because I need to know. Because I don't know if I want to live like this. Because..." She covered her face with both hands and turned away from him. She was a liar and a coward. She *didn't* want to die, and she knew it. But God, what was this alternative he'd given her? Blindly, sobbing, she took a few steps away, toward the mouth of the cave.

"Where are you going?"

"Away. Just away."

He followed, catching her shoulder. She jerked back from his touch. "Shannon, you can't just go off by yourself."

"Why the hell not?"

He stood there gripping her arm. "Please. Just sit down, give yourself time to adjust. Let me explain what all of this means...."

"Leave me alone!" She pulled away, stood facing him, breathless with shock and anger. "I swear to God, if you don't let me go I'll hate you forever. Does that even matter to you, Damien? Or was Bachman right about that, too?" She turned again, and raced off into the forest, into the night.

* * *

Damien didn't go after her. He couldn't. His grief over what he'd done, preserved her life, transformed her into something she couldn't begin to understand, his knowledge that he'd acted for reasons purely selfish, nearly paralyzed him with pain. He hurt, he ached, for her. For what she was suffering right now. The confusion. The fear. And yet he couldn't bring himself to regret what he'd done. He couldn't be anything but glad that she was alive when he rose tonight, instead of lying cold and lifeless, forever still on the chaise. That was the alternative. That was what he could have risen to see tonight, would have, if he hadn't acted.

So he didn't regret it. He only wished he'd done it differently, explained things to her earlier, before the decision had to be made, allowed her to choose.

He started after her, only to find his way blocked by a solid form. His eyes met Eric's and found understanding, even sympathy, there. "Let her go, Damien. She needs time. She has to explore this new realm she finds herself inhabiting, grow accustomed to it."

Damien shoved Eric aside and strode on. "How can I let her go? You said yourself what kind of bastard this Bachman might be. You think I want to see her captured for live study by that animal? And what about this rogue vampire that's on the rampage? How do you know she's safe from him?"

Eric kept pace easily. "I didn't say we couldn't watch her. We'll keep her in sight, but from a distance. Damien, you have to give her a chance to accept this on her own. You've forced it down her throat and she's choking. Can't you see that?"

Damien stopped. He turned to stare at the other man. Then felt his own shoulders slump in concession. "You're insightful, Eric. I'll give you that."

"I'm glad you think it. For I have a few other notions. I haven't wished to involve my mate in this for fear of the risk."

"Risk?"

Eric nodded. "I'd no idea what sort of temper you possessed when first I approached you, Damien."

"And now?"

"No worse than most. I believe Tamara can be of help to your Shannon."

"That might be true." Damien walked on, but his pace was slower. Part of his mind remained focused on Shannon, felt her tears, her confusion. Another part listened intently to what Eric suggested. "There's still Bachman, and this rogue we've discovered."

"I wouldn't bring her here if I had a choice, Damien. But the fact is, she's coming, whether I like it or not. She'll be at the house I rented within the hour."

Damien only looked at him, brows raised in question as he waited for Eric to finish.

"She worries about me. She found out about Bachman's presence here, and nothing could stop her from joining me."

Damien blinked, wondering what that kind of devotion must feel like. "You're a lucky man, Marquand."

"That I am."

"Go on to your house, then, and wait for your fierce protector. I'm going back to the mansion to watch over Shannon." At Eric's frown he added, "From a distance."

CHAPTER FOURTEEN

She tried not to notice how fast she was walking, or that she didn't get winded, or that her heart didn't even speed up. She ignored the fact that, while she felt the cold as she never had before, felt its crisp touch on every inch of her body, she didn't *feel* cold, or uncomfortable with it. She didn't get goose bumps or shiver. She tried to pay no attention to the incredibly flavorful *taste* of every breath she drew, or the scents of every plant and animal she passed, and of the air itself.

God, but she'd never been so aware!

When she reached Damien's house, she climbed the gate with no trouble, wondering about this new agility and strength. She walked inside, resisting the astonishing differences. The colors in the Turkish rugs that she'd never seen before. The intricate patterns. The smell of the fire. The taste of the wood smoke.

It would overwhelm her if she paid attention. She felt she could sit for hours and explore her heightened senses. The flames in the hearth . . .

My God, the flames. Look at them!

She stared, paralyzed by the beauty of the dancing tongues of light and energy and color. She had to force herself to break away.

Not now. Not now. She wanted only to gather up her belongings, toss them into her car and drive far away from here. Far away from Damien and Eric Marquand and this entire nightmare she'd fallen into.

She started through the round room, not intending to pause at all, when something stopped her. Some inner knowledge she couldn't understand made the hair on her nape stand up. And she went still, trying to find the source. Finally she turned around. Her gaze went to the arched doorway on the other side, and Bachman stepped out from his hiding place just beyond the beads, his gun pointed right at her.

Some hysterical person inside her began to laugh. It began as a chuckle and grew, gaining strength until she was gripping her middle with both hands, tears pooling in her eyes. She could easily have let it go on until she sank to the floor and the laughter led to hysteria and the hysteria to madness. But she didn't. She caught hold of herself. She stopped the laughter and eyed the weapon. "Bachman, what are you doing? You want me to take that one away from you, too?"

"Where is he, Shannon?"

She shrugged and wiped her eyes dry. "Not here. But you must already know that. You've been searching the place all day, haven't you?"

He frowned, scanning her face, and she stiffened, wondering what he saw. She waited, her breath halted.

"You've been crying. Why?"

She blinked, nearly limp with relief. He didn't see the change, he couldn't. Mindful of the marks on her neck, she lowered her head. When she lifted it again her hair hung down the front of her shoulders, hiding the wounds. "Oh, Bachman, why didn't I listen to you?" She let a few new tears dampen her lashes. "I thought I loved him, you know. But he left me. Just walked out."

"And you don't know where he went?"

She shook her head sadly. "I hate him now." It wasn't true. She didn't know what she felt for Damien anymore, but it wasn't hatred. She didn't think it ever would be.

Bachman nodded, but didn't put the gun away. His face softened a little. "Shannon, come with me to the institute. We might be able to help you there."

It was a lie. She knew it the second the words left his lips. She wasn't even certain Bachman *knew* it was a lie, but she did. Amazing. Not the slight intuition she'd felt when he'd lied to her before, but a glaring neon sign flashing in her mind. "Are there others there, others like me?"

He nodded, and for an instant she glimpsed a frightening image. Men and women imprisoned in cell-like rooms. Strapped to tables. Desolation in their faces.

She licked her lips. "I don't know." Fear gripped her heart. He might honestly think he could help her, but she knew he couldn't. If she went with him, she'd become a prisoner, a research object, a guinea pig. She took a step away from him. "I'll think about it, though. Give me until tomorrow to—"

His eyes narrowed and the gun's muzzle lifted a fraction. He shook his head. "No, Shannon. You're coming with me now."

She felt herself go cold all over.

"I'm not leaving here without you," he said softly, dangerously. "I wanted to wait until I had him, but he's gone. My chance to get him is gone. But I'm not going back to White Plains empty-handed. And I'm damned well not leaving you here to die." He shook his head. "Besides, I'm not sure you don't know where he is. Maybe I can convince you to tell me."

"I told you—I don't know. He's gone. He's not coming back." She defended Damien instantly and without any hesitation. Yes, she was angry with him for what he'd done to her. But this was instinctive and had nothing to do with the other.

"He'll come if you're in trouble, I think. I didn't want to do it this way, Shannon, but if I were to, say, shoot you, I think he'd know. I think he'd be here in a matter of minutes. Seconds, maybe." He worked the action of the gun.

Fear rippled through her and her mind sought wildly for an answer. But the sixth sense she'd felt before seemed to have deserted her. Was he bluffing or would he really do it? She couldn't just stand there and let him shoot her. She held her hands in front of her, palms out. "No, don't. I'll go with you. I'll tell you where he is—I will."

Bachman nodded, his frown altering, softening. "I figured you'd change your mind. Don't worry about him, Shannon. He won't suffer. That's if I decide to let him live long enough to take him in. I might not. He's a murderer. Someone has to stop him. Someone has to stop them all."

Then there were others. Others like Damien, hunted and persecuted by people like Bachman, and maybe even killed. Just as Eric Marquand's notes had said. It was too horrible to believe.

She lowered her head, chin to chest, and forced a couple of sobs. She took one faltering, weak-kneed step toward him, then another. She swayed sideways, catching herself on a table. Her palm pressed to her forehead and her eyes closed.

He strode to her, gripping her forearm none too gently. It hurt, though she didn't think he meant it to. Her skin seemed more sensitive than before. When he squeezed her arm, pain shot all the way to her shoulder.

She lifted her other hand, settled it on his shoulder as if for support. Her fingers clenched hard into his flesh. Her knee rose and connected. She'd expected him to double over in pain, giving her time to escape.

Instead he launched into the air, propelled by the simple lifting motion of her knee into his groin. He screamed aloud, a hoarse, gravelly yell, and he sailed backward, hitting the floor five feet away. The gun skittered across the marble tiles to stop near the hearth, well beyond his reach. *Then* he doubled over.

Shannon's hand flew to her mouth, and she felt as if her eyes would pop out of their sockets. "Did I do that?" she whispered. "Ah, hell, this is so frigging strange."

He struggled to his feet, rage in his eyes, even as Shannon thought that those thugs who'd tried to steal her car ought to try it again now. If they thought she'd given them what for last time... She halted that speculating as Bachman stood, took one staggering step forward, lifted a shaking hand, forefinger extended.

"You...you're one of them."

"Not by choice," she muttered. "Look, Bachman, why don't you just get the hell out of here before I really hurt you, okay?"

He glanced toward the gun, took a step toward it. She leapt, easily covering the distance in a single, gazellelike move, and put herself between Bachman and the weapon. He thrust a hand into a pocket and emerged with a blade. "Come on, Shannon. Come over here and try that again." He was panting, breathless, obviously in pain.

She held her hand up, telling him to stop. "Don't do this," she said softly. "Don't..."

"You think I *want* to?" He moved nearer, still brandishing the blade. She backed away, but he advanced. "I could kill you, you know," he rasped. "One little nick, honey, and then I could stand here and watch you bleed." She gasped. "Give it up, Shannon. Don't make me do it."

He lunged, and the blade swept toward her. She jumped back again and he missed—perhaps deliberately, she couldn't be sure—but now her back was against the mantel. There was no more retreat. Nowhere to go. He stood in front of her, grim-faced, and she recalled Damien's having told her how easily she could bleed to death.

Bachman lifted the blade. He pressed its pointed tip to her throat. "Say you'll come with me Shannon. Don't make me hurt you."

She'd die before she'd go with him. She had to do something. Her hand groped behind her, moving slowly, so as not to alert him. It bumped the glass cube that enclosed one of Damien's artifacts. She lifted the glass, set it aside and clenched her fist on the section of stone tablet.

And in that instant, that very instant as she felt the pressure of the cold blade increase, felt its tip press harder into her flesh, she sensed as clearly as if he'd spoken it, his intent to kill her unless she cooperated. And to kill Damien, as well. She knew only one thing. She didn't want to die. Damien had been right about that.

In a surge of strength brought on by panic, a surge she didn't try to gauge or temper, she swung the stone forward, catching him in the side of his head.

He fell sideways and his body slammed to the floor so hard she thought he'd cracked the marble. He didn't move, of course. She blinked, felt the bile rise up in her throat, wanted to retch. She tore away from the wall and ran to the door, flinging it open, racing through it—and colliding hard with a broad chest.

"Shannon—"

His arms closed around her, and she sagged against Damien, clinging to his neck, sobbing. "I think I killed him. Oh, God, I think I killed him."

"I'm sorry, Shannon. I came as fast as I could, the second I sensed something wrong, but—"

He broke off, threading his fingers in her hair, lifting her into his arms. He carried her back through the house, holding her face to his shoulder as they passed through his comfort room. He took her up the stairs, laid her gently on the bed. "Shannon, I'm sorry. I'm sorry. I don't know what else to say."

She searched his face, his beloved, beautiful face, and she didn't know what to say, either. Her fingers clenched, and she realized she still held the stone. She drew it up to her chest, rolled slowly to her side, facing away from him, and closed her eyes.

Sighing, Damien covered her with a blanket, and left her alone.

Damien went downstairs to check on Bachman's condition, but the man was gone. Shannon hadn't killed him after all. It would be a relief to her to know that.

Eric's voice came from the doorway. "Are you all right?"

Before Damien formed an answer, his lovely young mate came forward, with all the grace of a ballerina in the midst of a dance. She drew a flask from a pocket inside her coat, and offered it to him. "Here, Damien. You're white as chalk. Drink."

"Tamara, love, that isn't—" Eric began, but he paused, searching Damien's awestruck face. "What is it, my friend?"

A burden floated away from Damien's shoulders. "The need. The thirst. By the love of Inanna, it's changed. Altered. I don't feel..." He smiled softly at Tamara and took the small flask from her hands. He drained it, and by the gods, it assuaged the emptiness inside him. It satisfied his thirst as thoroughly as it had thousands of years ago. He didn't feel that raging need to take from a living being. Not even a twinge of it.

Eric studied his face, reading all of these thoughts, Damien knew. "Amazing," he whispered.

"Not so amazing." Tamara tilted her head, sending spirals of raven curls over her shoulder. Her black eyes glittered with knowledge and Damien shot her a searching glance. "I know about your problems feeding, Damien. Eric and I don't keep secrets. But honestly, you men are so dense about some things. Every species has to procreate. Nature gives them all urges that, when followed, lead to mating and reproduction. Is it so farfetched that we're burdened with the same urges? The need to drink from the living gets stronger, more maddening, more demanding, until you perform the ritual, the creating of another one of us. Then the need vanishes."

Eric shook his head in blatant amazement. "So, we must transform one of the Chosen once every thousand years or so, in order to preserve our sanity." He smiled, then laughed. "Makes perfect sense, Tamara."

Her brows rose in perfect arches. "Sure it does."

Damien paced to the chaise and sank into it. "One problem less to deal with. Why do I still feel like hell?"

"You ought to rest. It's nearly dawn. And your Shannon should be moved from that bedroom, with those big windows." Pretty young Tamara wrinkled her nose. "Although I don't think she's quite ready yet to wake up in a coffin."

"No. I think we'll be safe enough here today, in my usual place. I just wish I knew what happened to Bachman."

"You won't have to worry about him—for a while, at least," Eric said. "He staggered into the street and collapsed. A carload of teens found him and they sent someone for an ambulance. Even if Bachman comes to and starts talking, no one will pay much attention. A man with a head injury, raving about vampires, isn't exactly believable. It ought to be at least a day before he can contact DPI for reinforcements. You ought to be prepared to leave here then, though, Damien. They don't take these kinds of things well at all." He paced away. "What of Netty?"

"I bought her a ticket on a cruise ship that leaves at first light, paid her off enough to make her think twice about betraying me again."

"Good. Your troubles are dissipating, my friend," Eric said cheerfully. "You've whittled them down to two—Shannon's mind-set and this rogue in the city."

"And we'll deal with all that tonight." Tamara tugged on Eric's arm. "If we'd brought Rhiannon along, she'd have had that rogue for breakfast."

"Which is exactly why I asked you not to mention this either to her or Roland. Tamara, love, we have no idea of this renegade's age or strength. Rhiannon would charge in, fearless as always, and perhaps get herself killed."

Damien's mouth quirked up at one corner. "This woman sounds like someone I'd like to meet."

"Only in a good mood, believe me," Eric intoned. Tamara elbowed him and dragged him to the door. "Good rest, Damien."

"Good rest," he replied without thinking. He watched them go, then turned to tackle the problem of Shannon.

He came back, as she'd known he would. He just couldn't seem to understand that she needed time to herself. She rolled onto her back and faced him. Then she wished she hadn't. There was pain in his eyes when he looked at her.

She sniffed and sat up. "I felt strong before, but it's waning. Is it only temporary?"

"It's almost daylight." He spoke softly. "Day weakens us. We rest until dark, and wake feeling strong as ever." He approached slowly, as if waiting for her to object. When she didn't, he sat on the edge of the bed. "You must have a thousand questions."

She nodded.

"But it's almost dawn." He licked his lips, obviously nervous. "Shannon, you made it clear you don't want to spend eternity with me. Don't want to depend on me at all. There are others who can answer your questions. You don't have to bring them to me."

She swallowed hard, lowering her head. She'd hurt him by saying those things. "I didn't mean—"

He held up a hand. "I want you to stay with me through today. There's no time to find you another safe place to rest. I'm not trying to force myself on you, I promise. I just want you safe. There's another vampire in the city. The one who killed Tawny and the other woman. Eric and I will find him and stop him. After that you're free to go where you want. Run to the other side of the world—"

She shook her head hard. "I didn't mean—"

"Bachman isn't dead," he told her. "But he'll be out of action for a while. Still, there are others, that organization he works for—they'd like to eradicate us. And this other vampire, an evil bastard who hates me for reasons I still don't understand. It isn't safe for you to go out alone until I find him, but I swear, it won't be long. Eric and I will leave with the sunset to hunt him down. Then you can leave with my blessing."

She closed her eyes, knowing she'd hurt him deeply, maybe beyond repair. He held out a hand to her. She took it and rose from the bed. Without a word, he led her through the hall, up another flight of stairs and through a door on the third floor. He walked right into a closet, and she was surprised when the wall that was the closet's back slid open. He drew her inside, slid the door closed again, hit a button, and the lights came up. Music began, Sting, her favorite. An exotic incense filled the air. He touched her hair, then abruptly drew his hand away.

"You can have the bed," he said, his voice hoarse. "I'll take a blanket and lie on the floor."

"You'll be uncomfortable..."

"Not really." He smiled very slightly. "I sleep like the dead."

God, what was wrong with her? Wasn't this the same man she'd fallen in love with? Couldn't she find a way to forgive him for forcing her into an existence she wasn't sure she could bear?

She tried. She tried to judge her feelings for Damien. She'd been so sure before, just before all of this. When he'd made love to her, she'd known she was deeply in love with him. There'd been no doubt. And only the knowledge that she was dying had kept her from telling him so. She hadn't wanted to hurt him. But what about now? Could she love him now? Knowing what he was . . . what he'd made her?

She'd realized that she didn't want to die. But did she want to live? Like this?

"Give it a chance, Shannon," he whispered. "Don't walk out into the sunrise just yet."

"I wasn't thinking of that."

"Make sure you don't." She sat on the edge of the bed and he came to her, knelt in front of her, took her hands. "Hate me for bringing you over, if you have to. But don't hate yourself or what you are. You haven't changed, not really. You're the same beautiful, vibrant, wonderful woman you were before. You're still strong and capable, and as independent as you want to be."

"I have changed." She averted her eyes. "I thought I'd killed Bachman. I'm glad I didn't, but I could have, Damien. I don't think I can stand the thought of taking a life."

"You wouldn't have hurt him if you hadn't been forced. You don't know the extent of your strength yet, Shannon. And that wouldn't have happened if I'd been here faster. It was more my fault than yours." She didn't look at him, and he hurried on. "You hit the men who tried to steal your car. One of them could have hit his head and died. But you didn't find yourself questioning the value of your mortal life when it was over, did you?"

She blinked and met his gaze. "No."

"It was an unavoidable accident, Shannon. Self-defense. And Bachman is going to recover. You didn't kill anyone. Try to put it behind you."

"But don't you *have* to kill people . . . to live?" He closed his eyes as if that remark hurt him. She licked her lips. "You don't, do you?" Slowly, she shook her head. "No, you couldn't. You couldn't even bring yourself to kill that mouse. . . ."

"I cherish life, all life. I despise death, Shannon. It took away the dearest, most beloved friend I ever had, until you. It tried to claim you, as well."

As she listened to him, her mind grew heavy and foggy as it had been when she'd first awakened. She glanced down at the stone she still clutched, and blinked.

Damien was easing her back onto the pillows. She stared up at his face in wonder, and recalled the story he'd told her, the ending to the *Epic of Gilgamesh*. The one that had never been recorded, that he called his own personal theory.

"He found the secret," she whispered. "But it didn't make him a god, and it didn't give him the power to bring Enkidu back. It only condemned him to an endless existence, to watching death win over and over again."

The greatest king ever to rule, driven to the edge of insanity by the grief of losing his closest friend. She lifted a hand and pressed her palm to his cheek. "It was you."

His eyes fell closed. He lay down beside her, wrapping his arms around her. "You felt the power of the bond between Enkidu and me from the first time you read of it. You cried for it. I remember. You know how I felt about him, don't you?"

"Enkidu?"

He squeezed his eyes, but a tear slipped through anyway. "The brother of my soul," he muttered in Sumerian. Amazingly, she knew what he said. She heard the words pass from his mind to hers and the meaning was clear. "As much as I loved him, Shannon, I love you even more. How could I watch you die? How *could I,* when I had the power to save you? It was wrong. I know that. I knew it then. But Shannon, I had to do it. I'd do it again."

His arms tightened around her, almost reflexively, she sensed, as if he were reliving that moment when he'd chosen to cling to her—to do whatever he had to—to keep her with him. Her eyes should have been wide with wonder at this new knowledge of him, this new understanding. But instead they were heavy, lids dropping, sleep claiming her. She snuggled close to him, twisting her arms around his waist, not wanting him to keep his promise and sleep on the floor. She pressed her face into the crook of his neck, and she smelled his scent and tasted the salt of his flesh on her lips as she whispered, "Gilgamesh..."

And then she fell asleep, thinking of the lines she'd read in the epic, lines that returned to haunt her. Lines about grief:

It could go on for years and years,
and has, for centuries...
It yearns and waits to be retouched,
by someone who can take away
the memory of death.

He was gone when she awoke. She sat up slowly, blinking, realizing vaguely that the lights were still dim. They brightened gradually. The music began as if by itself, and only grew louder as she came fully alert.

"Quite a setup he has here, isn't it?"

She started, eyes flying wider. A woman stood in the room near the doorway. She was small, a pixie, with a tiny waist and cascades of raven curls that reached it. She smiled and took a step forward.

"I'm Tamara."

She'd heard the name, she was sure. She frowned. Tamara. Then she *was* real. "Eric's wife?"

"Well, not 'wife' exactly. We didn't do a church wedding or anything. 'Till death us do part' would be kind of meaningless for us. But our vows are just as binding. No, more binding." She strode to the stereo system in the back of the room, started pawing through the CDs.

She wore snug-fitting jeans and a green silk button-down blouse. A pair of shiny black flats on her feet. Even makeup. Shannon stared, gaping, until the woman turned and smiled at her. "I know—I don't look like a vampire, do I? Rhiannon does. She's all tall and elegant and has this haughty attitude. But I think she was like that, even mortal. She's a princess, you know. And I'm just . . . just me."

"I didn't mean to stare."

Tamara came forward, sat on the edge of the bed. "I've only been in darkness for a few years, Shannon. I know what you're going through." She lowered her dark, velvety lashes. "Well, sort of. In my case, I had to practically beg Eric to bring me over. I can't say for sure how I'd have dealt with it if he'd just done it, without asking how I felt first."

Shannon licked her lips. "I still didn't believe you existed. The next thing I know, I wake up and I'm one of you."

Tamara nodded, meeting Shannon's eyes with real concern in her own. "It's a tough adjustment under any circumstances. But I'll help you, if you want." She smiled a little, and her hand rose to touch Shannon's hair. "You're beautiful, you know. I've never heard of a fair-complected vampire before. You must be as rare as a flawless diamond."

Shannon felt herself blush at the compliment.

"It's probably because of the lineage. I think the darkness is inherited, along with the Belladonna antigen."

Shannon took that in, nodding. Then she glanced toward the door and gnawed on her lower lip.

"He and Eric went out to see if they could find this rogue vampire that's been raising hell around here."

She nodded again. She wished Damien hadn't left before she'd awoken. She'd hurt him. He thought she wanted to be away from him. That wasn't at all what she wanted. She wasn't sure exactly what she wanted anymore, only that she understood now. She understood his pain, his loss. She'd been half in love with Gilgamesh since she'd read his epic. And now she knew why. And she knew why he'd made the decision he had when she'd been dying in his arms. Being who he was, he couldn't have done anything else.

"You'll have time to tell him all that. He'll be back before dawn."

She blinked in surprise.

"We can hear each other's thoughts, Shannon."

"That's incredible."

Tamara smiled. *I'll teach you how to do it. You can surprise Damien when he gets back. For now, why don't you get up and shower and dress? There's so much I want to tell you about, show you....*

All of it, Shannon heard clearly. All of it spoken without Tamara's having uttered a sound. Her head spinning, Shannon got up and complied.

Tamara seemed so normal.

She'd been thrilled to ride in Shannon's car, more thrilled yet when Shannon let her drive it awhile. They took turns choosing CDs and they played them at ear-piercing volume, singing along until Shannon actually began to feel like herself again. Maybe Damien was right. Maybe she hadn't changed all that much.

They parked the car, then walked through the streets. As they did, Tamara urged Shannon to practice the telepathy,

and soon they were conversing almost totally in silence.
Shannon started attempting to read other people's thoughts
as they passed. The results were often hilarious.

Then, in a trash-littered, abandoned alley, Tamara stood
by Shannon's side. "Let's race to the other end."

A shiver of apprehension skittered over Shannon's nape.
"This isn't a very good place to hang out, Tamara."

"Think about it," she said. "Who's gonna bother us?"

Shannon smiled. She was right.

"You've got a lot of strength now, Shannon. And speed.
You won't believe it. Be careful not to hit the wall on the
other side. Pain hurts more now than before."

"I'd noticed that."

"On three," Tamara said, and then counted mentally.

They were off like bullets from a gun, and Shannon would
have collided with the wall if Tamara hadn't caught her arm
and brought her to a skidding stop.

For hours Tamara helped Shannon to explore her new
self. And as time flew past, Shannon began to think this
wasn't so bad after all. She could jump from the top of a
tree and land on her feet. She could see in the dark. All her
senses were honed to razor sharpness. She was strong, energized. And she could read minds.

"You think that's incredible, just wait until you... you
know." Tamara's pale cheeks pinkened.

"No, I don't know. Wait until I what?"

Tamara grinned and tilted her head to one side. "You and
Damien ... *you know* ... "

"Oh." Shannon bit her lip. "Is it... different?"

"Way different."

Shannon licked her lips. "I don't know when I'll find out.
Things aren't exactly... right between us."

"You love him, don't you?"

She thought about that, and found herself nodding em-
phatically. "I do. I really do. I lost sight of it for a while, a
really short, confused while. But I never stopped."

"Well, he's nuts about you. You'll work things out."

Shannon nodded, recalling his words to her before she'd fallen asleep this morning. He'd said he loved her even more than Enkidu. It awed her that he could feel that strongly about her.

They walked back to the car, only to meet a stranger there. A vampire. Surprising that she knew it at a glance, but she did, and she stopped short. He was tall, and almost emaciated. So slender. In his long face every bone was visible. His neck was like a reed, his shoulders pointy and hard.

He approached them slowly, and Tamara caught her breath, gripping Shannon's arm.

"No use," he said, and his voice reminded Shannon of a cobra's hiss. "I'm six thousand years old. You're a toddler and a newborn. Don't bother running."

And in the blink of an eye, he had them, his bony arms anchored around their waists, capturing their arms at their sides. Shannon struggled. She knew Tamara did, as well, but couldn't see her. He'd taken off at such incredible speed that everything was a blur. She thought they were airborne, but couldn't be sure. Tamara hadn't told her anything about flight.

Don't call out to Eric and Damien. Tamara's thoughts echoed in Shannon's ears. *It could be a trap for them. I've been through it before.*

"No matter," the monster who held them rasped. "I've left a note at the house for them. It's long past time for Gilgamesh to meet his fate."

CHAPTER FIFTEEN

They'd tried for hours to pick up some sense of the rogue in the city. They'd sought a hint of his thoughts, his presence, in the places where the victims had been found, and in the theater, and in and around Shannon's office. The sense of him should be stronger where his physical self had been. But their efforts got them nothing. He was concealing himself against them, and doing it well.

They returned to the house then, and Damien braced himself to come face-to-face with Shannon again, to see the despair in her eyes, the fear of him, the anger. Maybe this time there would be hatred in her amber eyes, as well. He had no idea what he could say to her. She despised what he'd done, hated what he'd made her. So how could she not hate him? How could she even bear to see him again, let alone sleep another day under his roof? What would she say when he told her he'd failed, and asked her to stay with him for one more day, give him one more night to make it safe for her to leave him? He couldn't let her go until this threat was removed, even though he was sure the hatred he'd felt emanating from this rogue had been directed at himself alone.

Hell, he didn't want her to leave at all, to be honest. He couldn't bear the thought of living a night without her vibrance to brighten it. Irony tasted bitter. He no longer had to fear he had become a ruthless killer, that to love her would be to endanger her. And he no longer had to fear that death would tear her from him. But he'd lost her all the same, hadn't he?

He felt Eric tense beside him. And then he sensed it. The feeling of something wrong, terribly wrong, of danger. The knowledge that the rogue had been here.

He ran to the front steps, up them, and found the note, impaled on the point of a dagger as old as time, pinned to the door.

Eric tore it down, leaving the blade where it was, and struggled to read, but he shook his head. "It's not in any language I know."

Damien frowned, taking the sheet of paper from him. "It's cuneiform script." The symbols on the paper were similar to those chiseled into stone aeons ago. A cold shiver racing through him, Damien translated aloud: "'Gilgamesh, king of Uruk, lord of a people long dead, vile betrayer of the gods, immortal, demon, murderer. For your role in the death of one who loved you, for your hand in her murder, for the life of Siduri, my betrothed, you will stand trial. In the temple of Inanna, you will be judged, that the gods might witness your sentence carried out. No longer does the temple lie buried beneath the burning sands of Uruk. Still buried, yes, but not there. Never to be seen by mortal eyes. Brick by brick did I move it. I await you there. Your lover waits at my side. Ready she stands to take your sentence upon herself in case you fail to heed my summons. Long have I anticipated this reunion, man of old. Anthar.'"

Damien looked up from the note, to see the fear, the wonder, in Eric's eyes.

"Gilgamesh," he muttered, staring at Damien. "My God."

"I'm no one's god, just an immortal like you. We have to go now, fast."

Eric's brows rose. "But how? You've no idea where you're going."

Damien gripped his arm. "Your Tamara—"

"Will stubbornly erect a fortress around her mind rather than lure me into what she must know is a trap." Eric closed his eyes. "I'll try, but if she really doesn't want me to know where she is..." He shook his head and tried to concentrate.

"What the hell *is this?*" Shannon watched the huge doors slide slowly open, then jerked against the hands that tugged her into an elevator big enough to hold an elephant. God, he was strong. His bony hand gripped her arm so hard she thought he'd break it. Tears streamed down her face. Her throat closed so tightly she could barely draw a breath. Her chest spasmed with sobs she tried to stop. And still she fought him.

She was afraid, terrified of what this skeletal man planned to do to her. But more than that was the fear of what he'd already done. To Tamara. They'd been airborne, soaring through the night at a speed that seemed impossible, with the wind stinging Shannon's face, screaming in her ears. So high the ground seemed no more than a fast-moving, colorful blur. And he'd just let Tamara go. Just let her go!

She hadn't even screamed. Not a sound. Nothing. And Shannon couldn't see where she landed, because the bony bastard had still been speeding through space, still been clutching her tight. But Shannon *had* screamed. And she hadn't stopped screaming until he'd hit her with a skinny fist and knocked her close to senseless.

And now she was in this elevator, going down at a sickening speed, deep into the bowels of some kind of structure that seemed to sit in the middle of nowhere.

The doors opened almost before they'd come to a teeth-jarring stop. The hand on her upper arm closed tighter, and wincing in pain, she stepped out into a stadium-size room where every step echoed a thousand times. In the center of the room, she saw it, a towering wonder of whitewashed brick, gleaming, immaculate. Her gaze traveled over the angular ramps and steps and corners, all leading upward. A squared spiral at least forty feet high, topped by what looked like a temple.

"What the hell is this?" she asked again.

"Who is this Anthar?"

Damien shook his head. "He must be from my time to know who I am and understand the cuneiform so well. The blade is ancient. Sumerian. And he must have known me once to have heard of Siduri."

"A woman?"

Damien nodded. "I'll explain later. We have to hurry." Already a cold knot of foreboding twisted inside his heart. He wished he could blink his eyes and be at her side. But he knew better. He was as attuned to her mind as he could get, and all he felt was her fear. It overwhelmed everything else. There was a dim sense of the direction in which she'd traveled, and Damien followed that sense, felt himself getting closer.

Anthar. Who the hell was he, and why this quest for vengeance? Damien didn't know. He knew only that if the bastard hurt Shannon in any way, no matter how small, Damien would kill him a little at a time. She must be so frightened. By Inanna's mercy, she must be twice as sorry he'd brought her over by now. She probably wished he'd simply let her die. He'd wanted to do so much for her. To show her happiness, to make up for all the sorrow in her life. Instead he'd brought her into a world of darkness, and so far all she'd known had been fear.

He'd get her out of this safely. He would, if it cost him his life to do it. And then he'd give her what she craved. Her freedom. No matter how much it would hurt him, Damien knew he had to let her go.

Eric had been silent for some time, and when Damien broke out of his own thoughts long enough to glance at the man, he saw turmoil contorting Eric's face. He stopped, facing him. "Marquand, what? What is it?"

His jaw tight, eyes moist, Eric kept moving. Then faster. And a moment later, he knelt beside a still form on the ground, cradling it in his arms and quivering with silent rage.

Damien ran forward. "Tamara!" Her left leg bent at an unnatural angle, and one arm was twisted beneath her body. Obviously broken. Damien's heart turned to ice as he saw Eric's pain. But her lovely black lashes fluttered, and she stared up at the man who held her with so much love in her eyes it hurt Damien to witness it.

"I'm... glad to see you."

"Tamara." Eric's voice wavered. He bent lower, kissed her face.

"Gently, Eric. It... hurts."

"I'll kill him," Eric whispered. "I'll kill him for this."

Damien felt tears choking him. When the hell had he become so attached to these people? "You're going to have to move her, Eric, pain or not. Find her some shelter before dawn."

Eric nodded and glanced around. "Where the hell are we?"

"Somewhere in Ohio, I think." Damien glanced around him. "There are houses. I can—"

"No." Tamara tried to lift her head, her good hand clutching Eric's arm. "Damien, you have to go on. Find Shannon before that beast hurts her." She drew a pained breath. "But be careful. It's you he wants."

"I know." Damien straightened and stared off into the distance.

"Go ahead, go after them," Eric said. "I'll take care of Tamara. We'll be fine."

"Are you sure?"

Tamara nodded. "I'll be okay after a day's rest, Damien. And we'll join you...with reinforcements."

Eric's jaw went rigid. "Tamara, you didn't—"

"I most certainly did. We have to end this bastard's killing spree, Eric. And we need all the help we can get." She relaxed a little, letting her head fall onto Eric's knees. "I pity that bastard if Rhiannon gets to him before Damien does."

Eric glanced back at Damien. "I wouldn't be too sure about that, Tamara."

"Neither would I." Damien turned, and started off again toward Shannon.

He was forced to seek shelter when the sun rose. But he resumed his search the instant it set, and he knew when he'd found her.

His best guess was that the structure dead center of a barren field had once been a missile silo. One of those sold by the government to private owners when arms-reduction deals took the place of the cold war. He approached the doors, and they opened. Then the bastard knew he'd arrived. Damien stepped inside what appeared to be an elevator, not caring if he was walking into a trap as long as he could get to Shannon. The car swept downward, clanged to a stop and opened as if to spit him out.

Damien stood frozen for a single moment, reeling at the sensation of having stepped back in time. The ziggurat stood as haughty and immaculate as it had been when it was new. This same temple had been the center of his city once. It had been filled with his people, his gods. A man-made mountain is what it was. A high, white monster of stairs and ramps, sharp corners turning this way and that, a path to the heavens marching its way to the cella at the very top. The temple proper. The chamber of the gods, where sacrifices had been offered.

He knew the temple well, remembered the way the white bricks had gleamed beneath a blazing desert sun. Now it stood in darkness. Appropriate. Ironic.

Mounting the first steps, Damien went upward, following the same path he had thousands of times so many years ago, only faster now, his strides more powerful than ever before. And more desperate. In seconds he stood at the entrance to the cella. He stiffened his spine and went inside.

A figure like a walking skeleton moved from sconce to sconce with a torch in his hand, lighting each as he came to it. The main room, sixty feet in length and lined with sconces on both sides, soon glowed with amber light as it had in days long past. Shadows fled the touch of the torchlight, ducking into the darkened doorways that lined the chamber. Every few yards a smaller chamber opened off one side or the other. But this was the room of worship, the room of the gods, the room of sacrifice.

Damien stepped forward, marveling that the place had been so well restored. The stone figures that depicted the worshippers were just as he remembered them, some standing as high as his knees, others smaller. Male and female, bearded and smooth skinned, eyes too large, hands folded in prayer.

Damien moved past them, tearing his gaze away from the figures that represented his people. Instead he focused on the emaciated man who'd stopped at the opposite end of the chamber, and turned to face him.

"I'm here, Anthar. I've done as you asked. Where is Shannon?"

Anthar only smiled, an evil expression, the flickering orange torchlight making it more so. He stepped aside, waving a hand beyond him to the life-size statue of the god Anu. Anu's golden hair and beard had been polished until they gleamed, and his eyes, inlaid with lapis lazuli, danced with fierceness in the firelight. At his sandaled feet, upon the stone offering table, Shannon lay wide-eyed, trembling, her hands bound at the wrists, clenched together on her stomach. Her ankles, too, were bound together. She was dressed in a white gown, fastened with a jeweled brooch at one shoulder, leaving the other bare. Golden bands encircled her arms. Her feet were bare.

As Damien's gaze met hers, he felt her fear, her absolute misery. He tried to convey reassurance, hope, comfort. Anthar stepped forward to ignite the torches near her head and at her feet. She cringed from him, and a sound of terror came from deep in her throat. Damien lunged forward, but Anthar stepped into his path.

"Look around you, Gilgamesh. See the gods you betrayed by seeking to become one of them." He lifted the torch toward each of the deities that towered at Anu's right and his left. "The goddess Inanna, whose name you cursed from the deathbed of your friend. Ea, of the fresh springs, friend to mankind. Even him you have offended. Enlil, god of earth, wind and spirit, whom you have defiled. Ninurta, god of war, furious with you now."

Damien held his temper in check with an effort. "It seems, Anthar, the only one I've offended is you. The gods haven't acted against me in all this time. I hardly think their justice would be so slow in coming."

"Their justice is at hand," Anthar said in a deep monotone.

Damien shook his head. "If that's true, then I'm ready for it. Let's get on with this, Anthar. Release the woman now. Whatever you have in mind, it's meant for me to suffer, not her."

"Not just yet, Gilgamesh."

Damien moved forward, meaning to free Shannon himself. But Anthar reached to a small stone stand and snatched

up a ritual dagger, its handle inlaid with glittering jewels—
emeralds and sapphires, diamonds and rubies. The blade
was honed to a razor's edge. He held it poised at Shannon's
throat and she screamed, her voice echoing endlessly in the
hollow room long after she'd gone utterly still. She stared at
Damien, her gaze clinging to his almost desperately.

"If you move, blasphemer, I will hurt her. Badly I will
hurt her. Likely she'll bleed dry before you can help her."

"I'm very old, rogue," Damien said softly, his voice
oddly hoarse. "Older than any, except Utnapishtim himself, who made me. You ought to be careful about angering
me."

"Utnapishtim made me, as well, great king of Uruk. Only
moments after you."

Damien looked quickly at the gaunt-faced man. "He
wouldn't have—"

"He had no choice. His exchange of blood with a young
madman left him weak. I forced him to repeat the ritual,
only so that I would live to see you die."

Eric's voice came into Damien's mind then, and he knew
his friend—yes, friend—was on the way, monitoring events
mentally, offering advice. *The blood was diluted then, when
this Anthar was made. You're still stronger.*

Damien nodded, sensing Eric guarded his thoughts from
Anthar. He tried to do the same. *Maybe.*

"What crime have I committed to anger you so much that
you'd follow me into eternity just to see me pay?"

"Do you recall Siduri? My beautiful Siduri, who gave her
heart to a beast?"

Damien nodded, stepping a bit closer, only to wince as
Anthar pressed the tip of his blade harder into Shannon's
neck. "Answer aloud, so that the gods present may know of
your sins."

He licked his lips. "I was half out of my mind with grief
when Enkidu, my friend, died. I went on a quest in search

of immortality, thinking I could somehow bring that gift back to him and raise him up again. When I came to Siduri's cottage by the sea I was near starved, sunburned, travel-weary and all but insane. She brought me inside, washed the sand and the sweat from my skin. She fed me and clothed me, restored my health and part of my senses.''

Anthar grimaced, his thin lips drawing away from his foul, uneven teeth. "Is that all she gave you, heathen?"

"She gave me comfort, Anthar. We shared a bed."

"She was my betrothed!" he screamed, nearly rattling the brick walls.

That declaration shocked Damien. But still it didn't seem reason enough for so much hatred. "I didn't know—"

"You used her as chattel and cast her aside to resume your mad quest. She begged of you to stay, but you turned a deaf ear to her tears."

"No. She knew I'd go on from the day I crossed her threshold. She knew—"

"You killed her. She thought herself in love with you, gave you all of herself as proof of it, even though she'd promised herself to me."

"And that was no crime!" Damien stepped forward once more, staring at this shell of a man. "You know as well as I do that in that time it was a king's right to take the virgin brides before their husbands did. Right or wrong, it was the law. So how can you say that I committed some crime by bedding your woman?" A flimsy argument, he knew, but all he could think of at the moment.

"Bastard, she lost her soul when you left her. But you wouldn't know, would you? You never looked back to see how she fared. You didn't know that she walked into the sea the very next dawn, walked and kept walking. Drowned herself for the love of a worthless king who would make himself a god!"

Eric's voice came again, like a solid hand clasping his shoulder. *It wasn't your fault. Don't let it distract you.*

But Damien felt the blow. He staggered a bit, then caught himself. "I didn't know. She...she was kind to me, Anthar. I cared for her. I am sorry. More sorry than I can say."

"Your sorrow will not suffice, Gilgamesh. You must suffer as I did."

Incinerate him.

Damien shook his head quickly, responding to Eric in the silent form of communication he'd so recently mastered. *I'm not sure it would work, and it takes an unbelievable amount of energy to incinerate anything. If it failed, I'd be practically helpless.*

Damien had gone utterly still, watching the way the firelight played on Shannon's skin, in her hair, a terrible fear of what this bastard intended settling like ice water in his veins. "What are you going to do, Anthar?"

"I'm going to take your woman as you took mine." He glanced down at Shannon as he spoke. "And then I'm going to drain her, and let her die. And you are going to stand witness to it, Gilgamesh. For I want to see you suffer, before I kill you."

"You haven't got the strength to kill me."

"We'll soon see."

The man, blade still in his hand, bent over Shannon, and she screamed.

At the same instant there was a tremendous crash and a rain of footsteps at the entrance. Damien knew without turning that four immortals had entered the cella. A powerful female voice echoed like that of Inanna herself. For a second Damien wondered if the statue of the Queen of Heaven had come to life. "Exactly what kind of death wish do you have, you sorry excuse for an immortal!"

"You're in for it now, Anthar," Tamara stated flatly.

The rogue was distracted for a bare instant, and that was all Damien needed. He spun in a circle, becoming a blur, and an instant later, a massive wolf launched itself at the evil vampire, sending him crashing to the floor, the knife skittering away.

Shannon tried hard to cling to her sanity as the horror played out before her eyes. The wolf snapped at the man's throat, but then they rolled, and a second later the wolf backed away from a coiled king cobra, cape unfurled, poised to strike. The wolf leapt into the air, and as it hurtled earthward, it became a hawk that swooped and dove, drawing the snake away from her. She rolled her body off the stone table, pulled herself to her feet, both hands working as one, and began hopping toward the two who fought. The snake had the hawk cornered now, and would strike at any second. She had to stop this.

But a tug at her hands brought her to a stop. The woman, tall and slender, regal as a queen, with her ebony hair all swept to one side and diamonds and onyx dripping from her ears, leaned over the rope at Shannon's ankles. "You fledglings are nothing but trouble." With a flick of her scarlet-painted, dagger-tipped fingers, she freed Shannon's ankles, then her wrists. "I'm Rhiannon," she said, as if she were saying "I'm Queen Elizabeth." She pulled Shannon toward the corner where Eric and Tamara waited with another man Shannon didn't know. At their feet, a sleek black panther crouched, watching the struggling beasts with predatory eyes.

"None of them for you, Pandora." The woman stroked the cat's head lovingly, but her eyes were on the floor where the two battled.

Shannon whirled, half expecting to see Damien dead on the floor. But there was a lion now, and a jaguar, ripping at each other's throats, rolling in a tangle of claws and teeth.

"Do something!" She screamed.

Tamara touched her shoulder. "I don't know what we can—"

She broke off when Shannon jerked away from her touch. Shannon had spotted the glittering dagger on the floor, and she lunged for it, falling to her knees to snatch it up. Rising slowly, her gaze on the combatants, she started forward, lifting the blade high above her head, giving a little growl she'd never heard herself utter before.

The tall woman caught her shoulders. "Fool, you'll be killed! Come with us. Damien wants us to take you out of here, someplace safe."

Shannon turned on her, the blade between them an unspoken threat. "I'm not going anywhere. You try to force me and you'll wish you hadn't, lady."

Tamara's eyes went saucer-wide. The two men, who'd been talking urgently, went silent.

The woman eyed Shannon for a moment. "I'll forgive that fledgling. Once."

Shannon ignored her imperious words and turned once more. The forms on the floor had become men again. They stood, facing each other, panting, bleeding from various wounds. Eric and the strange man both lunged forward, but Damien held up a hand to stop them.

"Get Shannon out of here, for the love of Inanna!"

"I won't go!" she shrieked.

"Anthar, stop this at once. You're no match for all of us!" It was the stranger who shouted it.

"Care to put that theory to the test?"

Anthar whispered. He looked at the stranger, his gaze hardening, intensifying in a way Shannon had never seen. It was as if an energy pulsed from his sunken eyes.

"Roland!" Rhiannon threw herself at the stranger, sending him sprawling to the stone floor just as a ball of flame exploded in the air where he'd stood.

She rose, facing Anthar, rage in her eyes. "Oh, now you *will* pay—"

He laughed at her, and Shannon thought the woman's rage was so full-blown it made the air around them quiver.

Anthar turned away from her and lunged, shoving Damien onto his back on the floor. He yanked a blade from his boot and lifted his arm to plunge it into Damien's throat.

"Noooo!" It was a battle cry, emitted as Shannon launched herself. She landed squarely on the man's back, both hands gripping his wrist, pulling it away from Damien with every ounce of strength she possessed.

Anthar flung her from him like a dog ridding itself of a flea. She felt herself fly through the air. She landed brutally hard. Her head connected with the stone offering table, sending her senses reeling. Dizzy, her head exploding with pain, her body weakened by it, she forced her eyes open.

Damien growled his rage, flinging the man away from him, then focusing his eyes on the bastard as he struggled to get to his feet.

The man seemed to feel that heated gaze. He froze for an instant in time, and turned to face Damien. "Can you do it, do you think?" His thin brows rose, and he moved forward, menacingly. The black panther growled deep in its throat, crouching low. "Better question, can you do it fast enough?" Anthar sprang forward, arm swinging in a deadly arc, the knife he clutched on a collision coarse with Damien's neck. He'd behead him!

Damien stood his ground, staring harder, not backing away even an inch, and Shannon shrieked at him to move.

Just before he reached Damien, Anthar's body froze. It began to tremble, then vibrated head to toe. His eyes bulged and a wisp of gray smoke writhed from his hair. A tremor rocked the temple floor, and then a roar, as Anthar burst into a blinding ball of white flame. His keening came more loudly than the blast, and seemed to echo within the temple chamber even after he was silent. It died slowly, an eternal prisoner of the cella walls. And there was nothing, just nothing. Anthar was gone.

Damien sank to the floor as if the act had drained every ounce of his energy. Shannon struggled to her feet and ran to him, fell to her knees, not caring that the stone floor scraped them raw. She pulled him to her, her hands cradling his head. She couldn't speak. She only moaned softly and rocked him against her as the tears flowed. God, she loved him. She hadn't realized just how much until she'd thought he might die trying to save her. If he had, what would she have done? How could she have gone on?

His arms went around her waist, his face nestling in the white linen that covered her, nuzzling her belly. His hands stroked her back again and again. "It's over now, Shannon. It's all right. You're safe now." He pulled himself up a little, pressed his lips to her wet cheeks, to her burning eyes. "Safe now," he whispered again, as her arms encircled his neck. "And free of me. You'll leave with the others. One more day, Shannon. You'll recover from all of this while you rest tomorrow, and then I want you to go. I just hope you can find some kind of contentment in this life I've condemned you to live."

She blinked, her tears ceasing abruptly.

CHAPTER SIXTEEN

"We're stuck here for the day," Tamara observed, her voice soft with relief. She sat on the cold floor, her knees drawn to her chest, and watched as Eric approached Damien. Shannon had withdrawn suddenly, going silent after Damien had told her she could leave him soon. He couldn't look at her to judge her mood, whether she was happy at the news or angry to have to wait through one more day. He couldn't stand the thought that he might see her eagerness to leave mirrored in her eyes. Eric reached out a hand and Damien clasped it, letting Eric help him to his feet. "I wasn't much help, I'm afraid," he said aloud, and silently he said more. *For God's sake, Damien, she jumped on the bastard to save you.*

"You were more help than you know." It was true, Damien thought, a little surprised. Not just the distractions their arrival had provided, breaking Anthar's concentration more than once and probably saving Damien's life. But the feeling of support. The warmth of friends. It was something he hadn't felt in centuries.

And she tried to help me because she feels she owes me, for saving her life in the past.

"Well, at least I can patch up the worst of these injuries for you." Normally, Damien would have turned away, insisted he could take care of himself. But not now. He stood still while Eric ripped a sleeve from his own shirt and began tearing bandage-size strips.

"Tamara's right, you know," Damien observed, loudly enough so everyone, including Shannon, could hear. He wanted her to understand that he wasn't deliberately prolonging her presence here. "We couldn't make it far before sunrise, and who knows what kind of shelter we could find out there? It's best to stay here, rest tomorrow and leave at dusk."

He chanced a peek at Shannon to see if she understood. But she was kneeling now in front of Tamara, and a second later, hugging her. "I thought you must be dead."

"I almost wished I was when I landed." Tamara smiled at her. "But I'm fine now."

Shannon shook her head slowly, mutely. The newcomer, Roland, stood with his back against a stone wall, while regal Rhiannon tore a strip from the hem of her floor-length satin dress and used it to make a sling for his arm. He must have injured it when she'd knocked him to the floor. He winced in pain, and Damien saw the woman wince along with him. Her eyes were dark with concern when she looked at him. Jealousy stabbed Damien. Why couldn't Shannon look at *him* like that?

She did a second ago. Eric again. The optimist.

No, she didn't.

"He should see a doctor," Shannon whispered. She glanced back at Damien, who was currently using pressure to stop the bleeding of a small cut on his forearm, while Eric wrapped a makeshift bandage around it. "And so should you, Damien."

Tamara ran a soothing hand over Shannon's hair. "Any injuries we have heal while we rest during the day. Hasn't anyone explained that to you yet?" She shot Damien a slightly accusing stare as she asked it.

He only shrugged. "Shannon has a lot to learn, and plenty of time to do it." Damien glanced at his watch. "It'll be dawn in a few hours. I think I'll move to one of the smaller chambers now. After that battle, I don't feel like doing anything but lying down." He avoided Shannon's eyes. The truth was he didn't want to see her anymore. It already hurt too much knowing she'd leave him so soon.

Rhiannon left Roland's side to approach Damien as he turned to go. She wasn't smiling. She seemed to float over the stone floor rather than walk, until she stood before him, chin lifted, eyes blazing. "Not until we've been introduced, at least."

"Rhiannon..." Roland's voice held a warning.

She ignored it. "So, you're the great Damien I've heard about."

"And you're Rhiannon, princess of Egypt." She was beautiful. Not as beautiful as Shannon, of course, but lovely just the same. Elegant. "I've heard of you, too."

"You nearly got my friends killed." It was a simple statement of fact.

"It wasn't his fault, Rhiannon." Tamara's voice didn't douse the hint of fire in her eyes. But Roland's good hand closing on her shoulder, his words, spoken low and near her ear, did.

"I don't think it's my imagination, Damien. The wolf I just saw fighting a cobra looked awfully familiar to me. We've met before, that wolf and I. Haven't we?"

Damien averted his eyes. Rhiannon frowned hard at Roland. "Wolf? You mean..."

"In France, my love, when you'd been captured by Lucien and I lay immobilized, watching the sun come up to fry me. The wolf that came to me, pulled me into a cave as I clung to its furred neck. That wolf with the wisdom in its eyes..."

Roland let his voice trail off. Damien said nothing, only nodded once, and turned to go into the nearest chamber. He'd gone against his vow of seclusion to help Roland back then. But he'd been in the area on tour and sensed the man's distress, loud and clear, though he hadn't been listening. Even when he'd decided to step in, knowing he couldn't let someone die when he had the power to save him, he'd done it in disguise. He'd wanted no one's gratitude. No one's friendship.

He'd been wrong. He had their friendship now. Even Rhiannon's. Her hand rose and cupped his face. She leaned forward and pressed her lips to his cheek. No words were needed. Damien nodded a confirmation to himself. He had their friendship, and he was better for it.

But he didn't have what he wanted most. Shannon. Not just her, but her heart. Her love. And he couldn't deal with the fact that he was about to lose her in front of them, friends or not. "You should all find a place to rest, be sure no light can penetrate." He turned once again and walked into the first darkened room within reach.

Roland lowered his head and disappeared into another one. The cat left Rhiannon's side to lumber toward Shannon. She stood, her back to the wall, a little thrill of alarm jingling her nerves. It sat on its haunches in front of her, lifted a forepaw and playfully batted Shannon's hand. She felt her eyes widen, but she stayed still as the cat rose and moved forward, shoving her head against Shannon's hand and pressing upward, eyes closed. She stroked the animal, blinking in shock.

"Her name is Pandora. She's…usually a very good judge of character."

Shannon met Rhiannon's almond eyes, saw the ruby lips curve just slightly.

"Not everyone has the courage to shout defiance in my face. Barely anyone, actually."

Shannon lowered her head. "I'm sorry about that. I know you were only trying to help me, but I…" She glanced toward the chamber where Damien had gone, a lump forming in her throat. "I couldn't leave him."

"You threw yourself onto the back of a creature that could have killed you."

"I had to try."

Her lips curved a little more. Her eyes glittered. She sent a meaningful glance toward the chamber doorway. "Yes. A woman in love always has to try." And then, the picture of elegance, she floated into the room where Roland had gone. The cat trotted along behind her, a slight limp in her feline gait.

Shannon glanced down to the stone floor where Tamara sat, Eric now resting on her opposite side. Their hands were joined, fingers interlaced. Tamara met Shannon's eyes and nodded once.

Licking her lips, squaring her shoulders, Shannon turned and entered the dark chamber where Damien had gone.

He heard her come in, knew she was there even before he heard her. He felt her presence. He groaned inwardly, but there was another voice in him, one that was thrilled to have these few moments with her, alone, before she left him forever.

He'd brought a torch in here, mounted it in the sconce on the wall near the back of the room. He sat on the floor, back to that wall, watching the play of shadows on the small carved figures and the play of light on their eyes. They seemed alive.

She crossed the room, sat down beside him. By Anu's power, she was a goddess come to life, still dressed in the sacrificial gown, with the golden bands on her arms. She didn't look at him, so he was free to study her until it hurt. Her golden tresses tumbling over her shoulders, her satin skin, her velvet lashes.

"I've lost count now of the number of times you've saved my life."

He said nothing. She was sitting very close to him, but not touching. He longed to reach out, to run his hands through her silken hair, to bring her face to his and taste her mouth one more time. He clenched his hands into fists that trembled. She was here out of gratitude, he told himself. Nothing more.

"I've been thinking," she whispered. "About a lot of things. About you, mostly. The man I got to know, and the man I know now. And I realized that you're the same. Damien or Gilgamesh, mortal or immortal, you're the same."

Still he said nothing. Only watched her struggle for words, waited for her to continue, to tell him why she would leave him.

"I was afraid of something I didn't understand, and angry because I felt you'd taken control." She tugged at the tip of her right index finger, picked at the nail. Nervous. "I'm afraid to let other people have any authority or control in my life. It terrifies me."

"Because of your childhood," he said softly, unable to keep silent on the subject. "It's understandable, Shannon. If the man who tried to abuse you wasn't already dead, I'd kill him myself." He blinked, fighting down the rage that had risen inside him. "I knew how you felt. I had no right to act without asking you. No right at all, and I knew it."

She nodded slowly. Her tongue darted out to moisten her lips. "And what would my answer have been, I wonder?" She drew a deep breath, and released it slowly. "I've been thinking about that a lot, too. And you know, I think if I'd known all there was to know, if I'd had a chance to get to know these people, to accept what seemed impossible to me, I think I would have agreed. I think... No, I *know* I would have wanted this."

He turned his head sharply, staring down at her eyes, torchlight in amber.

"When you were fighting with Anthar...God, I was so afraid he'd kill you. And I started wondering what I would do, how I would go on without you."

"You don't have to be dependent on me, Shannon. I never meant to make you feel that way. Any of them can teach you all you need to know."

She shook her head, staring into his eyes, an intensity building in hers. "But I don't *want* any of them to teach me. I want you to do it, Damien."

He lowered his head. It was too painful to stare into her eyes for another second. "So you've decided you can bear to be immortal. You've decided you'd like me to teach you. But, Shannon, *I've* decided... that I just can't do it."

"No?"

"No." He met her eyes again, forced himself to. "I can't be around you and not be *with* you, Shannon. I want you too much, and I'm not strong enough to fight it anymore. I love you, Shannon." He got to his feet, frustration urging him to beat the walls down with his bare hands. But it wouldn't help.

She stood, too, facing him. Her expression so solemn that he had to look at her, had to wonder what she was working up to, here.

She lifted her hands to the brooch that held the white gown in place.

"No, Shannon..."

A second later, the garment was a soft white cloud settling around her feet. "I don't want you to fight it right now, Damien."

He wanted to close his eyes. But nothing could make him turn away. She was too beautiful, standing naked before him, torchlight flickering over her pale skin. He reached out with hesitant hands, and paused. But he couldn't stop himself, could he? Whether it was gratitude or just ordinary desire, he couldn't turn her away. Not when he knew so well it would be the last time.

He touched her arms, ran his palms slowly up and down over them. "Shannon . . ."

"I told you, I would have taken this option if you'd offered it before I got so sick," she said. "But you haven't asked me why."

He ran his palms over the perfect curve of her back, pulled her close to him, bent his head to kiss her neck, her jaw, her face. Ah, she tasted like ambrosia! He caught her earlobe between his teeth. She wanted to drive him insane, didn't she?

Her fingers traced invisible patterns in his hair. "Ask me why, Damien."

He took her mouth, fed on it, and she responded in kind. Dammit, but he wanted her. Even knowing it would only result in more pain when she left him. He fell to his knees to suckle her breasts, and his blood heated when her breaths quickened and her hands held him to her. He kissed a path over her belly, tongued her navel, then bent lower to taste her secret sweetness. He wanted all of her, every bit. He'd commit her to memory and never forget.

She gasped, her hands trembling on the back of his head as he worked her into a frenzy with his mouth and tongue. She whispered his name, and he used his teeth, smiling when she shuddered in response. Her knees buckled, but he followed her down, climbing up her body with his mouth as his hands worked to open his pants. He'd have her, one last time. He'd be sure she never forgot him, either, even if she lived ten thousand years, a hundred thousand!

He reached her face, parted her mouth with his tongue and made love to it, even as he urged her thighs wider and nudged into her moistness. She arched her hips to take him inside, and he went, eagerly. Her slick entrance clenched him, squeezed him as he drove deeper, filling her up and re-treating. Holding back, teasing her until she bounced beneath him, before he plunged into her once more. It was heaven. It was hell. It was slow, burning torture.

He rode her hard on the path to ecstasy, and when he hovered at the brink, he felt her teeth at his throat. She took his essence into her body, as release pounded through her. His own climax was his reply, and she clung to him as if she were drowning. Then relaxed beneath him. He felt her muscles unwind, one by one. She sighed long and low and her fingers wound in his hair again.

"That was like nothing I could have imagined." A bare whisper. A new wonder in her voice.

He rolled off her to lie on his side, lifted her head to pillow it on his arm. "Your senses are heightened. You feel everything more thoroughly than before." He kissed her cheek. It had happened too fast. He should have taken more time, made it last, drawn it out. It was over. Dammit, already it was over.

"You can say that again." She opened her eyes to stare up at him, the laughter vanishing from the amber. "Ask me why I would have chosen to live, Damien."

He swallowed hard, a small candle of hope igniting in his dark soul, just from the touch of the light in her eyes. He hated that glimmer. It would only make the impending disappointment harder to take. But he asked her. He grasped at the straw she dangled. "Why would you have chosen to live, Shannon?"

"Not just because I was afraid of death. Not for eternal life and health and youth. Not for all this strength and energy, or even for the chance to avenge Tawny's murder."

She paused, her head lifting until her lips hovered a hairbreadth from his. Her eyes shot amber sparks at him, and the candle inside him flared brighter. "But because I love you."

"Shannon..." He caught her head in his hands, kissed her, tasted her, dug into her mouth with his tongue.

"I'll never leave you, Damien. Gilgamesh. I'll be with you for always. You will never have to walk alone again. And neither will I."

He kissed her again, deeply, and the slow healing of his oldest, deepest wound began.

> ... it yearns and waits to be retouched
> By someone who can take away
> The memory of death ...

* * * * *

Dear Readers,
This time, DPI's agent Bachman got away intact. But on his next assignment, he'll be fighting for his life *and* his heart. In October, look for "Beyond Twilight," Bachman's story, in *Strangers in the Night*, the Shadows short story collection.

Love,
Maggie Shayne

And now for something completely different....

SILHOUETTE

SPELLBOUND
R O M A N C E

**In January, look for
SAM'S WORLD (IM #615)
by Ann Williams**

Contemporary Woman: Marina Ross had
landed in the strangest of worlds: the future.
And her only ally was the man responsible for
bringing her there.

Future Man: Sam's world was one without
emotion or passion, one he was desperately
trying to save—even as he himself felt the first
stirrings of desire....

**Don't miss SAM'S WORLD,
by Ann Williams, available this January,
only from**

INTIMATE MOMENTS®
Silhouette

SPELL6

Bestselling Author

Elise Title

Anything less than everything is not enough.

Coming in January 1995, Sylver Cassidy and Kate Paley take
on the movers and shakers of Hollywood. Young, beautiful,
been-there, done-it-all type women, they're ready to live by their
own rules and stand by their own mistakes. With love on the
horizon, can two women bitten by the movie bug really have it
all? Find out in

HOT PROPERTY

 MIRA **The brightest star in women's fiction**

METHP

Now what's going on in

 ?

Guilty! That was what everyone thought of
Sandy Keller's client, including Texas Ranger—and
American Hero—Garrett Hancock. But as he worked
with her to determine the truth, loner Garrett found he
was changing his mind about a lot of things—especially
falling in love.

Rachel Lee's Conard County series continues in January
1995 with A QUESTION OF JUSTICE, IM #613.

MONTANA
Mavericks

Stories that capture living and loving
beneath the Big Sky, where legends live
on...and mystery lingers.

This January, the intrigue continues with

OUTLAW LOVERS
by Pat Warren

He was a wanted man. She was the beckoning angel
who offered him a hideout. Now their budding
passion has put them both in danger. And he'd do
anything to protect her.

Don't miss a minute of the loving as the passion
continues with:

WAY OF THE WOLF
by Rebecca Daniels (February)

THE LAW IS NO LADY
by Helen R. Myers (March)

FATHER FOUND
by Laurie Paige (April)
and many more!

Only from **Silhouette®** where passion lives.

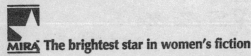

MEN MADE IN AMERICA

Fifty red-blooded, white-hot, true-blue hunks
from every State in the Union!

Look for MEN MADE IN AMERICA! Written by some
of our most popular authors, these stories feature some
of the strongest, sexiest men, each from a different state
in the union!

Two titles available every month at your favorite
retail outlet.

In January, look for:

WITHIN REACH by Marilyn Pappano (New Mexico)
IN GOOD FAITH by Judith McWilliams (New York)

In February, look for:

THE SECURITY MAN by Dixie Browning
(North Carolina)
A CLASS ACT by Kathleen Eagle
(North Dakota)

You won't be able to resist MEN MADE IN AMERICA!

SILHOUETTE... Where Passion Lives

Don't miss these Silhouette favorites by some of our most distinguished authors! And now you can receive a discount by ordering two or more titles!

SD#05786	QUICKSAND by Jennifer Greene	$2.89	☐
SD#05795	DEREK by Leslie Guccione	$2.99	☐
SD#05818	NOT JUST ANOTHER PERFECT WIFE by Robin Elliott	$2.99	☐
IM#07505	HELL ON WHEELS by Naomi Horton	$3.50	☐
IM#07514	FIRE ON THE MOUNTAIN by Marion Smith Collins	$3.50	☐
IM#07559	KEEPER by Patricia Gardner Evans	$3.50	☐
SSE#09879	LOVING AND GIVING by Gina Ferris	$3.50	☐
SSE#09892	BABY IN THE MIDDLE by Marie Ferrarella	$3.50 U.S. $3.99 CAN.	☐ ☐
SSE#09902	SEDUCED BY INNOCENCE by Lucy Gordon	$3.50 U.S. $3.99 CAN.	☐ ☐
SR#08952	INSTANT FATHER by Lucy Gordon	$2.75	☐
SR#08984	AUNT CONNIE'S WEDDING by Marie Ferrarella	$2.75	☐
SR#08990	JILTED by Joleen Daniels	$2.75	☐

(limited quantities available on certain titles)

AMOUNT	$_____
DEDUCT: 10% DISCOUNT FOR 2+ BOOKS	$_____
POSTAGE & HANDLING ($1.00 for one book, 50¢ for each additional)	$_____
APPLICABLE TAXES*	$_____
TOTAL PAYABLE (check or money order—please do not send cash)	$_____

To order, complete this form and send it, along with a check or money order for the total above, payable to Silhouette Books, to: **In the U.S.:** 3010 Walden Avenue, P.O. Box 9077, Buffalo, NY 14269-9077; **In Canada:** P.O. Box 636, Fort Erie, Ontario, L2A 5X3.

Name:_____

Address:_____ City:_____

State/Prov.:_____ Zip/Postal Code:_____

*New York residents remit applicable sales taxes.
Canadian residents remit applicable GST and provincial taxes.   SBACK-DF

Silhouette®